CW01203353

Acknowledgements

Thanks to Dawn Spears the brilliant artist who created the cover artwork. My wife who is so supportive and believes in me. Last my dogs Blaez and Zeeva and cats Vaskr and Rosa who watch me act out the fight scenes and must wonder what the hell has gotten into their boss. And a special thank you to Troy who was the Grandfather of Blaez in real life. He was a magnificent beast just like his grandson!

THANK YOU FOR READING!

I hope you enjoy reading this book as much as I enjoyed writing it. Reviews are so helpful to authors. I really appreciate all reviews, both positive and negative. If you want to leave one, you can do so on Amazon, through the website, or also on Twitter.

About the Author

Christopher C Tubbs is a dog-loving descendent of a long line of Dorset clay miners and has chased his family tree back to the 16th century in the Isle of Purbeck. He left school at sixteen to train as an Avionics Craftsman, has been a public speaker at conferences for most of his career and was one of the founders of a successful games company back in the 1990's. Now in his sixties, he finally writes the stories he had been dreaming about for years. Thanks to inspiration from great authors like Alexander Kent, Dewey Lambdin, Patrick O'Brian, Raymond E Feist, and Dudley Pope, he was finally able to put digit to keyboard. He lives in the Netherlands with his wife, two Dutch Shepherds, and two Norwegian Forest cats.

You can visit him on his website
www.thedorsetboy.com

The Dorset Boy, Facebook page.

Or tweet him @ChristopherCTu3

The Dorset Boy Book 8: La Licorne

The Dorset Boy Book 8: La Licorne

The Dorset Boy Series Timeline

1792 – 1795   Book 1: A Talent for Trouble
Marty joins the Navy as an Assistant Steward and ends up a midshipman.

1795 – 1798   Book 2: The Special Operations Flotilla
Marty is a founder member of the Special Operations Flotilla, learns to be a spy and passes as lieutenant.

1799 – 1802   Book 3: Agent Provocateur
Marty teams up with Linette to infiltrate Paris, marries Caroline, becomes a father and fights pirates in Madagascar.

1802 – 1804   Book 4: In Dangerous Company
Marty and Caroline are in India helping out Arthur Wellesley, combating French efforts to disrupt the East India Company and French sponsored pirates on Reunion. James Stockley is born.

1804 – 1805   Book 5: The Tempest
Piracy in the Caribbean, French interference, Spanish gold and the death of Nelson. Marty makes Captain.

1806 – 1807   Book 6: Vendetta
A favour carried out for a prince, a new ship, the S.O.F. move to Gibraltar, the battle of Maida, counter espionage in Malta and a Vendetta declared and closed.

The Dorset Boy Book 8: La Licorne

1807 – 1809   Book 7: The Trojan Horse
Rescue of the Portuguese royal family, Battle of the
Basque Roads with Thomas Cochrane, and back to the
Indian Ocean and another conflict with the French
Intelligence Service.

1809 – 1811   Book 8: La Licorne

Marty takes on the role of Viscount Wellington's Head
of Intelligence. Battle of The Lines of Torres Vedras,
siege of Cadiz, skulduggery, espionage and blowing
stuff up to confound the French.

The Dorset Boy Book 8: La Licorne

Dedication

This book was mostly written during the long evenings of the Covid 19 virus pandemic and I would like to dedicate it to all those care workers who gave everything in support of the rest of us. A special dedication goes to my eldest sister Teena and Uncle Gordon both of whom died within a week of each other in April that year.

The Dorset Boy Book 8: La Licorne

Contents

The Dorset Boy Book 8: La Licorne

Chapter 1: A New Role

The Formidiable slipped into the mouth of the Tagus quietly and without fanfare, she fired no salute, just dipped her flag to Admiral Smith's flagship as she passed.

Smith, who was on deck getting some exercise at the time, watched the frigate ghost by and smiled. He had talked extensively with Wellesley and agreed wholeheartedly with him on the appointment of their talented friend as his Head of Intelligence. The war that would be fought on the Peninsula would be as much about intelligence as the armies that would fight it.

The world is changing, he thought as he raised a hand to the figure on the Formidiable's quarterdeck, *we need quick minds who can play the game better than our enemies.* That not only meant having better intelligence gathering than them, but effective counterintelligence as demonstrated in Malta and London.

"It helps that Martin is the luckiest man I have ever met," he chortled, causing his flag lieutenant to ask,

"Milord? Do you need something?"

"No, nothing, thank you, just thinking out loud." He smiled as the Formidiable faded into the mist.

A week before in his office, Marty had been nervous. Everyone seemed to be gleefully dropping him in deep water and waiting to see if he floated or sank. Ridgley had followed up the revelation of his next mission with a packet of double sealed orders that had, "Not to be opened until at sea," written on them. That was bad enough but there was a second written order to report to

Admiral Cotton 'at his earliest convenience'. The old boy was soon to be replaced and the rumour was it would be by Pellew, which pleased Marty a lot.

Marty was sad not to see Collingwood's name on the summons as he had finally succumbed to the cancer that was eating away at him. The heart-breaking fact was the poor man never made it home alive. He repeatedly requested the Admiralty to return but they had delayed and delayed until he finally passed away just off of Mahon on his way home. The irony wasn't lost on Marty.

"Captain Stockley, sah!" announced the marine guarding the admiral's door.

"Enter!" ordered the admiral.

Marty stepped inside and presented himself in front of the desk where the admiral sat going through a paper.

Cotton waved a hand at him,

"Sit down, Captain, if you please. I won't be a minute."

Marty perched himself on the edge of one of the padded armchairs that faced the desk and waited.

Cotton scratched his signature on the paper with one of the new steel tipped pens, placed the paper in a tray to his right, after blotting it, and wiped the pen's nib with a cloth before replacing it on a stand.

"Sir Martin, it's very good to see you again," he smiled. They had met at several functions in London and at the Admiralty. The admiral was also a friend of Hood's and therefore an ally.

"You should have received some sealed orders by now," it was a statement not a question, "and I have been asked to set you on your way, so to speak."

Marty nodded and waited; the old boy would get to it in his own time.

"Your successes against the French intelligence service have not gone unnoticed and you have supporters, and enemies, at almost all levels in the government. Even Pitt cannot gainsay you, even though you are known to be contemptuous of his ally Admiral Gambier. A view held by the majority of the service I may add."

Marty smiled quietly at that- he frankly didn't give a shit what people thought of him and was gloriously ambivalent to politics.

"I am told that your good lady wife has been dabbling in politics and seems to have established somewhat of a power base in your support," Cotton said with a grin.

"Has she? I wasn't aware," Marty replied, genuinely surprised. He knew Caroline had pocketed a couple of MPs but had no idea what she had been up to recently.

"Yes, she does it quietly, but she uses your wealth wisely and has established strong ties with some very influential people. Be that as it may, you need to get yourself to Lisbon as soon as you can. Your orders will explain what you will be doing. I have been asked to make sure that you keep your Flotilla intact and to provide any assistance I can if you need it.

I believe that your new role will give you significant powers. I have been asked to provide you with advice and council should you need it as a favour to Admiral Hood."

"I am honoured and grateful, sir," Marty said with genuine gratitude and affection for his mentor back in London.

"I would have done it even if he hadn't asked." Cotton smiled, "Now, let us have a glass to the future and the defeat of Napoleon," Cotton concluded and called his steward.

Marty sat at his desk in his cabin and opened the double sealed packet; one seal was the Admiralty's fouled anchor, the other was the portcullis of the Government.

Inside were two letters; the first was from the Admiralty signed by the First Lord himself and after the usual preamble said,

You are hereby commissioned to take the position of Head of Intelligence on the staff of Viscount Wellington, Lieutenant General Wellesley, and to take responsibility for both intelligence and counterintelligence operations. You will maintain command of the Special Operations Flotilla and, at all times, conduct yourself in the best traditions of the Navy.

That was the meat of it. There were other minor details but that one paragraph gave him an open remit answerable only to Arthur.

The second was a letter commanding whoever read it to lend all assistance to the holder by the command of Spencer Perceval the Prime Minister himself.

"Ppff," he said to Troy, who sat at his usual place beside his desk, "this is more than a bit of a challenge."

"Adam!" he called and a second later his steward appeared from the pantry.

"Sir?" he enquired.

"Pass the word for Mr. Ridgley to attend me please and make some coffee. I think this will be a long meeting."

Now, as Marty stood on the quarterdeck and returned Sir Sidney's wave, he braced himself for the meeting that would launch this next phase of his career. It would make him or break him; of that, he was sure.

He had discussed with Ridgley the existing spy network they had established, where it needed strengthening, and how much it could be trusted. Likewise, they had gone over everything they knew about the French intelligence network and the military hierarchy in Spain.

What he had was an embryonic mainly amateur spy network with a good foundation that needed expansion, and on the other side was a professional French intelligence network that he needed to frustrate.

Now, he needed to know what Arthur expected. Only then could he plan ahead and see how he could help make this as short a war as possible.

A pilot came aboard and guided them to a berth against the stone dock usually reserved for commercial transports, and as they tied up a group of horsemen trotted up. Marty immediately recognised Arthur on his big mixed-blood stallion with his glittering honours and bicorn hat worn fore and aft.

Wellesley was happy and somewhat relieved to have gotten the alert that the Formidiable had entered the Tagus. He had just been elevated to Viscount Wellington and given sole responsibility for the Peninsula. He had gotten his peerage for beating the French at Talavera but after that, he was forced to retreat back into Portugal. Now he was in the process of fortifying a line from the Tagus to the coast that passed close to the town of Torres Vedras.

What he wanted to keep secret was the fact that there were two more lines of defence being constructed behind that one. He wanted, no, needed to stop Marshal Masséna at the first line and use Lisbon as an impregnable beachhead to push the French out of Spain.

The Formidiable was finally tied up and a gangplank put into place. He dismounted, left his horse in the care of his groom, and led his small cadre of officers up onto the main deck of the Frigate.

"Martin! I am so pleased to see you again," he greeted as Martin stepped forward.

Marty watched the tall, hook-nosed, and haughty-looking general step down off his horse and come up the gangplank followed by three staff officers

"Pleased to see you again, Arthur," Marty responded and was faintly amused by the frowns of the staff officers at the familiarity. He was dressed in his simple captain's uniform without any of his honours.

"Gentlemen, may I introduce Captain, Sir Martin Stockley, Baron Candor," Arthur introduced him,

"Martin, this is Lt Colonel Sir Richard Fetcher- my engineer, General William Beresford, and General Roland Hill.

Martin, can we retire to your cabin so we may talk privately?"

"If it's privacy we need, Wolfgang, please warp us away from the dock and anchor us a cable out," Marty asked his first.

Wolfgang touched his forelock, sketched a bow to the worthies, and started bellowing orders. Troy had come up on deck and positioned himself by Martin's knee.

"Is that the same dog you had in India?" Arthur asked as they walked down to his cabin,

"His son. The old boy is at home with Caroline and the children. Ship life is a bit much for him nowadays."

"Same mean streak?"

"Just as protective." Marty grinned.

They settled in the coach around the dining table, Adam brought in coffee and tea.

Chapter 2: Lisbon

"We have constructed a line of mutually supporting, small earth redoubts along two lines, here, from the River Tagus to the coast," Fletcher explained, pointing out the defences on a map he produced from his document case. "Each is manned by two to three-hundred men supported by six cannon."

Arthur pointed to an area to the North,

"Masséna has around forty thousand men advancing towards Sobral and we have 25,000 Portuguese militia, 8,000 Spaniards, and 2,500 British gunners and marines manning the line. Behind that, we have a combined Anglo/Portuguese force of some sixty thousand men."

"Sounds to me you have the situation under control. What do you need from us?" Marty asked.

"I need to know what Masséna will do after he comes up against our wall, if he is able to bring in reinforcements, and whether he will try and shift his point of attack. We need time to be able to mould the army into an effective force."

Marty was about to answer when there was the sound of a boat bumping against the hull. He called for Sam, who entered from the steward's pantry.

"Find out where that boat is from and who is on it," he ordered. Sam nodded and left.

"He wasn't with you in India," Arthur observed.

"Tom retired and Sam took up his mantle," Marty replied, "he joined me in the Caribbean."

There was a knock at the door. Sam poked his head through and announced with a huge grin,

"The rest of the team has arrived," then stepped in followed by Francis Ridgley and a cloaked and hooded figure that barely came up to his chin.

Marty stood with a beaming smile of welcome and held out his arms. Linette threw back the hood and embraced him, kissing each of his cheeks in turn.

Arthur and his men stood in surprise and were reminded of how low the ceiling was to muttered curses as they banged their heads. Linette smiled dazzlingly at Arthur and held out her hand to him. He bowed elegantly over it and brushed it with his lips, his Generals and Fletcher just bowed in greeting.

"Gentlemen, may I introduce a valued member of our team and member of the British Intelligence Service, Linette," Marty introduced her.

"I thought you were busy in France?" he said as he offered her a seat.

"I was but Monsieur Canning asked that I come 'ere to 'elp you," she replied.

Marty saw that the men were looking a little concerned as they heard her French accent.

"Linette and I have worked together many times in French territory. She is French, speaks Spanish, and is one of our most experienced operatives," he reassured them then, remembering Francis who stood looking a bit peeved at being ignored. "This is Francis Ridgley of the foreign office, controller for this region." The soldiers snapped him bows without rising.

Arthur decided it was time to get back to business.

"Do you require a base for your operations?" he asked.

"I will embed myself in your headquarters if I may. That way, we can set priorities and organise missions as required. Francis will manage his agents in Spain and Portugal from his place in Gibraltar when he isn't here."

Ridgley, who was quiet up to then, added,

"I will find somewhere I can base myself while I am here; Martin can use that if he needs somewhere away from prying eyes."

"I have my mobile office as well," Marty grinned, waving a hand at the cabin, "this is the most secure location in Portugal."

"Which brings us to the subject of keeping our fortifications secret," General Beresford prompted.

Francis surprised the military men by informing them,

"I have agents embedded in the Spanish and Portuguese populations here in Lisbon. They have identified a number of suspected French agents and are keeping them under surveillance. Do you want us to remove them or use them to feed false information to the French?"

Arthur looked to his generals, who both shrugged, obviously uncomfortable with all this undercover nonsense.

"May I make a suggestion?" Linette interrupted. "The French must already have a good idea about the forces you have here. What they do not know is what you are going to do next. Keeping them in the dark at this stage will be more frustrating for them than false information."

"What will you do?" General Hill asked.

"Oh, that's easy. We eliminate them," Marty grinned wolfishly. "There is nothing worse for a spy master than having his sources all dry up at once."

Hill looked outraged at the thought of wholesale 'eliminations,' which in his mind sounded like 'assassinations' and was about to say something when Marty held up his hand.

"We will, however, thin their ranks down so we can concentrate on a few who we can manipulate. In the meantime, we will gather information to help you plan your next move."

"You have people who can do that?" Hill asked.

"Several, but in this case, I think I will send a couple of 'Spaniards' who can wander up and down the border without attracting too much notice."

Linette smiled expectantly at him, "Ryan and me?"

"Yes, I will be far too busy to accompany you, as much as I would like to. You can take Garai as your 'servant'."

The meeting broke up with Marty promising to visit Arthur's headquarters on the morrow.

Lisbon was quiet. With the sixteen thousand aristocrats and wealthy commoners still in Brazil, the economy had slowed to almost a standstill. The remaining citizens were short of money, and with the French camped to the North and a sixty-thousand-man army camped on their doorstep, short of food. Any shipments coming in were destined for the army, leaving the citizens short of victuals.

Marty decided to do something about that and had a word with a couple of merchant captains, paying them to sail to Poole and return with cargos of grain, cured meats, and other foods that would survive the one-week voyage and be sold in the market.

He sent letters to Caroline and his brother Alfred alerting them to the opportunity to ship foodstuffs, including live cattle and sheep as the market was wide open. This was not entirely charitable. He fully expected to be paid for what was shipped but he would be happy to cover his costs and set up some valuable trading relationships in the process.

Their network of agents noticed an anomaly. One of their suspected French agents was a merchant who had a private fleet of ships, but the amount of goods he sold at the markets didn't tally with the amount seen going into his warehouse on the docks. He was also rumoured to be very wealthy, which begged the question why he stayed when all the other rich people had left. A sneaky look in the warehouse had shown it to be almost empty. Where did the balance of the goods go?

Marty walked through the streets, Sam and Troy at his side. He wore civilian clothes and a wide-brimmed hat. They were headed to the house of that particular merchant, located in the Alfama region of town near to the docks but far enough back to be comfortable.

As they approached the house, Marty nodded to Matai who was leaning nonchalantly against a wall in a place where he could watch the front door, Antton and Chin were watching the rear of the house, and John Smith was following a discreet distance behind him.

He walked up to the door and pulled a brass knob set into the wall, which rang a bell somewhere inside. A servant opened the door after a short delay, and Marty asked to speak to Señor Jose Correia Mendez in Spanish. He was admitted and shown into a grand reception room decorated with expensive ornaments, which made him wonder how he had avoided being pillaged during the French occupation.

He waited and after about ten minutes, the merchant arrived.

"Good afternoon, sir," Marty greeted him in Spanish and when the servant closed the door, he switched to French,

"I am told you have valuable information and supplies available for the French cause."

"I am sorry, I do not speak French," Mendez replied in Spanish, looking startled and glancing at the door and windows, *"I only speak Spanish and Portuguese."*

"Oh, come now," Marty persisted, *"I have it on good authority you speak excellent French."*

"I'm sorry, I do not understand you!" he replied in Spanish and repeated it in Portuguese.

"You are Señor Jose Correia Mendez?" Marty asked in Spanish.

Mendez confirmed that was who he was and looked worried and frightened.

Marty looked at Sam and sighed in French,

"We are wasting our time here. General Masséna must have been mistaken. Kill him so he cannot identify us, and we will move on to the next name on the list."

Sam, who was primed to react to the general's name, pulled out a wicked, long knife and advanced on the now terrified man. He grabbed him by the collar and dramatically raised the knife, his eyes wide and staring.

"Stop! Stop! I speak French and I am the one the general named!" the frightened man cried in French.

Marty held out his hand. Sam lowered the knife but kept hold of Mendez's collar.

"Now why didn't you say that before? My friend here is going to be very disappointed. He does enjoy cutting throats."

"I thought you may be trying to trap me."

"Aah, well, I should introduce myself, Armand Clavell, Department for Internal Affairs at your service." Marty waved a hand at Sam to let Mendez go. *"I have replaced your previous contact as he suspects he was identified by the British."*

"This is Samuel, he doesn't speak, and this is Troy, he likes to bite people." He smiled. He was enjoying the playacting as it had been a while since he was undercover.

"Now I would like a report on the supplies you have stored away for when the general arrives." Marty rolled the dice to see how they would come up.

"I have done as asked by Mr Plagnol and ensured that the secret warehouses are full of both food and cloth for uniforms and boots. We have managed to keep it all from the British and the Portuguese army. As far as they are concerned, my warehouses are empty," Mendez boasted.

That was excellent - they now had the name of the French spymaster.

"They don't inspect them?" Marty asked.

"Why should they? They don't see the goods arrive- we have tunnels from the docks to the secret warehouses and it is all moved underground. Half of every cargo is

diverted to those warehouses; the other half stays in the warehouse at the docks for selling at the market."

There was a noise from outside, and Sam moved to the window to have a look. He saw Matai leading a man away at gunpoint. He turned back to Marty and nodded.

"Show me the warehouses," he demanded rather than asked.

"Certainly, please come with me," Mendez replied and led them out of the room. They moved deeper into the house until they came to a door that looked like any other. Mendez took a lantern from a niche and lit it with an ornate tinderbox.

"Mind the steps," he said as he unlocked and opened the door, which led down an ancient stone staircase. The temperature dropped as they descended two flights, around thirty feet. Mendez walked ahead, the lamp providing enough light for Marty to see that the tunnel was carefully made and well finished.

"Has this been here long?" he asked.

"The tunnels date from the time of the Roman occupation. It is thought they linked palaces to the garrison to allow the ladies to dally with the soldiers. We think the warehouses are the cellars of the Roman garrison."

This was all news to Marty, who knew the British were totally unaware of the tunnels and cellars, which explained why no one had inspected them.

They emerged after quite a long walk into a vaulted room lit by lamps hanging from chains and stacked to the roof with crates and bagged goods. Mendez proudly told him,

"We have six of these and have stored about one hundred and fifty tons of grain, about the same of salted beef and dried peas. We bought the beef and peas from a corrupt supply officer in the British Navy. It's all new and means the stupid British sailors will only get old stock."

Marty made a mental note to extract the name of that officer from Mendez in the future and exact some retribution, either officially or unofficially, on behalf of his shipmates.

Mendez was oblivious to Marty's growing anger and continued,

"We have leather for boots and tack, material for uniforms, canvas for tents and sundry other useful items for the Army when it arrives."

"Excellent!" Marty congratulated him, *"Do you have weapons as well?"*

"French muskets with bayonets, ball, and cartridge, pistols and army pattern swords. We smuggled those in from Santander whilst it was under French control."

"It was a genuine treasure trove," Marty told Arthur the next day when they met up at his headquarters, "the damn man has been building his stock up since you booted the French out of Porto."

"Who was the man Matai intercepted?" Arthur asked.

"Aah, now. He was the real French controller, one Paul Plagnol, who went by the alias of Gregor de Quintas, a merchant. He is now sitting in the brig on my ship." Marty almost crowed in delight. "We never expected to flush him out so quickly, but he was on his way to Mendez to warn him that there was a new head of British Intelligence in town when Matai stopped him.

He was obviously trying to visit Mendez while I was there, but I had left orders not to be disturbed. When I returned, I thought I heard something odd in his accent, so we checked up on him and found out where he lived. A thorough search revealed some papers hidden in a fairly cleverly concealed compartment behind the stove in his kitchen. They were encoded using a fairly common cypher, identified him by name and linked him to the Department."

"A happy chance then," Arthur dryly observed, thinking that some people have all the luck. "Where are the hidden warehouses located?"

"Under the Alfama Old Quarter. It appears that it is built on the ruins of the old Roman town."

"What will you do next?" Arthur asked.

"The boys are out rounding up the French agents on our list. We were going to leave a couple loose but now that we have Plagnol, we don't need to."

"Mendez as well?" Arthur asked in anticipation.

Marty laughed, "I will collect him myself along with around forty marines. We don't want him destroying those stores. Then you can hang him after we have rung some more information out of him."

"Excellent, we need to make a show of distributing them and hanging him to show the locals that we have their best interest at heart," Arthur concluded then changed the subject,

"What about the intelligence gathering on the French Army?"

Chapter 3: Reconnaissance

Linette, Ryan, and Garai took the Eagle and sailed up to Bilbao. Their plan was to start in the North at Santander and try to plot the French forces surrounding Portugal.

When they got there, they established a base in a hotel and looked for transportation. They needed something either totally bland and unmemorable or something loud and flamboyant that couldn't possibly be suspicious.

Garai came up with the answer.

"Gypsies. They move around. Nobody takes any notice of them, apart from locking up their valuables and daughters, and they go largely unnoticed. I can contact a local group and talk to their leader; us Basques and the gypsies are both oppressed peoples and get on fine."

Ryan and Linette thought it was a great idea, and Garai left in the morning to find out if there were any nearby. He returned after lunch slightly tipsy and reported he had got a meeting set up for the next morning.

This all got Ryan thinking,

"Could we use the gypsies as a spy network?" he asked Linette as they lay in bed.

"The question is could we trust them to provide reliable information and not just make things up to get the gold," she replied and snuggled closer.

"There is that," he admitted, "Garai said the old guy who ran the band here," he paused and pondered, "is it a band or a tribe? Anyway, the old guy is shrewd and crafty, and he would only trust him so far."

"We could offer them gold for information and if they come up with anything interesting, get another agent to check it out," Linette suggested.

"Well, we will meet him tomorrow; we can see what he says then." Ryan concluded and kissed her.

Early the next morning, they walked about a mile outside of town to an area of common ground and approaching the camp. They spotted men on guard around the perimeter who were concealed well enough that an untrained person wouldn't notice them, but Ryan spotted them straight away. They were armed with muskets, long knives, and were alert.

The camp was a ring of horse-drawn caravans and carts with canvas awnings set up on the inside. In the centre of the circle was a large communal firepit. Horses were corralled just outside the camp, goats wandered around freely, browsing on the scrubby vegetation, attended by small boys. Several men and a couple of women sat around the fire eating breakfast. A more roguish group would be hard to find. The men were dressed in colourful shirts and baggy trousers with wide sashes tied around their waists and bandanas on their heads covering their hair. The women were dressed in wide skirts with multiple petticoats, laced up boots, blouses, and Spanish-style short jackets. Many of them smoked pipes.

Other members of the band sat around on the steps of caravans or under the awnings on cushions. Weapons were conspicuously displayed and within easy reach of every man and woman.

"This is the Englishman interested in spying on the French?" the leader asked.

"Yes," Garai answered, *"Señor Danior, this is Señor Ryan."*

"Welcome to my fire," Danior greeted them and indicated they should sit, *"take some breakfast with us."*

That was a good sign. Garai had told them that if they were offered food and drink, they would be safe for as long as they were in the camp.

They were given bowls of coffee, strong and black, and churros, the fried bread/pastry favoured by the Spanish for breakfast. There were also delicious slices of ham and spicy sausage. As they ate, they talked,

"What do you want to know about the French?" Danior asked.

"Troop numbers, movements, supply routes and times, when and how they are paid, strongholds, who is commanding them, things like that," Ryan replied as if it were nothing.

"We can do much ourselves, but we cannot cover the whole of the border region on our own," Linette added.

Danior ignored her and spoke to Ryan,

"What is this information worth to the English?"

Linette bristled and was about to say something else when Garai placed a hand on her arm and shook his head.

"We would pay in gold for good information," Ryan replied.

"Like you do the smugglers?" Danior grinned, delighted he had gotten one over the English man.

Ryan was surprised and gave Garai a questioning look. He shook his head in reply. He hadn't told Danior about any arrangements with the smugglers.

"How do you know about that?"

Danior and the others laughed. This was obviously something they had saved up for a big reveal. Well, if they wanted to play Ryan would let them.

"We work with them to move their goods across the country. The Roma are ignored and spat on by many, but the smugglers know our worth. We know who they sell to and know they sell more than just wine and ham."

"Would you sell information as well?" Ryan asked.

"For a price," was the reply, and Danior leaned forward expectantly.

What followed was a spirited negotiation, which ended with both men spitting on their hands before shaking to seal the bargain.

Ryan wrote in his report.

We purchased a caravan and horse with all the accoutrements they carry for living and were accepted as honorary members of the band for a fee to be paid per month. The leader agreed to collect and pass information to us for five hundred Real in advance and a further payment depending on the value of the information.

This, of course, is as a matter of trust but I made it clear to him that we would be checking on the important information ourselves and it wouldn't be a good idea to double cross us."

We (Linette, Garai, and I) will take the caravan and work our way around to Santander and down through Portugal. We will link up with the smugglers and gypsies to collect as much information as we can about the size and constitution of the French Forces in and around Portugal.

Marty read this with a certain amount of satisfaction. The cover story was good and provided them with a freedom of movement that others couldn't. The information would be fed back through the existing smugglers network and be sent to him on a regular basis. It was all working out quite well. Ryan was using his head and not trying to do it all himself. Money was no object as this was being funded from the treasure left on the docks, they 'rescued' when the refugees fled Lisbon for Brazil.

The caravan was pulled up on a road outside of Santander, and Ryan, now called Pedro, was busy sharpening swords. The swords belonged to soldiers who were enrapt watching Linette, who was going by the name of Rosa, dancing along to a tune played by Garai on an Asturian gaitera, a bellows-powered set of bagpipes. She had several knives on display to dissuade any amorous soldier boys who got ideas.
As he ground the edge, he chatted to the men in pidgin French,
"Why don't you get your armorers to do this?"
"Those dolts don't know how to put a proper edge on a sword, they can only sharpen axes."

"I can put an edge on good enough to shave with!" Ryan boasted. *"Where did you get this nick in it? If I grind it out, it will weaken the blade?"*

"Leave it. It's a souvenir from fighting the Portuguese and British at Porto," the young officer puffed himself up in pride.

"You look like a killer! You will be heading on down there again then," Ryan flattered him.

"No, the fight is over in Portugal the British are penned in Lisbon and will leave as soon as Masséna engages them."

Will we really? Ryan thought amused at the arrogance as he put the final touch to the sword before handing it back and receiving his twenty centimes in payment.

He took another sword and looked up into the face of an older officer, probably a major, who looked at him disdainfully.

"Sharpen it and don't grind the blade away in the process," he barked, his moustache bristling.

"Yes sir," Ryan simpered and sharpened it quickly to get the man away as soon as possible. Once done, he handed it back hilt first. The major took it and held the blade across his forearm so he could look down the edge.

"That is very well done," he sheathed it and tossed Ryan forty centimes. *"Get yourself down to Olivenza if you want to make some more money."*

"Thank you, sir. I will, sir," Ryan fawned.

That's interesting. He obviously knows something the young cockerel doesn't, Ryan noted as he took another sword.

Sharpening swords all day gave Ryan a backache and he lay face down on their bed in the caravan while Linette rubbed on a concoction of oil and mustard, infused with chilli and herbs that had a warming effect to ease the muscles.

"I could have made a fortune today if I was a whore," she teased him.

"You would have to be busy at twenty centimes a go," Ryan tossed back and groaned as she dug her fingers in extra deep in vengeance for the tease.

"Very funny. What did you learn with all your grinding?"

"That this army is heading to Olivenza to try and invest the town. It's on the border between Spain and Portugal opposite Lisbon. He is obviously trying to consolidate the border."

"That makes sense," she answered. "By the way, I overheard two officers being very rude about General Soult. They were saying he had ambitions to be the next King of Portugal. I don't think they like him very much. They were gloating that his plan had been ruined."

"Yes, that's the general impression I got as well. Some of the regular soldiers even talked about how the old republican officers downright hate him. They were laughing about how they grumble behind his back but don't have the guts to do it to his face," Ryan murmured as the massage was having the desired effect and sending him into a doze.

Linette wasn't having that. She had other ideas for their evening entertainment! She reached down and tickled his balls. There was a delay then Ryan suddenly rolled onto his back, eyes wide, mouth wide open, and grabbed his groin.

Linette sat back in amazement then realised what she had done, and tried very, very, hard not to giggle while she got him a cold wet cloth.

The next morning, they broke camp and headed West. Garai rode a horse while Ryan and Linette rode on the caravan. Their next stop was Gijón, a fishing village one hundred miles along the coast. They had arranged to rendezvous with the Eagle there and give them their next report

They stopped off at Ribadesella for the first night, met up with a band of gypsies outside of town, and were surprised they knew who they were. Apparently, the gypsies had an efficient messaging system. The general opinion was the French Army in the region was looking like it was settling in for a long stay.

They were eating their supper when a group of men entered the camp. They were heavily armed and looked like a genuine band of cutthroats.

"Señor Pedro, this is Juan, the leader of the local guerrilla band. Juan, Pedro has connections to the British."

Ryan looked at Linette in surprise and concern at the lack of security, but she just shrugged and whispered,

"It is the way it is here."

This is going to be a tense trip! he thought but feigned a relaxed pose and said,

"Greetings, you are resisting the French?"

"We do what we can, but we need help," Juan replied and plonked himself down next to Ryan while leering at

Linette. Ryan saw Garai moving to a position where he could cover Juan and his men and that he had four pistols pushed into the sash around his waist.

"What kind of help?" Ryan asked.

"Guns, powder, money."

Ryan looked at him then at his men and saw they carried a random selection of guns of different calibres. He returned his gaze to Juan and asked,

"I see some French muskets and pistols."

"We take them off the bodies of soldiers."

"Are the French guns good?"

"They are better than the bird pieces many have."

"Well how about we get you some more of those and cause the French some grief at the same time. Stephano, you said the French were settling in for a long stay, they must be setting up supply depots?" he asked the leader of the gypsies.

"Yes, they have a big one at Léon about two days South of here. It is well guarded."

Chapter 4: Arming the revolution

There are two ways to feed a man: give him food or show him how to go get it himself. Marty likes to do the latter, Ryan thought as he left Linette at the camp, and he and Garai joined the guerrillas to travel to Léon.

This was a sparsely populated part of Spain with mountainous terrain and few roads. They rode at a reasonable pace that the horses could maintain for long periods at a time and arrived in the area of the depot in good time. Ryan, Juan, and his lieutenants crouched on the top of a hill and looked down into the valley that the French had fortified.

He could see why the French had chosen this village to locate the depot compound as it was on the junction of six roads that headed out in a star from the centre. On closer examination, Ryan could see it was actually a distribution point where supplies were brought down from the coast on the North road then sent out to the various garrisons the French had established in the Northwest of Spain.

Ignoring the impatient urging of the Spanish, he took his time and made a sketch of the compound, its fortifications, where the sentries were positioned, the number of troops, where the barracks and kitchens were, and anything else he considered relevant. While he watched, a train of covered carts came down the North road escorted by a strong cavalry escort. They entered the palisade by the main gate and were immediately unloaded by thirty-eight (he counted them) men, who swarmed out of the barracks to the shouts of, probably, a warrant officer. The cavalry stayed long enough to eat then headed back the way they came.

The last two carts were moved to an area in the far corner of the compound. He watched them unload the first cart, long boxes suitable for carrying muskets were stacked by the cart and some heavy barrels, probably containing shot, were moved off somewhere he couldn't see. The second cart was unloaded with much more care and the casks were taken into a store that was walled off by a pair of high earth berms and entered through a pair of offset gates.

He had seen enough and after a short talk with Garai, he gathered the leaders of the guerrillas around him. Garai slipped away with one of their men and headed down towards the compound.

"Most of the compound contains general stores; food, clothing, boots, that sort of stuff, but this area here is the magazine where they store the guns and ammunition. You will notice it's as far away from the barracks and kitchens as they can get it without putting it outside the fence. The earth walls are to protect the rest of the compound if there were to be an accident and it blew up."

"Why do they need two walls?" one of the more observant asked.

"That's so they can offset the entrance like this," Ryan answered, sketching it to show how they had to negotiate a dog leg through offset gates to enter the magazine. *"That way there isn't a direct path for an explosion to get out."*

He looked around the men as they exchanged comments and figured they understood well enough. It was now midday, so they settled down for a meal and discuss options while they waited for the scouts to return.

Around mid-afternoon, Garai and his fellow scout returned and gave their report around mouthfuls of bread and cheese. The palisade was well made and there was a second gate to the rear. The lookout posts were built into the wall and had no blind spots that they could see. All the soldiers were housed in the compound. There was no evidence that there was a garrison outside that could interfere.

Ryan explained that they had two options; either break in and get what they wanted or ambush a shipment that was on its way in or out.

"The problem in ambushing a convoy is you cannot be sure that it is carrying what you wanted unless you are patient and watched the depot for several days or even weeks" he explained.

As the guerrillas didn't want to spend days waiting, (they didn't have that long an attention span) they would have to raid it. A plan emerged after Ryan asked what the different members of the band were good at and what they had done before they were guerrillas.

"The South gate is the least protected and closest to the Magazine so that is where we will enter and leave. To distract the French, we will fake an attack on the North gate," Ryan explained. *"Garai will lead a team of five men who will make as much noise as possible to drag as many of the French to defend the gate as they can. Get a cart from somewhere, which can be run down the hill into the gate to set it on fire. You need to attack at three AM. Garai has a watch."*

There were nods and grins from the five men that were part of the North gate team. They would acquire a cart from one of the local hill villages and immediately set out.

"The rest of us will go for the magazine. Stefano and Miguel are both expert shots with a sling and will take out the lookouts in the two towers. Me and Angelo will use ropes to get over the wall and open the gate to let the rest of you in. The rest is simple, you quietly kill any Frenchman you see, no shooting, knives only, make your way to the magazine where we will liberate at least two cases of muskets, a cask of balls and a cask of cartridges. There are usually ten muskets to a case, so that should be plenty. You have no more than ten minutes to do this. I will set a fuse to blow up the magazine five minutes after we leave. That will cover the theft and our escape."

He spent time making sure every man knew the layout of the compound, where they had to go, and where they would meet afterwards. It was all he could do. They would roll the dice and see where they fell, but as he thought about it, he knew that the element of surprise should shift the odds in their favour.

The teams split up; Garai and Ryan made sure their watches were synchronised and wound before they parted. Ryan's team circled through the hills and took up position near the South gate. At three AM, there was a flare of light from the North as a burning cart full of brush wood ran right into the North gate and shooting started at the sentries in the lookout towers.

That was their signal; the slingers slunk forward and took up position near the two towers by the south gate.

At the same time, Ryan and Angelo swung ropes with hooks attached, up and over the wall, set them, and started climbing.

Ryan was used to clambering up ropes and fairly scampered to the top of the wall, paused, and checked the tower nearest to him just as the sentry slumped over the rail, the side of his head stove in by a stone. There was a narrow walkway on the inside of the wall, and he moved over to where Angelo was struggling to come over the top. He reached down, grabbed a handful of coat collar, and hauled him up.

A glance showed the guard in the second tower outlined by the light of the flames, still standing and breathing. *Damn,* Ryan thought and ducking down into the shadows, scuttled along until he got to the tower entrance. There was a thunk and a knife quivered in the tower roof support next to the guard's head, causing him to spin in Ryan's direction.

Shit! he thought and moved at the same time, slashing backhand with his dagger across the guard's throat stifling his shout as it started. He followed up by diving over the rail and slamming the man to the floor with him on top, thrusting his knife through his heart.

He climbed off the now still man and turned to look at Angelo, who was sheepishly pulling his knife from the support. Ryan raised his hand and thought about saying something, restrained himself with an effort, and instead just beckoned him to follow.

There was a ladder to ground level, and Ryan slid down it, his feet on the outside. Angelo tried to emulate him and landed in a heap with a curse. He picked himself up and followed Ryan to the gate, which was secured by a large beam in metal hooks.

The two of them struggled to lift the bar, which must have been at least eight by eight inches thick and ten feet long. After a minute of sweating, they managed to push it out of one of the hooks. *Where is Wilson when you need him,* Ryan thought. Then they had to work the other end up and out of its hook and shove the beam out of the way so the gate could be opened.

A glance showed him that the French were rushing to man the southern palisade and shooting into the dark to fend off the diversionary attack. He opened the gate and the rest of the guerrillas streamed through; Ryan led them to the magazine. The earth-covered store was secured with a thick wooden door held closed by a large padlock. A prybar made short work of the lock and they stepped inside.

There was a flash as one of the men struck a flint and Ryan's heart nearly stopped. The leader grabbed the tinderbox and threw it outside, cursing the man in a hoarse whisper. By feel, they found the cases of muskets and two were taken outside followed by a couple of casks of cartridges. The balls weren't in the magazine. Ryan instructed the men to get what they had out through the gate and pulled the plug out of a cask of powder so he could set a timer.

Outside, he grabbed Angelo and quickly searched the piles of stores nearby. No luck, and he knew they had all but run out of time. He turned to head back to the gate only to see a pair of French soldiers, guns levelled, stood just a few feet away looking straight at them.

"Put your hands up and turn around," one ordered and gestured with his gun.

Ryan put up his hands and Angelo followed suit. They slowly turned around. The guards prodded them in the back with their bayonets to start them walking forward. Ryan had been counting in his head since the last time he checked his watch and as he reached sixty for the third time, he shouted in Spanish, *"DOWN!"* and dove to the ground and covered his head.

Angelo hesitated for half a second before he followed him, so he was about halfway down when the magazine exploded.

The guards were blown off their feet and Angelo ended up the other side of Ryan from where he started. Dirt, bits of timber, and stores rained down on them until they were buried.

A plume of fire from the crater that had once been the magazine illuminated the wreckage of the southern part of the compound. A pile of debris moved and was pushed aside as a body pushed itself upright followed by a second.

Ryan shook his head to try and clear the ringing in his ears and looked around. The berms hadn't done their job very well and had been blown out when the magazine went up. The palisade wall also disappeared and all they had to do was walk out.

He stepped forward and felt something soft under his foot. He looked down and saw he was standing on the hand of one of the soldiers. He bent down, pulled aside some wood, and saw that it was just an arm with no body attached, a musket laying right beside it. He picked the gun up and checked it over; it was at half cock and still primed.

He looked around one more time and spotted a cask with the top slightly askew, wandered over to it, and grinned at the sight of grey musket balls.

Back at the Gypsy encampment, Linette wiped the blood off her knife blade and smiled at the older woman who sat next to her on the step of her caravan.

"I am sorry I had to cut him," she apologised to the woman.

"It is no problem," the woman replied with a sigh, *"young men can only learn the hard way and my son is no different. I told him not to bother you as you were attached, but he wouldn't listen. Now I expect your man will want to challenge him."*

"I don't think so," Linette reassured her, *"he knows I can look after myself and will be satisfied that I took care of the situation."*

The woman looked relieved. She knew men and had recognised a seasoned fighter in Ryan and to be honest, she didn't give her son a rat's chance if he took him on.

They heard horses and a column of riders came into the camp, four of the horses were pulling travois loaded with objects covered in blankets. For a moment, she thought they might be bodies, but a quick headcount showed all the men were present and correct.

Two pulled aside and walked their horses towards her. She almost didn't recognise Ryan as he had a bandage around his head and his clothes were torn and filthy.

"Hello man," she greeted him, hands on hips and head cocked to one side in question.

"Hello woman," he replied with a lop-sided grin and tossed her the musket he was carrying. She caught it, checked it, and saw it was French military issue.

"Successful then,"

"Yes, got everything we needed."

"Did you bring me a present?"

"Yes, me in one piece." He threw his leg over its neck and slid off his horse.

She stepped up and put her arms around his neck.

"Are you sure everything is working? You look like shit."

"There is only one way to find out," he grinned.

She laughed and kissed him on the nose.

"Not until you have a bath, you stink," she replied, wrinkled her nose, spun away with a swish of her hips, and walked back to their caravan.

Back in Lisbon, Marty was having a secret meeting with a man who was introduced as the leader of the resistance in the South of Portugal. He was obviously an educated man, as he spoke English, and probably a landowner. He had also read too many dramatic novels.

Dressed all in black with a basket hilted rapier at his side, O Dragão (The Dragon) had dark hair swept back into a ponytail, a neatly trimmed goatee beard and moustache. He would stick out like a sore thumb in any crowd as he had assumed a swagger when he walked and posed for effect when he stood still. Marty decided that he would humour him and see where it took him.

"I have fifty militia ready to throw out the French in the Vale de Pedra and contacts with other leaders who are waiting for the word to rise up," he boasted.

As far as Marty was aware, there weren't any French troops in that region to be thrown out, but his men could be used to harass and delay any French movements.

"That is excellent!" he praised, "how are your men armed?"

"That is one thing I came to discuss with General Wellesley," he replied and looked expectantly at Marty as if he expected to be taken to the general immediately.

"He delegates these matters to me," Marty replied, suspecting what would come next.

"Senhor, with all due respect, I will talk with the General not one of his clerks," O Dragão replied grandly.

Marty sat back and gave him a flat look.

"With all due respect, Senhor, you should be sure of who you are talking to before you insult them."

O Dragão suddenly looked unsure of himself,

"and you are?" he asked

"A captain in his Majesty's Navy and the man who may get you your guns," Marty replied and then continued conspiratorially, "we must keep our real identities secret, mustn't we, Senhor Laurenco."

The revelation that the man across the room from him knew his real name shocked and knocked some of the arrogance out of him. Francis told Marty that he would get a visit from O Dragão and given him the man's real name and background.

"Now, you say you have fifty men, so we need to get you fifty muskets with flints, cartridge and ball. The muskets will be French, so you can replenish your stock of balls and cartridge from any troops your men kill.

"Why not British guns?" O Dragão asked.

"Different calibre," Marty replied, "French ball are smaller. Do they all have swords?"

"Aah, no not all of them," he replied, still stunned.

"So, thirty swords would be enough?" Marty asked, making a note on a sheet of paper.

"Yes, that would be excellent."

"And how do you propose to get them to your valley?" Marty enquired.

O Dragão looked at him in confusion, he hadn't thought that far ahead.

Marty relented,

"We will bring the weapons to you up the river Tagus by boat. They will be with you in a month." They would, in fact, be part of a much larger shipment sourced from the secret stores they had captured, that would be distributed along the Tagus valley to different militia bands.

There was a knock on the door, and Francis stuck his head through. He already knew who Marty was with and grinned at him.

"General Wellesley's compliments old boy. Can you attend a meeting of the general staff at two this afternoon?"

Marty grinned back at him,

"Tell Arthur I will be there," he responded.

The fact that it was a request and the familiar use of the general's first name by a mere captain registered on O Dragão, and he quickly revised his attitude.

Chapter 5: A Poor Defence

Marty was asked to give a report on the security situation around Lisbon and on the efforts to prepare the country for when they broke out of Lisbon and took the war to the French.

"We have rounded up all known French agents and are interrogating them to discover if there are any we have missed," he reported.

"You can be sure you have them all?" General Beresford asked sceptically.

"There is always a chance that there are agents who are deeply undercover, who will stay inactive until they have an opportunity to pop up and do damage, but we are taking every precaution to minimise that chance," Marty replied honestly.

"What we can say is that we have eliminated the French controller and his network that was active. He has been interrogated on my ship and we will continue that until we believe we have gotten everything he can tell us out of him."

Since his capture, Paul Plagnol had been held in a cage in a British warship. It was dark and he hadn't been allowed to sleep for three days. All that time, no one talked to him. His food was barely enough to keep him alive and consisted of bread and water, which made him incredibly constipated. He wasn't allowed out to exercise and the cage was only six feet to a side.

He had been ready to be tortured, he was familiar with the methods used by the Department, but this was different and today it took a turn for the worst. A pair of burley men came into the cage, forced him into a kneeling position with his hands trapped between his thighs and calves, a hood placed over his head. Any attempt to move was met with a blow and growled order to stay still.

The men were silent. He knew they were there, but they said nothing. Suddenly, he was hauled to his feet, a man either side. He had been in pain as he knelt from the strain on his back and knees, now shafts of pain shot down his legs and back as he was forced to move.

He was dragged roughly out of the cage and down a corridor to another room where he was pushed onto a hard-wooden chair. The hood was ripped off and bright sunlight seared into his eyes. A man sat across the other side of a table from him silhouetted by the sun which shone through the windows of the cabin.

Marty put up with the heat of the sun on his back to achieve the effect he was after and looked at the man sat across from him who stank of his own filth. It would take days to air the smell out of his cabin.

"What is your name?" he asked quietly in French.

"Gregor de Quintas,"

"Liar. What is your real name?"

He didn't reply. The hood was pulled over his head, and he was dragged back to the cage and forced to kneel again.

He couldn't tell how long he was held like that without food or water, he was just aware of the pain. An indeterminate time later he was dragged back to the other cabin.

"What is your name?"

He answered again,

"Gregor de Quintas"

His tormentor didn't answer. The hood was pulled over his head and he was forced into the kneeling position again.

Sometime later, a voice said softly in his ear,

"What is your name?"

He found himself answering,

"Paul Plagnol,"

"Where do you live?"

"On the Arco de Graça," he replied and wondered why he had lost control of his mouth. He was lifted on to the chair, the hood removed, and a metal cup of water placed to his lips. He tried to lift his hands to hold it, but someone stopped him. He was fed like a baby.

"Where do you come from in France?"

The man behind the desk asking the questions kept them coming, sometimes spoken softly, other times shouted, and he kept answering. He was rewarded with sips of water until they asked him about his network and then it was back to the dark and the pain.

The next time he was questioned, two men threw questions at him sometimes so fast he didn't get a chance to answer one before another was fired in. He was exhausted, confused, disorientated, and he cracked.

It took Marty and Francis a week of questioning to get all they wanted out of him then he was handed over to the Army. Not a single drop of blood was spilled, nor overt force used. Paul Plagnol was a broken man as effectively as if they had pulled his fingernails or put him to the rack.

"Where is he now?" Arthur Wellesley asked.

"In the custody of the Army at St Georges castle," Marty replied.

"Can we put him on trial now?" General Beresford asked.

Marty nodded and the generals looked satisfied. They enjoyed a good hanging.

"The arming of the various militias is progressing. We are supplying boots, weapons, and ammunition. We are also sending marine 'advisors' in to give them some minimal training like we have in Spain."

"Are your instructors well received?" General Hill asked.

"In general, yes. We have had occasional resistance, but we make the supply of weapons conditional on the training, so it's accepted in almost all cases. We are encouraging them to attack the French supply lines, what they aren't stealing they are burning."

"What's happening in the North?" Wellesley asked.

"Ryan and Linette are up there and have made contact with the Roma gypsies and Spanish Guerrillas. They report that Soult doesn't seem to have any intention of moving his army South to directly support Masséna and is moving to invest the town of Olivenza in Spain. In fact, most of the troops he had in Santander are moving there now."

"You are sure they won't come down here?" Arthur asked.

"From what they have gleaned, it would seem that Soult once fancied himself as the next King of Portugal and that put him at odds with the old republican guard.

He wanted a power base at Porto to rule the country from, but you spoiled that by kicking him out last year."

"How on earth do your people get this information?" Beresford asked.

"Now, if he told you that, he would have to kill you," Arthur quipped straight faced. He was known for his severity which people took for a lack of a sense of humour. In fact, he had a very dry one, which was often used to bring people to heel.

Meanwhile, in the French encampment North of Sobral, Masséna raged. He had no information on the force he faced except what he could see along the line of fortifications in front of him. The golden rule for attacking a defensive position was to outnumber the defenders four to one, but he knew they at least matched him in numbers. On top of that, the fortifications were well designed to support each other, forcing any attack to pass through areas that were saturated with artillery fire.

Worse, he was running out of food. The damn militia bands were attacking his supply lines and only a trickle was getting through overland and the British Navy were effectively blockading the coast. If this kept up, he would have to retreat to the Spanish border as autumn was upon them and his men would freeze as well as starve come winter.

He made his decision; they would probe what he estimated was the weakest part of the line at Sobral de Monte Agraço.

Antton sat on a hill just outside of Sobral on a rug he found in the market in the village of Vermoas where he took a room. He had been on that hill every day for the last week. He was well supplied with a bottle of Dao wine and a basket with a picnic of bread, sausage, cheese fruit and paté. He could have been mistaken for an artist as he had a board with a sheet of paper pinned to it and was scratching away with a piece of charcoal.

Anyone who approached would soon find out that he didn't want to be disturbed as there was a Baker rifle leaning against the rock he was leaning on and a pair of pistols beside him on the rug.

He looked through a telescope, supported on a small tripod, at the valley to the North and watched the French marching up and down keeping their men drilled in their camp.

Good luck with that! he thought and grinned as he noted down another regiment, its numbers, and disposition. He had sketched the flags he saw carried by the troops or flying over their tents, counted the men, cannon and horses and come to the conclusion that there were around thirty-five thousand men in the force.

Given that the fortifications were held by a similar number of troops reinforced with cannon, he didn't give the French much of a chance of breaking through. Their only chance was if they were massively reinforced from Spain.

He was surprised when the VIII corps, a division he had identified as being commanded by General Junot and the largest in the French force, formed up and started moving in the direction of the British line. He grabbed his guns and ran to his horse.

Marty got news that the French were on the move when Antton's message arrived via the semaphore chain and decided to ride up to the first line to see what was going on first-hand. Sam and Troy went with him of course, and he took Sergeant Bright and five marines as an escort at Arthur's insistence. He had his Durs Egg carbine over his shoulder and was dressed in civilian clothes.

They pushed the horses to cover the twenty miles in good time, knowing the beasts would get a rest at the other end and there would be remounts available if they needed them.

They arrived in time to see the skirmishers of the 27th Foot, an Irish rifles regiment known for their love of a fight, engage the French Voltigeurs of Junot's VIII Corp. They soon discovered it was the entire Corps they faced and were forced into a fighting retreat back to the strong point. The French were only three hundred yards away advancing in columns.

Marty watched from the top of the wall and was impressed by the orderly way the Irishmen retreated, working in pairs one firing while the other moved.

He spotted a French soldier flanking one pair who were engaging three others as they backed up. The Frenchman was working himself into a positioning where he could pick the British men off and had just gotten into range of Marty's carbine at about two hundred yards.

Marty checked his priming, and wrapping the shoulder strap around his left forearm, brought the gun to his shoulder. He took a deep breath and focused in on the Frenchman, he allowed a touch of left for the wind and aimed just over his head to allow for the range. He let his breath out slowly and when it was out, he squeezed the trigger.

The bullet took the man just behind the ear, throwing him to the side. He must have cried out as one of the skirmisher's turned his head and saw him fall. The threat removed, the British pair made it back to the line and safety.

Marty was surprised when a short while later, a broad Irish accented voice said from behind him,

"Excuse me, sor, but it was you who was after takin' out that French feller, was it not?"

Marty turned and recognised the skirmisher and his mate.

"I had the pleasure of lending you a hand, yes."

"Well we, me and Mick here, wants t' t'ank ya, and tell ya dat was a foin shot." He held out his hand sheepishly, which Marty took and almost instantly regretted it as the man had a grip like a vice.

"If der be anyt'ing we can do fer you, just ask for Pat Mulligan of the 27th Inniskilling," he grinned gap-toothed, touched his cap, and walked off.

 Sam was grinning as Marty shook his hand to get the blood back into his fingers, their attention returned to the front when Troy suddenly stood on his back legs, front feet on the parapet, and barked. Marty looked and saw the French were charging en mass to storm the wall. Some were carrying ladders all were carrying guns and were angry.

The cannon on the wall and the guns of their supporting redoubt, fired and cut swathes through the advancing hoard, but there were too many of them. They kept on coming and were at the wall before the guns fired again. It was their sheer weight of numbers that pushed the British and Portuguese out of the strong point, forcing them to make a fighting retreat.

If the French had followed up with an immediate attack out from the captured fortification, they would have probably been able to roll up the line. However, they stopped to 'consolidate' their position which gave Marty and the officers of the 27th time to organise a counterattack.

Marty found himself, Sam, and his marines leading a platoon of skirmishers whose lieutenant had been wounded. They would work their way undercover of the rocky terrain to a point where they could lay down suppressing fire. This was a concept worked out by Arthur Wellesley who had formed the skirmishers into independent units.

They made their way forward making use of the available cover. Marty led them down a gulley, keeping their heads down as the French were shooting at anything that moved. At the end, they had to move even closer to the redoubt. This involved a lot of scuttling, a fair amount of crawling, and a bit of dashing but they got there and were settling into position to be able to rake the top of the wall when he heard a familiar voice,

"Well how about that, Mick, we're here wid de man again."

He smiled as he brought his carbine to his shoulder and focused on a French sentry on the wall.

"Marines prepare to fire with me. Second rank fire a count of twenty later. Volley, fire for two more rounds each, then fire at will. Is that clear?" he said over his shoulder to the men. "Aye, aye, sir," responded Bright and, "Yes sor!" came the familiar voice of Pat.

A drum sounded, beating out the advance, the signal for the start of the counterattack, and he pulled the trigger. The man fell, and he cranked the lever to raise the breach to reload. His marines fired as he did, each had picked a target and took his time. The skirmishers fired twenty seconds later and were just as careful to select their targets, a sense of calm purpose pervaded.

Marty's breach loader let him keep up a rate of fire that no other man could match with their Baker rifles, and he fired with every volley.

"Would you look at that, Mick!" came Pat's familiar voice as he fired for the third time as his marines fired their second. "The man's a platoon all on his own!"

He couldn't help but smile as the second rank fired another volley. They kept up a constant hail of bullets at the top of the wall, keeping the French from mounting more than a token resistance as the British main force advanced.

He wasn't about to be left out of the fight, though, and as soon as the advancing men passed his position, Marty gave the order to charge. Skirmishers are chosen to be nimbler and more mobile than regular troops and they soon overtook the main force and were up and over the low rear wall of the fort and laying into the French at the fore of the attack.

Troy worked with Marty just as if they were boarding a ship. He would take on the nearest threat, usually the man in front of his boss, dragging him to the ground for Marty to finish off. Sam had Marty's back and took out anyone who got within reach of his spear. The marines formed up either side of the three of them and did sterling work with their bayonets. It was cut and thrust, kill and move on, business as usual.

The fortification was back in British hands and General Lawry Cole arrived to survey the aftermath. He approached Marty, who was sitting on a wall cleaning his gun.

"Captain Stockley?" he asked, his Irish origins evident despite his educated accent.

Marty put aside his gun and stood.

"Yes, that's me," he replied.

The general introduced himself, held out his hand, and they shook,

"General Wellesley sent me a message that you were heading up here. Didn't expect for a minute you would get stuck in, but I thank you and your men for helping out."

He paused and looked around at the skirmisher platoon that had attached itself to Marty and were mixing with his marines.

"Never had the honour of fighting alongside the Navy before. Thought you men were all about broadsides and the like."

Marty gave a low laugh,

"To be honest, this wasn't much different to boarding a ship, a lot of shouting, screaming, slashing, and dying."

"That just about sums up every battle I've been in," the general said and looked at Sam, who was cleaning blood off of Troy's coat by sponging him off with a bucket of water.

"Your dog?"

"Yes, he likes a fight," Marty replied, looking fondly at the two of them, "Sam is my Cox and looks after both of us."

The general looked around the men again and spotted Mick and Pat,

"Are you sober, Mulligan?"

Pat leapt to his feet and stood rigidly to attention,

"Yes, sor! As sober as a judge, sor!"

"Good, then you can escort these men back to the second line sergeant."

Pat's face broke into a grin and he started forming up the skirmishers into two ranks.

"Broke him last month for being drunk, promote him back to sergeant today and will probably break him again in a week's time, but he is one hell of a fighter," the general confided sotto voice then straightened and said,

"Thank you again. Will you join me for dinner? You can bring your dog."

Marty guessed there was more he wanted to discuss and agreed to join him that evening. In the meantime, he made sure he had Antton's report in his pocket.

Sir Galbraith Lawry Cole had a large villa in Santo Quintino and had a complete staff to look after him. When Marty arrived, he was greeted by a uniformed steward and shown into the library where he was greeted by the General and his dog. For a second he thought Troy would start a fight then realised it was a Mastif cross bitch who had other things on her mind than fighting.

"She will be in season in a few days," Lawry Cole informed him as they took glasses of whiskey from a servant, "I had it mind that she would make a good cross with your dog."

Troy and his new girlfriend were flirting, him showing off how big he was, standing stiff legged and head high, her bouncing around and inviting him to chase her.

Marty smiled.

"You are looking for a fighting cross?"

"That was the idea. Her mass and his agility will make a fearsome combination."

"I'm sure Troy will be more than happy to oblige, General," Marty agreed.

"Call me Galbraith. I understand you are a Baron and a Knight of the Bath?"

"Yes, Baron Candor, but please call me Martin."

"Excellent, now let's get the business over before we eat. I understand you have had someone checking on the French strength?" Galbraith asked.

"Yes, one of my men has been able to carry out a survey. The French general is running out of options and I think today's effort was probably his last roll of the dice," Marty said and handed over the copy of the report.

"Won't Soult reinforce him?"

"I have agents in the North as well and they report that Soult is moving on Olivenza and has no intention of helping Masséna kick, what he believes is, a beaten force out of Lisbon," Marty informed him as he savoured the smoky taste of the amber fluid in his glass. "Where does this come from? I don't recognise the taste and it is delightful."

"It's from near my home in Enniskillen, an Irish Whiskey. I can let you have a couple of bottles if you wish. Consider it payment for the use of your dog."

"My thanks, you are too generous," Marty responded, delighted to take some with him.

They discussed the possible lines of retreat of the French Army and the possibility of 'hurrying them along', Marty told Galbraith about their activities with the Portuguese militias and added,

"I have the intention to take some of my marines into the countryside and set up a harassing action as Masséna retreats."

Galbraith asked how they would operate and offered,

"If I may, I would like to offer some of my skirmishers. I think they would work well with your men and are well used to working in the wild as it were."

Chapter 6: Harassment

Two weeks later after they had repelled another probe by the French, Antton, who was still out watching the French camp, sent a message via a farm boy that the French were getting ready to move out. Marty immediately sent a message to Galbraith and before the end of the day a mixed platoon of Irish Riflemen and Portuguese Caçadores led by Sergeant Patrick Mulligan and Corporal (newly promoted) Michael O'Malley marched into his camp.

With his marines he now had a force of forty men plus him, Sam, Chin, Antton, and two local militia guides.

"Time to go play hell with the French," he told Troy, who gave him a big grin and a lick on the nose.

He had the men pack rations for several days and organised resupply from the river. The weather was unusually cold for Portugal and he had everyone issued with extra heavy coats.

They set out in a loose formation with scouts out ahead and to the sides. A guard's sergeant major was heard comment, "Look like a complete rabble."

He was probably right but their long dark coats over their green and grey uniforms made them hard to spot as they moved out into the countryside. Antton arrived and informed them the French were heading West towards the river, which made sense as the terrain was so rough that there were limited options.

Troy loped ahead, putting himself on point alongside the militia guides. Marty watched him carefully as the slightest threat would illicit a reaction ranging from stopping and focusing on it with a front leg raised to bounding forward on the attack. He was mated with Galbraith's bitch the day before and now considered himself the cock of the walk and had a decided swagger to his gait.

They moved fast, much faster than the French, who were encumbered with their baggage train and set up an ambush where the road from Corregido turned North and had to pass through a gorge before it entered the village of Galp.

It was a simple crossfire setup with men on both ridges firing down into the gorge. Marty brought grenades and distributed them amongst the men, they would be as good as artillery in the confined space below them.

The scouts came back and announced that the French column was about a mile away and progressing at a walk. They waited, Marty wanted the column well into the gorge and to attack the centre. That way, the troops would not be able to just turn and run as they would be hemmed in on both sides by their own men.

The sound of a drum echoed up the walls of the gorge and the advance elements of the French wandered into view. They were just advanced scouts, so they left them alone and stayed undercover. Marty looked across at the other ridge and spotted Sergeant Mulligan, who was looking straight back at him, waiting for the signal.

A couple of minutes after the scouts came the front ranks of Infantry. The men looked starved and were dressed in rags, which were totally inadequate for the winter weather.

Marty let the first two divisions pass, then came a column of cavalry. *Oh, that's perfect,* thought Marty and raised his hat into the air. The lead riders passed below him. He counted ten and waved his hat from side to side. There was a fizz from beside him as Matai lit the fuse of a grenade and heard him count to three before tossing it over the side. He saw the smoke trails from another twenty loop out from the rocks and fall gracefully onto the ranks of horsemen.

Horses screamed and men cried out as the grenades exploded, sending out wicked shards of shrapnel in all directions. Marty fired and reloaded his carbine as fast as he had ever done and his men followed his example, albeit at less than a quarter the speed.

In the gorge, it was as if hell had opened up and swallowed them. The explosions had panicked the horses and those that could, bolted, causing absolute chaos in the ranks of infantry in front and behind them. Bullets were raining down on them and those that didn't hit flesh of some kind ricocheted of the rocks and whined away until they hit something soft.

"Capitan, the French are making their way up the sides of the gorge at the end," reported one of their Portuguese guides some five minutes after the ambush had started.

"Time to go then," Marty grinned. He stood and waved his hat at Mulligan, who noticed it when Mick pointed to Marty from beside him. He gave a thumbs up, shouted some orders, and the men on that side slid away into the rocks.

Marty ordered the retreat, and his men left their positions. Keeping low, they moved back into the hills.

They had the odd skirmish with outlying French troops but got away relatively unscathed apart from one of the Irish troops who slipped and got his leg broken when it dropped into a crack in the rocks. The whole force met up in the foothills just outside of the village of Azambuja on the edge of the Tagus' floodplain.

"He will need to be evacuated back to the lines and your surgeon," Marty told Mulligan, "that's a complicated break of the lower leg and the bone is sticking up, pushing out his calf."

"Well, god help him, then. He will lose his leg," Mulligan stated with a frown, "the bloody surgeon only knows how to cut them off."

"In that case, we will get him back to my ship and my physician can deal with him," Marty decided, "get him on a litter and we will get him down to the river and rendezvous with the supply boat."

It was two miles across open country, and they moved as fast as they could while keeping the injured man comfortable. The only pain killer they had was a half pint bottle of rum that one of the marines sheepishly supplied, earning a raised eyebrow from Marty as he forbade alcohol on shore actions.

"To keep the cold out," was the mumbled excuse.

Sergeant Bright was seen to lean towards the contributor and say something which made his face blanche. Marty decided to leave it to him to deal with it.

The cutter and barge were already heading to the rendezvous as scheduled.   Along with a squad of marines, they were fitted with boat guns in the bows for defence, the rest of the free space being taken up with provisions. They were commanded by Stanley Hart and Shelby, the ship's surgeon, who had invited himself along as,

"The sooner I can start treating any wounded the better chance they have," he stated emphatically when Wolfgang Ackermann asked him why. If he was the slightest bit honest with himself, he would have admitted he was bored with just sitting on the Formidiable in harbour while Martin was away playing spy chief. Lisbon was a nice enough town except there just wasn't anything interesting to do!

Stanley had masts rigged and got them under sail for the journey upriver, so they made good time to the stretch of river between Carregado and Muge that Marty had designated as their patrol area. All they had to do now was sail up and down until they saw Marty's party on the shore.

Shelby was on the verge of regretting his impetuous decision to come along as it was absolutely freezing on the river and it didn't seem to make any difference how many layers of clothing he put on, he just didn't get any warmer. He was longing for a warm fire or a stove, but they didn't go ashore even at night, just anchored in mid-stream and slept in the boat.

He was roused out of his reverie by a call from the bowman,

"Shore party on the North bank! Looks like they have someone on a litter."

Stanley pushed the tiller over, and they closed in on the shoreline, which as the tide was out, had a wide band of mud between the water and the bank.

"Take the sail in, out oars," he commanded.

"Captain is indicating he wants us to head upstream for a bit," the bowman reported.

Maybe a better landing spot, Stanley thought to himself. Sure enough, about three-hundred yards upstream, the riverbank was on the outside of a curve and had been cut away to make it easy to dock against.

A pair of marines were ready to grab the bow ropes of the boats, so they were soon secure, and Marty was shaking Stanley's hand in greeting.

"Good to see you, Mr. Hart," Marty smiled.

"A pleasure, sir," Stanley replied politely then barked to the crew of the cutter, "pay attention to the surgeon there! It will take a week to dry him out if he falls in!"

"Mr. Shelby is here?" Marty exclaimed in surprise, "well we have business for him. Where is he?"

"I am right here!" what looked like a mobile pile of clothes muttered.

"Good grief! A talking laundry basket," Marty laughed.

"You have no idea how cold it is just sitting in the middle of that damn boat," the pile replied as it started shedding layers.

"Now where is the casualty? Gun shot? Sword slash?" he asked as he emerged from his cocoon.

"Broken leg, nasty complicated fracture, bone sticking through the calf."

"Treatment?"

Just then a rich tenor started to sing in Gaelic,

Lá na mara
Lá na mara nó rabharta
Guth na dtonnta a leanadh
Guth na dtonnta a leanfad ó

Lá na mara nó lom trá
Lá na mara nó rabharta
Lá an ghainimh, lom trá
Lá an ghainimh

"Rum?"

Marty nodded.

"Well let's take a look."

On their way to the patient, Marty ordered pickets to be posted two hundred yards out.

Rifleman Shamus O'Flanigan was pleasantly pissed and continued singing right up to Marty and Shelby's arrival. As he saw them, he broke off and said,

"To be sure, it be a pleasure to see ya, Captain! And who is this foyn fella you have wid ya? I could do wid a drop more of dis exshellent rum ya know."

Shelby examined his leg and grimaced,

"Can I barrow your knife, Martin?"

Marty slid his fighting knife out of its sheath and handed it over. O'Flanigan saw it, and the colour drained from his face as Shelby bent over his leg. He fainted as Shelby slit his trouser leg down the seam.

"I want you to bring up three of the chests in the barge and stack them on a flat piece of ground side by side to make a table and then place our friend on top of it. Oh, and please light a fire."

Marty didn't want too much smoke, so he had a bucket from one of the boats filled with dry sand from the riverside then poured lamp oil on to it. He piled some primer powder in the middle and ignited it with the flint from one of his pistols. There was a small puff of smoke as the powder fired then the oil burned relatively cleanly.

"That's a new trick," Shelby commented as he opened his medicine chest after warming his hands.

"A little trick I learnt in India. Saw a man selling food do it to cook his pakora," Martin grinned in reply.

Shelby put some raw alcohol on a clean cloth and washed down the leg, O'Flanigan twitched.

"I want two men to hold him at his shoulders and another across the top of his legs," he said to Martin.

"Pat, Mick, and Stevenson," Marty pointed to the two Irishmen and one of the marines.

Shelby organised the volunteers so that his patient was immobilised.

"The break itself is nice and clean, so I am going to open it up so I can manipulate the bones into line. Martin, once I have done that, I want you to hold his foot still, so they do not move while I stitch his leg back together and splint it.

If we are lucky and we can keep it in place, it will heal, and he will keep his leg."

The soldiers that were not on picket duty stood in a circle to watch; they had never seen anything like this before.

Shelby used a scalpel to open the leg and a retractor to hold it open. He then gently pulled on the foot and worked the bones back into line.

"Take the foot please, Martin,"

Once he was happy Marty had the foot secured, he checked the alignment of the bones and that the ends were together. He dusted the wound with sulphur, stitched the muscles and finally the skin together before splinting the leg with four pieces of wood and wrapping it with bandage to immobilise it completely.

During the entire exercise, not a sound was heard, or word spoken from the spectators, and after he finished, any comments were made in hushed and awed voices. The marines boasting of their man's prowess and miraculous abilities.

Patient and doctor were returned to the barge to be sailed down to the Formidiable and the stores were distributed to the men. Marty wanted them to travel fast, so he restricted them to just three days rations and fresh ammunition. The French had a day's head start on them and they needed to catch up.

Chapter 7: A Fighting Repost

Masséna was furious that his troops had so easily walked into an ambush. The fact that they were cold and hungry was no excuse in his mind, the scouts had simply not done their job. He wondered at the unconventional manner it had been carried out. Grenades were not commonly used by the army anymore as they went out of fashion at the end of the last century.

Masséna had been told by the political officer on his staff that the intelligence people suspected that the British may have brought in a notorious naval officer who had been a thorn in the Empire's side for a number of years now. His reputation was of a cunning fighter and fearless opportunist who was not above assassination, theft, and spying to achieve his ends.

He wondered; was this man behind the ambush? The Navy still used grenades for clearing ships after boarding, so it could be.

He doubled his flankers and forward scouts, resulting in their rate of progress slowing to less than ten miles a day as every possible ambush site was thoroughly checked before they advanced through it.

He selected a contingent of the 4th Hussars as a rapid counterattack unit who were notorious for their ruthlessness. They were armed with carbines and sabres, rode fast, light horses and would attempt to flank any ambush, drive the ambushers away and pursue them if possible. If they got as much as a sniff of the British, they would annihilate them.

In order to trap the ambushers, he ordered his Voltigeurs not to engage but to inform the Hussars then try and encircle the enemy.

Marty and his men had worked their way ahead of the French again and were making the most of the mountainous terrain to stay hidden. It was unfortunate that a rare shaft of sunlight broke through the persistent cloud and reflected off the bayonet of one of the marines, who for some reason known only to himself, had it fitted to his rifle. The resultant random flash was noticed by one of the French scouts, who with his comrade, worked their way to some high ground where they could watch the British making their way into position.

One scout stayed to observe the enemy while the other left to tell their commander what they had found. He, in turn, sent a message to the Hussars, then set about deploying his troops to encircle the British force to the North and East. The hunters were becoming the hunted.

A company of Hussars is around one hundred men, which meant the British would be outnumbered by four to one. Major Jannot was confident that his men would ride right over them, and was looking forward to an opportunity to exercise his sabre.

Fortunately for Marty and his men, the French weren't anywhere near as good at concealment as they were and the Voltigeurs were spotted as they tried to move into position.

Knowing the game was up, Marty immediately ordered the men to retreat East, towards a small wood and the river which was three and a half miles away.

They stayed together in a loose group, retreating in an orderly fashion with scouts ahead and a rear guard behind.

A pair of Voltigeurs were caught at the edge of the trees and dispatched by the lead marines in a brutal hand to hand fight. Marty's policy of training all his men in close combat paid dividends as the French, used to fighting with musket and bayonet, were unprepared for a knife fight.

They approached the trees and became aware of the thunder of galloping horses. The rear guard appeared, running for all they were worth and shouting that the entire French cavalry were coming.

They needed to get into the trees. Marty yelled at his men to move and get into cover. They were lucky that the edge of the woods was well defined by tree felling and there was a band of stumps about twenty yards wide at its edge providing a natural obstacle to horses.

He set up a rank of riflemen just inside the tree line to send a volley into the advancing cavalry and another ten yards back into the trees to cover their retreat. Grenades were quickly prepared; they came with a long fifteen second fuse, which was normally cut to whatever length the thrower desired. Marty ordered them left as they were. The second rank were to light them and leave them amongst the trees before they retreated.

The Hussars caught sight of their prey running like hell towards the trees. They were two hundred meters away and Major Jannot immediately ordered the charge. At one hundred meters, the tree line blossomed puffs of smoke and men either side of him were plucked from their saddles by musket balls.

They continued the charge, the loss of ten or fifteen men meant nothing. A horse screamed as its leg broke against a hidden tree stump. The rider pitched over its head and under the hooves of the following horses. Others suffered the same fate, which slowed the advance.

There was a second volley from back in the trees and more men fell, but now they were at the edge of the woods and forced to slow to avoid getting swept out of their saddles by branches.

Once inside the trees, Jannot smelt burning gunpowder and at first thought it was the residual smoke from the muskets, then he heard a hissing noise. His eyes widened as he realised what it was just as the first of the grenades exploded send hot metal shards hissing through the air.

Horses reared and screamed as they were hit and men fought to stay mounted.

"Sound the retreat," he ordered his bugler, "this is no place for us to fight,"

"The British are in the woods and that will be their graveyard," he told his officers and the commander of the Voltageurs.

"I will set a cordon of half of my men along the North and South sides of the woods then your Voltigeurs will drive the British through to the river plain. The other half of my men will be waiting to grind them into dogmeat."

Marty climbed down from the large beech tree he was perched in to see what the French were doing; he was not going to run headlong into the unknown if he could help it. He also got reports from his scouts. It was just after midday.

"The French are going to try and drive us onto the open land by the river where we can be trampled by their cavalry. They are sealing off the North and South sides of the woods with Hussars and the Voltegeurs are massing along the West end to act as beaters."

He looked around at the gathered men, they didn't look afraid and just waited for the brilliant plan he was bound to come up with.

No pressure, just think, he told himself.

"Well, we aren't going to do what the French want. We will go back the way we came, where there is cover and break up into six-man teams to make our way back to the rendezvous. Now this is what I want you to do…"

A bugle blew a signal and the Voltegeurs, in their light blue jackets and black hats, advanced into the trees. They couldn't really feel it but there was a slight breeze blowing towards them from the East. Their non-commissioned officers shouted at them to stay in a line and they advanced with their muskets advanced, bayonets fitted, feet crunching on the dry leaf litter under the trees.

Every five paces, they would let out a yell, "Vive Napoleon!" partly as a war cry and also to let the Hussars know where they were. Suddenly, wisps of smoke drifted towards them. Men exchanged questioning looks but the NCOs pushed them on.

The smoke got thicker and soon men started to cough and their eyes water. A man cried out that he could see fire but was suddenly quiet. Another called out to him by name, there was a scream, and he too was silenced.

The smoke was so thick that the Voltegeurs could barely see each other and now flames could be seen advancing towards them. Several fell as they were hit by musket balls, but there were no shots! They were starting to panic; they weren't front line infantry, so they were not used to standing in line and they couldn't fight what they couldn't see. One found himself facing what looked to him like a wolf. He fired his musket, missing his target by a mile, then turned tail and ran for his life. That triggered a collapse in discipline and more men broke, running back the way they had come, triggering a general rout.

Under cover of the smoke, Marty's men made their way to the Western edge of the woods and followed the retreating Voltegeurs out through the stump field. From there, it was a flat run to the rocky hillside.

Marty found himself with Sam and Troy, a Portuguese guide, and three marines. Following his own orders, they melted into the rocky slope and the gathering gloom as the sun dropped behind the hills.

He didn't know if they had lost any men and that played on his mind. He wouldn't find out what the bill was until they got back together and to do that, they needed to get back to the place where they had met the boats.

They headed deeply into the hills and made a cold camp for the night. Moving again as soon as it was light enough, they headed South towards the village of Cartaxo. Troy was out ahead as usual and as they rounded a rock outcrop Marty saw him stood, back flat, head down, hackles up, right leg raised, intent on something ahead.

Marty signalled for the others to stop then made his way silently up to the side of the big dog and looked across the hillside. A line of Hussars was stretched out ahead of them and making their way slowly towards them. There was no way forward.

"We are blocked that way. We will have to go back and try and work our way around them," Marty told his men when he and Troy re-joined them.

"Senhor, there is a trail that runs the other side of this hill, it is very narrow and dangerous, and they will not be able to follow on their horses," the Portuguese guide told him.

"That's a sheer rock face!" one of the marines exclaimed as he looked down.

"Sim, but there is a trail," the guide responded.

Marty shrugged. They didn't have many options.

"Lead on!"

The path, when they got to it, started out at as a game trail and rapidly turned into a ledge that was no more than eighteen inches wide at best and only nine in places. They moved down it, hugging the rockface and trying not to look down. They had gone a couple of hundred yards when there was a shot from above and a ball whined off the rock-face near to them. They were spotted.

"Keep moving!" Marty ordered and when they came to a broad section, he let the rest of the men pass him, so he was bringing up the rear. He had Sam take Troy, he didn't need him getting in the way of what he needed to do.

Marty got himself into a position where he could wait and watch the back trail to see if the Hussars would try and follow them on foot.

A scuff of boot on rock alerted him that someone was coming. He cocked the right barrel of his double-barrelled Manton pistol and watched the track where it curved around an outcrop intently.

A shoulder appeared followed by the rest of the richly uniformed Hussar. He had his back to the wall and looked terrified as he worked his way around the outcrop on the narrow ledge his eyes fixed on the path just ahead of his foot.

Marty waited. The soldier was followed closely by a second man and once they were in line with him, he sighted and pulled the trigger. The ball took the Hussar in the neck, passing clean through and hitting the second man in the face. Both fell forward into the gorge without a sound. Another soldier glanced around the corner but pulled his head back before Marty could fire.

Marty knew he needed to catch up with his men, so he pulled a grenade out of his shoulder bag, quickly cut the fuse to around ten seconds, and lit it from the lock of his spent barrel. He lodged the grenade into a fissure in the rock at around waist height and retreated down the track.

Marty didn't care whether the grenade killed anyone or not. The fact that it was there would slow up the pursuit and buy them time. It went off with a satisfying bang and must have scared the hell out of the French because he made it around the safety of the next curve without getting shot at.

The trail stayed narrow for almost a thousand yards before opening out into a series of rock steps then a shale slope that ended by a stream at the bottom of the gorge. They looked back and couldn't see any sign of pursuit. It appeared that the French had given up.

Marty sighed in relief and stepped over to the stream to get a drink of the fresh mountain water. He went to one knee and bent to cup some in his hand when there was a tug on his coat and a splash in the water ahead of him followed by the sound of a shot.

He spun and saw a pair of Hussars knelt at the top of the steps and dived to the side as he saw a puff of smoke come from the second one's carbine.

His marines responded immediately, and their rifles barked almost in unison spinning one the Hussars around as he took a bullet in the shoulder. The other ducked back behind a rock.

They had to be dealt with, so he beckoned to Sam and they started back up the slope while the marines kept up a steady suppressing fire.

Troy moved ahead, his body low to the ground, and soon left the two men behind. He knew where the enemy was and slipped from cover to cover as he made his way closer. The wind shifted and he smelt the sharp iron smell of blood, his lip curled up in a silent snarl baring his inch-long canines.

He slunk forward, totally focused on the rocks ahead as a bullet from below ricocheted away. He could now smell the sweaty odour of the men hidden behind them that was laced with garlic and essence of horse. He jumped up on top of the rock in front of him and the firing from below stopped. One man was lying slumped, wounded, the other was ramming a new charge home in his carbine when he looked up straight into Troy's eyes. He swore and tried to swing the gun around and up, but he was far too slow, and Troy sprang forward, going for his face, jaws agape.

Marty and Sam saw Troy leap from the rock and heard a scream as he attacked the Frenchman. A Carbine fired and a ramrod flew through the air, bouncing off the rock face. They hurried to a background of snarling and screaming. By the time they climbed up and could see what was going on, it was pretty much over.

Troy had savaged the Frenchman, biting a huge chunk out of his face and ripping his arms to shreds. Marty called him off and without hesitation, shot the man in the head. It was the kindest thing he could do. There was a gurgle from behind him and he didn't need to look to know that Sam had finished off the second one. They left them there after smashing their carbines, the crows would eat well today.

They made it to the rendezvous and found two of the other parties already there. They had managed to avoid the French and had been there for a day already. There were three groups still out and all he could do was wait for them.

The next party arrived carrying one of their men, a couple of others were sporting bandages. They were a man short. They had run into a squad of Voltigeurs and fought their way through, killing and wounding many, and forcing them to retreat. The remnants of the squad had dogged their trail for a day before they had lost them by travelling overnight.

All his ship's boats turned up with fresh supplies and reinforcements under the command of Paul la Pierre, his Captain of Marines. Shelby was there too, having left the wounded man in the care of his loblolly boys on the Formidiable. He went straight to work on the wounded.

"You have a message from General Wellesley," Shelby told him and handed over a sealed envelope.

Marty opened it and read that he was requested to return to Lisbon and attend a meeting with the general staff. He wondered what was afoot. Lisbon was now secure, and Arthur could wait for his reinforcements to arrive from England.

Well, he wasn't leaving without his men, so Arthur would just have to wait for a day or so. That afternoon, another party led by Mulligan arrived muddy, tired, but unharmed. They had hidden in ditches and travelled only at night to avoid the French hunters.

The last group led by Sergeant Bright were being hounded by a larger force of Voltigeurs and were firing and retreating in two groups of three. This was enough to hold off the foot troops, but it was only a matter of time before a troop of Hussars would join in an then it would be all over.

They were about half a mile from the rendezvous when the Hussars appeared, almost out of ammunition and now facing at least twenty horsemen as well as a dozen Voltigeurs the odds were not good.   Running wouldn't help as they were in the middle of a field of waist high grass.

"Form up, lads," he ordered and got his men into line, thinking that at least they could take a half dozen of the scarlet uniformed bastards with them.

They knelt to make themselves smaller targets and to make aiming their rifles easier. If they got a volley off early enough, they might get a second off before they were overwhelmed. It was, all in all, a forlorn hope if ever he saw one.

The Hussars moved forward and they could see the glint of their sabres as they moved out into a line. They started forward at a walk, which moved into a trot, then a canter, and finally a gallop as they charged, yelling war cries.

"Ready lads," he said, gauging the distance, "steady, steady, FIRE!"

Their six guns barked as one and a couple of the red uniformed horsemen were plucked from their saddles.

"Reload," he ordered unnecessarily as all the men were reloading as fast as they could.

Six guns came up when the French were less than one hundred yards away and the ground shook with the beat of their hooves.

"FIRE."

There was the ripping sound of forty guns firing at once and the chuff of at least two swivel guns. He looked in amazement as the cavalry charge dissolved as men and horses tumbled to the ground. He looked around to see a line of marines and riflemen arrayed just behind and to either side of his men. A grinning Paul la Pierre stood, walked over to him, and held out his hand.

"Took your time, Sergeant," he teased as he helped him stand.

They got all the men into the boats and set off for Lisbon. Marty reflected on the earlier action. He had placed lookouts out in an arc a half mile from the rendezvous and they reported the approach of Sergeant Bright when they were still a mile away.

Paul had immediately seen the opportunity to ambush the French and had the men crawl forward in the long grass to a position that turned out to be just ten yards behind the good sergeant's men when they stopped to make a stand. He had swivels loaded with canister brought along with pole stands and positioned them at either end of his line.

Paul let the French get to seventy-five yards of the group when he ordered his men to the kneel and at fifty yards, as Bright shouted fire, the volley was devastating.

It was all quite satisfying really, Marty reflected. The Hussars were all but annihilated in the brief hand to hand that followed and the Voltigeurs had run for their lives. He only lost a couple of men in the whole action from beginning to end and he caused the French significant discomfort and disruption.

Chapter 8: Fresh Orders

Back in Lisbon, he took the time to bathe and get into uniform on the Formidiable before he accompanied the Irish Riflemen, who had been entertained by his men, back to shore. The Portuguese left as soon as they reached the port.

"If I may, sor?" Sergeant Mulligan asked once they were safely on the dock and his men were formed up in ranks.

"What is it, Sergeant?"

"Me an' the lads would like to say how we is proud to have served wid you and to t'ank yous for taking care of dem that was wounded and dat if ever you be in need of any good fighting oyrishmen den we are your boys," he said in a rush like he had to get it all out before he forgot any of it.

Marty smiled, shook his hand, and taking in all the men replied,

"It has been a pleasure fighting with you men at my side and I am sure we will meet again. I will make sure that the general hears about your valour."

"Three cheers for the captain!" Mulligan cried, and his men responded with enthusiasm, much to Marty's enjoyment and slight embarrassment.

A carriage took Marty to Arthur's headquarters, and he was announced by a lieutenant that couldn't be more than twenty years old and fresh out of Horseguards. By his accent, which was decidedly plummy, he came from an aristocratic family which had probably bought his commission.

"Martin welcome back!" Arthur smiled, "you have met Lord Ashley-Cooper, I see."

Marty looked around and realised he was referring to the lieutenant and raised his eyebrows questioningly to the young man.

"Sebastian Ashley-Cooper, fourth son of the Earl of Shaftesbury," he introduced himself with a bow and lopsided self-deprecating smile.

"The Lieutenant is here to get him away from the temptations of the fleshpots of London," Arthur added with a stern look at the young rake. "His father procured his commission after a rather embarrassing duel. Over the honour of a whore, wasn't it?"

"I prefer to think of her as a courtesan, but yes, you are essentially correct, sir," Sebastian replied without a hint of regret.

"Did you win?" Marty asked, amused in spite of himself.

"He crippled his opponent, who just happened to be the nephew of the Earl of Pembroke," Arthur barked in a tone that said the subject was closed.

"You missed the meeting of the General Staff yesterday," Arthur said, looking down his nose at the two of them.

"Sorry, but we were extracting ourselves from the welcoming arms of the 4th Hussars at the time," Marty replied and handed over his written report, which Arthur put to one side.

"Well, be that as it may, we have a new job for you," he was unusually brusque, and Marty guessed it was for the benefit of the lieutenant rather than directed at him.

Arthur paused and looked at the large map of the peninsula pinned to his wall.

"We have a foothold here but what we don't need is their Army currently besieging Cadiz to reinforce Masséna." He stood to look at the map more carefully.

"Soult, as you have already reported, is showing no sign that he would be interested in helping Masséna as he has his own agenda in the North, but here at Cadiz, Marshal Victor isn't achieving much as we can resupply the city from the sea. The French have already occupied Grenada, so Cadiz is all that is holding him there."

Marty nodded as he understood Arthur's concern.

"What we need is for the Spanish guerrillas to pin down Victor there until we can send a force to raise the siege and drive him and his men off for good."

"Then you want me to go there with my men and stir the Spanish into action,"

"Yes, and while you are there make sure that the French Navy do not blockade the port."

Marty knew enough and rose to leave.

"Oh, and one more thing," Arthur said over his shoulder, "take young Ashley-Cooper with you. He needs seasoning."

Marty looked steadily at Arthur, who just looked back in his haughty way.

"Get your gear, Lieutenant, you are going on a short voyage," he said to the surprised youth. The lieutenant did not see Arthur and Marty share a smile behind his back as he hurried to leave.

Lord Ashley-Cooper had an extensive set of baggage at his rented rooms, which Marty took one look at and told him to select one trunk, fill it with essentials, and put the rest into storage. He would only need one uniform and civilian clothes.

"What about personal stores, sir?" the bemused young man asked.

"You can bring two cases of wine and any preserved foods that you carry."

"And my batman?"

Marty sighed and resolved to get his own back on Arthur someday soon.

"One servant if he can fight."

They arrived at the Formidiable and Marty asked Ackerman to have the carpenter prepare a 'cabin' for the lieutenant. What he got was a dog box six by five feet with just enough room for a cot and his chest. The batman got put in with the mids in the cockpit.

They set sail with a minimum of fuss and followed the current out of the Tagus into the Atlantic. Smith and his squadron had moved on as there was no longer any need to blockade the port. Marty experienced a moment of regret that he hadn't had a chance to meet with his friend again.

There was a pile of correspondence waiting for Marty mainly made up of the usual letters from the Admiralty demanding reports and the status of his stores etc. There were also personal letters from Sir Sidney and Thomas Cochrane, and more importantly, letters from Caroline. To his sheer delight, he also received, for the first time, letters from James and Beth, who were now eight and six respectively.

He read the official stuff first. One was from Hood and brought him up to date on political happenings at home, which he noted but otherwise ignored except one point which mentioned some concern over the influence his votes could have in parliament. This confirmed what the Admiral said. He would have to have a word with his wife when he saw her next.

Caroline's letter didn't shed any further light on it, just talked about their lands and how well their trading fleet were doing, how much she missed him, and what the children had been up to. The twins had, apparently, developed a unique way of talking to each other that only they understood and were mischievous and constantly getting into things they shouldn't. James and Beth were being tutored at home and she asked whether he wanted to put James' name down for the Naval College at Portsmouth. If he didn't, she wanted to put his name down for Charterhouse where he could go when he was ten years old.

Marty's opinion was that James should go to school until he was fourteen and then to the Naval College until he was sixteen when he should go to sea as a midshipman. He added this to his letter and promised to discuss it with her when he got home next.

James wrote in a childish but neat hand that he had learned to ride, and mummy had gotten him a pony. He wanted a gun so he could go hunting with the gamekeepers and Uncle Tom, but mummy wouldn't let him have one yet and said he had to wait until he was ten years old.

Beth wrote about learning to fight with a sword with mummy and Don Aldo. Caroline added a note saying that she stood at the back of the room imitating their moves as the Don put Caroline through her paces. She was also learning to ride and had a Shetland pony called Smudge because he had a black patch on his face that looked like a soot smudge.

Marty read the letters twice then finished off the letter he had been writing to Caroline and started letters to the children as well.

They sailed to Gibraltar and anchored in Rosia bay next to the rest of the flotilla much to Lieutenant Ashley-Cooper's surprise. He knew nothing about the Flotilla, he only knew that Marty was something to do with Intelligence. He was even more surprised when they went ashore, and he saw their headquarters.

"Is it normal for the Navy to carry so many marines for just four ships?" he asked la Pierre.

"No, these are chosen men and are specialists in Amphibious landings, infiltration, guerrilla warfare, and general mayhem," Paul replied with pride. "The cream from almost every gaol in Britain. The captain has asked that you train with us. You can join my lieutenants over there."

What followed was the hardest two days of the young man's life. He discovered many things and had his illusions as to his own prowess dispelled in the most brutal of fashions. Everyone was a better and faster shot than him. He knew nothing about hand to hand combat and his swordsmanship was revealed as being mainly form over function. He was bruised physically and mentally and was angry and hurt.

"I must protest!" he said as he stood in front of Marty in his office.

"You must protest what?" Marty replied, knowing what was coming.

"My treatment at the hands of your marines!"

"Have they abused you?"

"No, but..."

"Then they have mistreated you or not respected your rank?"

"No," he suddenly felt silly.

"You are indignant that they don't make allowances for your social rank and treat you just as they treat each other during training?"

"Well..."

"Let me explain something that they would never teach you at school or Horseguards. The French don't give a toss what your rank is or your class. They just want to kill you because you are British. The fact you wear an officer's uniform just makes you a target for their sharpshooters. The men will only respect someone who is at least as good as they are and prepared to stand beside them or in front of them when the shit starts to fly.

You have just discovered you are lacking in some key skills because, for once, no one will hold back because you are the Earl of Shaftesbury's son and gentlemanly combat means nothing when you are fighting for your life."

He looked the young man over, pulled a throwing knife from his boot, and hit a knot in the door over Sebastian's right shoulder with a smooth throw.

"Gentlemanly conduct and fair play are things that belong in your childhood. Viscount Wellington sent you with me to educate and hone you as a soldier. I suggest you get back to the marines and learn how to stay alive."

Sebastian stood for a long minute taking in what he had just been told then saluted and turned to leave.

"Attend me at weapons practice this afternoon at three," Marty ordered as he opened the door, "and give me my knife back."

Because of meetings with Ridgley and some of his agents, this was the first chance Marty had to practice with weapons since they had gotten back

"Lieutenant, please fetch your sword, and leave your coat in your room," Marty instructed as soon as he saw Sebastian stood beside the practice square. Sebastian went to the room he was allocated as his shore quarters in the officer's block and selected a fine 1803 pattern footguards officer's sword from the three in his chest. It had a curved thirty-two-inch blade that was sharpened on both sides for six inches behind the point, shagreen wrapped hilt with a brass cross guard, and steel knuckle guard. He left his jacket on the bed and removed his cravat as he saw that Marty was wearing an open necked shirt.

It was mid-afternoon as he walked out onto the square and squinted to get his eyes used to the sun. He could smell the dusty odour of the sand and the body odour of the men as he passed them. He realised the captain was already in the square with the Chinese fellow that was part of the team known as the Shadows.

"Lieutenant, this is Chin Lee. He will be your blades and open-handed combat instructor. We will spar and afterwards, he will help you improve your technique."

Sebastian nodded and barely avoided a sweeping slash from Marty's hanger, which appeared as if out of nowhere. He stepped back and brought his sword to the ready. Marty grinned at him and twirled his blade at the wrist.

He didn't know how it happened, but for the next attack, he was suddenly facing two blades, the sword and a bloody great knife! His sword felt heavy and clumsy. He couldn't believe that even though he had more reach with his longer arms and a longer sword, he couldn't get anywhere near the captain.

Marty ended the contest by stepping past his guard and slapping him on the thigh with the flat of his hanger.

"Not bad. You need to get a lighter and shorter sword for ship work, but you are steady on your feet and move well," Marty complimented him. "Chin, did you see enough?"

"Yes sir, I have something to work with. He will probably live to see his next birthday,"

Marty laughed and slapped Sebastian on the shoulder as he walked away. Sebastian realised he hadn't seen him sheath either the knife or his sword but there they were on his belt.

They sailed the next day with the entire Flotilla but instead of heading towards Cadiz, they turned East into the Mediterranean and Malaga. Marty knew he needed to enlist the guerrilla groups they had trained in Granada if they were to tie down the forces blockading Cadiz.

Once they anchored in Malaga bay, he, Lieutenant Ashley-Cooper and Paul la Pierre went ashore for a meeting with the Council.

"I will loan you Midshipman Williams as an interpreter once we have the agreement of the Spanish," Marty offered to Paul as they walked through the town.

"That would be most satisfactory," Paul replied, "the boy has a quick mind and proved most useful in dealing with the Spanish in Gothenburg," he continued, referring to the evacuation of the Spanish force that defected from Napoleon's Army of the North.

"Just try and bring him back in one piece. He has a tendency to advance before he thinks in combat situations," Marty smiled.

They came to the doors of the Ayuntamiento the Moroccan-style, richly decorated building that the council called home and were met by Don Andreas Carlos de la Borda, the Minister for Justice who they had met before.

"Greeting, Sir Martin," he smiled and shook their hands warmly, *"your ships were observed approaching the bay and the council has convened in anticipation."*

That's useful, Marty thought as it would save a lot of time. They followed the Don into the building and to the same room that Marty had been to before. Nothing had changed. The same eight men were seated around the table.

After the usual formalities, Marty got down to brass tacks,

"The French have invested the city of Granada and are blockading Cadiz. We, the British and our Portuguese allies, have secured Lisbon and will use it as

a beachhead to build a force that will not only reclaim Portugal from the French but then help our Spanish allies to push him out of the peninsula!" he paused and looked around the room and saw hope on some faces and discontent on others. He had to sell this to all of them,

"The one thing that can stop this is if the French manage to take Lisbon. If they achieve that, it may be years before we can establish another secure beachhead to launch our forces from. While Viscount Wellington only faces the army of Masséna, we are secure but if the Army commanded by Victor, currently besieging Cadiz, reinforces him, we stand a good chance of being forced out."

"How can we help?" the head of the military, Don Louis, asked.

Marty bowed his head to him in thanks and continued,

"Captain la Pierre, is the commander of my marines, and this is Lord Ashley-Cooper, a lieutenant in the Guards, what we propose is a joint force of marines and guerrillas to pin down Victor at Cadiz."

Don Louis looked thoughtful.

"Even a combined force could not hope to raise the siege of Cadiz."

Marty smiled at that.

"That is the last thing we want to do. What we propose is to pin them in place by threatening their rear and disrupting their supply lines. A classic guerrilla tactic." Marty moved to a large map that adorned one wall.

"Cadiz is a hundred miles away over mountains. How can we fight there?" asked one of the unhappy faces.

"That is where my ships come in," Marty replied, *"We will transport your men to this bay here at Barbate and land them with all our marines."*

"And you propose that your captain is in command?" said the same man.

"He is very experienced, but no, he will be an advisor to your commanders, his marines there to assist."

Every man in the room knew this was fiction, but it salved Spanish pride and allowed the British more freedom.

"How many marines will you 'lend' us as 'advisors," the same man asked again. Marty knew this was the Minister of Finance. Francis Ridgley warned that he had certain sympathies for the French that Marty should be wary of.

"Don Osuna, I will give you one hundred marines, the complete force carried by the Hornfleur. We will also provide supplies for the joint force so they do not have to live of the land. The locals around Cadiz are suffering enough from the depredations of the French army."

The Minister looked surprised that Marty knew his name and sat back in his chair with a harrumph. The chairman gave him an undecipherable look and turned to Marty.

"We can supply three hundred men, most trained by your men, led by regular army officers who have also been trained in guerrilla warfare. If you are able to

keep them supplied with food and ammunition, then a four-hundred-man force should be adequate."

Marty translated for his two companions, and Paul agreed that this would be enough. He would break them into two divisions each made up of ten, twenty-man squads. Marty understood, he was setting up a flat chain of command with maximum flexibility. This should work!

Gathering the men took close to a fortnight as they had to be called in from the countryside, they were equipped and allocated to ships for transportation.

"We have a small problem," Paul reported on one of his regular visits to the Formidiable, "there is a certain amount of distrust between some of the guerrilla bands."

Marty raised an eyebrow in query.

"Is it a problem?"

Paul continued,

"There are two bands who have an ongoing feud. We will have to keep them apart and put them in separate divisions."

"Any idea what caused it?"

"I asked Williams to look into it. Apparently, it's all about a bull."

"A bull?"

"A young prize fighting bull. It was to be sold by the family who dominated one band to the family who dominated the other. But as it grew, it showed extraordinary fighting prowess, so they reneged on the deal to keep it for breeding."

"God, they'd start a vendetta over that?"

"Well, not exactly. The matriarch of the family who didn't get the bull confronted the leader of the bull's owners at a market and gave him a piece of her mind. He told her to fuck off, which got him a punch in the mouth from her husband and it went downhill from there. Knives were drawn and, well, you can guess the rest."

Marty rolled his eyes. What was it about the Italians and Spanish that made them want to start carving lumps out of each other at the drop of a hat?

"Well, if you think you can handle it, I'll leave it to you. How is Sebastian shaping up?"

"He is raw and inexperienced but show's potential. We just need to knock the illusion that his breeding will automatically get the respect of his men out of him. I will keep him close for now."

Marty nodded in agreement. If anybody could mould the young Lord into a proper leader, it was Paul.

The gathering and loading completed, they set sail East for Barbate some one-hundred and twenty sea miles away against a West-South-Westerly wind and a heavy sea. Marty was worried that by the time he got them to the landing, the Spaniards would be too weak from seasickness to be an effective fighting force.

They tacked back and forth for two days and barely cleared the strait against the crank wind. They got lucky in the end when the wind shifted to the Northwest as they approached the bay, so it was sheltered for the ship's boats to ferry the men and supplies ashore. Marty smiled when he saw men fall to their knees and kiss the ground thankful that their ordeal by sea had ended. They stayed on station until the force had formed up into its two groups and melted into the hills a short way inland.

The Hornfleur sailed back to Gibraltar to load up with supplies and the other three set off North towards Lisbon. Marty had arranged for a guide to meet him there to take him to rendezvous with Ryan and Linette.

The smell of woodsmoke and cooking mixed with a tinge of tobacco and the sweet smell of herbs was the first hint that they were close to the camp. The wind was from the South, so he followed his nose.

They dismounted and walked the horses forward until Troy froze, head down, right foot raised, teeth bared. He didn't snarl or bark, just let his boss know there was something ahead. Marty stepped forward, arms out to the side and called,

"I am Señor Alphonso Cartagena. I have come to see Pedro the knife sharpener."

A gypsy stepped out of the shadows, his gun at full cock and pointing at Marty.

"What does Troy want to do?"

"Bite your balls off."

The man grinned, lowered his piece, dropping the hammer back to half cock, and gestured them to follow him.

The camp was as Ryan had described in his report, a circle of wagons around a central campfire. Every man was armed, and he suspected, so were the women and older children. Ryan sat with Linette and the band's elders closest to the fire. There was an empty pile of cushions beside them. Garai was with a group of young men and women sitting around a second smaller fire.

"Good evening, captain," Ryan greeted him, "come, sit and warm yourself." Marty had the distinct impression he was expected.

Marty leant over and kissed Linette on the cheeks French style, then folded himself down onto the cushions, which were very comfortable. Sam and Troy were gathered up by one of the women in Garai's group. Sam and the guide were offered a flask of wine with a long spout called a 'porron' from Spain. This peculiar shaped vessel allowed one to drink wine without putting any part of the flask to your lips, but the downside was it also got a lot of wine down your shirt until you got the knack.

Marty noticed that Sam had quite an audience and more than one woman admiring his muscular physique. Troy just chewed happily on the large bone they threw him.

"Well, what is the state of the French siege of Olivenza?" Marty asked after they exchanged pleasantries.

"About ten thousand troops arrived a day ago, we don't know where from, we suspect from Santander. To be honest, he will not have much of a problem taking the town once his artillery arrives, as the walls are practically falling down on their own. Word has it that his main goal is Badojez, but we also got a report that a week ago another ten thousand troops were seen moving Northwest towards Santarem."

"Where did they come from?" Marty exclaimed in surprise.

"We aren't sure, but we have identified that they are from Soult's 1 Corp," Ryan admitted.

"Damn! Then they are from Cadiz," Marty exclaimed.

He considered and realized there was only one reason Soult would do that, to try and draw Arthur into sending troops to relieve the siege thereby weakening his defence of Lisbon. Their assumption that Soult wouldn't help Masséna was wrong!

"That devious bastard is trying to tempt Wellesley out of Lisbon so Masséna has less troops to face at Torres Vedras," he described the lines of fortifications and told them of the battles they had fought.

"I need to get back to Lisbon as fast as possible."

The next morning, Marty and Sam were back in the saddle escorted by two of the gypsy band and the guide. They had over a hundred miles to cover and would need to change horses regularly to do it in good time. The gypsies had that covered, the route they took ensured that they passed farms and regular camp sites where they could get fresh mounts. They did the trip back to Lisbon in less than two days.

Marty saw ranks of soldiers being formed up ready to March and went straight to Arthur's offices walking in without knocking.

Arthur Wellesley was in discussion with two officers one British the other Portuguese. They were discussing the route for the relieving force to be sent to Badojez. A glance at the map and the activity outside told Marty that Arthur was about to make a terrible mistake.

"Martin, you look exercised and exhausted. Do you have news?" Wellesley asked as he glanced up from the map.

"My Lord," Marty started which got Wellesley's immediate attention, "I have come directly from Olivenza."

Wellesley nodded for him to continue.

"There is only one reason for Soult to attack Badojez and that is to weaken you here so Masséna can press home an assault."

"Not possible. He doesn't have enough men," Wellesley barked.

"What if he had another ten thousand?"

Wellesley looked shocked and sat down with a thump.

"He's been reinforced?"

Marty nodded and let himself down into another chair, the other two soldiers just stood and watched. Marty's arse hurt from being in the saddle for two days and he was spent.

"Where from?"

"As far as we can make out, Cadiz. They must have left before we got the Guerrillas in place."

"So that was a wasted exercise then."

Marty shrugged; he would evaluate that later. For now, he thought he would leave them there; it was excellent training for both the marines and the Spanish, and he needed to get some sleep.

The next morning, he was rested but still sore, and he had to meet with Arthur at ten. He looked at Troy, who had run as far as he could with the horses until his feet were too sore to run any more, at which point Marty slung him across his saddle in front of him. Undignified for Troy, but he wasn't about to be left behind. The big dog was curled up in a corner resting his torn pads, which had been treated with sulphur powder and ointment by Shelby when he came to check on Marty.

Marty ate his breakfast and thought about what happened. He had gotten lucky and been in the right place at the right time and he knew he couldn't rely on that happening again. He needed to talk to Ridgley, but first he had to face the general.

Arthur met him outside his office.

"Walk with me, Martin," he commanded.

He looked calm and, if anything, content.

"I want to thank you for your timely intervention yesterday. I was under a lot of pressure from the Spanish to send troops to Bodojez to counter Soult's move."

Marty was surprised. He expected a roasting for getting Soult's intentions wrong in the first place.

"You did the journey from Olivenza to here in two days?"

"Yes, and my backside is continuously reminding me of it."

Arthur laughed, a rare sound.

"And your dog is recovering?"

"Yes, for once Troy is forced to stay still for a while until his paws heal. He probably ran forty miles."

"An impressive feat of endurance in itself." Arthur smiled, impressed.

They strolled along in the sun for a while watching the soldiers marching and drilling on the quadrangle.

"What do you plan to do now?" Arthur asked as they approached the stables.

"I plan to go to Gibraltar and work out, with Francis Ridgley, how to expand our intelligence network in Spain," he looked at Arthur out of the corner of his eye, "are there any particular places you want us to focus on?"

They had reached the stall where one of Arthur's horses was stabled. He pulled an apple from his pocket and offered it to the handsome beast. He had a fine Arabian head, which Arthur preferred, and looked like there was more than a little thoroughbred blood in him.

"It would be good to know what Soult is up to and what Victor is doing around Cadiz as we will have to do something about both of them soon. After that, we will take the war to them in Spain."

"Well, I have time then. We will increase our efforts to train and direct the guerrillas to disrupt and use up French resources as well."

Arthur nodded in agreement, then asked,

"When was the last time you saw your family?"

Marty was surprised and had to think before he answered,

"It's been a while but that's not unusual in the Navy."

"It would be good if you took a trip back to London and coordinated your ideas with Canning and Hood. There are a lot of politics flying around about this war. The coffers are almost empty, and the politicians are tightening the purse strings."

"I will go to Gibraltar first. The good thing is I don't think we will need to ask either of our esteemed friends for more money," Marty replied with a smile, remembering the pile of gold and valuables the

Portuguese aristocrats had left behind when they fled Lisbon the year before.

That afternoon, he wrote to Caroline to tell her he would be back in London in probably three weeks' time and Hood, the same. The letters left on the packet that sailed that evening and he instructed Wolfgang to have the Formidiable ready to sail in the morning for Gibraltar.

Marty met Francis Ridgley, the local Foreign Office spy master, in his office at 17b Devil's Tower Road in Gibraltar. The office was actually in a soundproof and hidden garret above his living quarters where he posed as a wastrel in exile.

They entered through a door disguised as a bookcase, opened by a key that looked like a pendant, turned in a lock that looked like a knothole. All this cloak and dagger stuff made Marty smile every time he visited.

Inside the office, the soundproofing layer of cork on the walls, floor and ceiling made everything sound dull. Marty noticed a new rug on the floor and lifted it.

"I couldn't get the stain out, so I got the rug to cover it up," Ridgley explained as Marty identified it as blood. Some unfortunate hadn't survived an interrogation from the look of the size of it.

Marty shrugged and put the rug back in place before pulling up a chair.

"We need to strengthen our informant network in Spain especially around Cadiz and anywhere Soult has forces," Marty opened. "Ryan and Linette are getting good information from the Gypsies in Portugal and along the border, but we almost got caught out when Victor sent ten thousand men to Masséna."

"Yes, I heard," Francis replied as he busied himself making tea from the steaming silver samovar in the corner. "Milk? Sugar?"

"Just black please. I won't be able to keep the guerrilla force there for long now that we know that they sent troops before we got there. They will be better used back in Granada. So, who can we use in that area?"

Francis had a sly smile on his face as he handed Marty his tea then plonked himself down in a chair beside him.

"I have just recruited a man in Cadiz who has free access to both sides in that conflict."

Marty returned the sly smile.

"A smuggler?"

"Of sorts, he finds himself in a situation where Cadiz itself is awash with food and luxuries thanks to the fact we hold the port (the Navy is doing an adequate job of keeping it open) and a ready market for those goods with a French besieger that is practically starving."

"A strange situation for a siege where the tables are usually the other way around," Marty responded. "However, I will put a golden guinea on his customers being confined to the officer classes."

"That's no bet, fraternity and egalitarianism hasn't reached your common French soldier yet," Francis sniggered.

"So, who have we got to verify this good gentleman smuggler's, sorry, trader's information," Marty fired back.

"No one yet, I have to admit, but I am looking for someone," Francis replied.

"Have you tried the fishermen?" Marty asked.

Francis's look was all the answer he needed.

"I will send James down in the Alouette and see if he can cultivate some of them. The French are encamped on the coast after all," he continued. "He can get a message to Paul to start withdrawing his force as well."

"Sounds like a good idea. What about keeping an eye on Soult?" Francis asked, pleased that he didn't have to find another spy near Cadiz.

"Ryan and Linette have had a lot of good results from their association with the Gypsies. They will try and expand that network then we can make better contact and relations with the guerrillas," Marty said as if he was thinking out loud.

"I have a man who can go undercover in Spain, Spanish mother, English father like Ryan. I will send him to Ryan and they can work together," Frances offered.

Marty nodded.

"How is the situation in Malta?" he suddenly asked as a thought struck him.

"Good, why?" Frances replied, surprised by the sudden change in track.

"Didn't the new man there have mixed blood or something?" Marty asked, frowning as he tried to remember.

"Yes, Indian and English, made him look like your typical Mediterranean type. Oh! I see where you are going. Problem is he only speaks Italian," Francis replied, realised his teacup was empty, and rose to get a refill.

"That gives me something to think about," Marty mumbled just loud enough for Francis to hear.

"Wolfgang get the Formidiable ready to sail for England," Marty ordered two days later. He and Frances had worked out a strategy and he had spent some time writing letters and encoding them for Ryan, and in plain English for Arthur.

He also wrote up a plan then rewrote it twice, putting himself in Canning and Hood's positions. He didn't know whether they would want it, but he would have it in his pocket if needed. He then called Antton in,

"You Basques are on both sides of the French Spanish border, aren't you?" he asked.

"Yes, we all come from the French side."

"But when we were in Bilbao, you seemed to have an affinity for the Basques that live there," Marty persisted.

"Naturally, we all speak Basque. They just speak Spanish as their second language rather than French," Antton admitted.

"Could you and Matai go there and recruit some to spy on the French?" Marty asked with an intent look. "Do they hate the French as much as you do?"

"They might. They also hate the Spanish, so we will just need to sweeten them." Marty understood what he meant, reached over, and took a leather bag off his desk, which he tossed it to him. It was surprisingly heavy for its size and chinked musically.

"That might help." He grinned.

The Dorset Boy Book 8: La Licorne

Chapter 9: A Rear-Guard Action

In Cadiz, Paul received the message to pull out and started organising the men so that the Hornfleur could ferry them back to Malaga in groups of fifty. The last to leave would be his marines and it would take two trips to get them all off with all their equipment and supplies. They wouldn't leave the French anything.

"You will go with the last group," Paul told Lieutenant Sebastian Ashley-Cooper, "I will go with the second to last. I want you to take command of the rear guard. The French have been scouting in force towards the bay and we think someone has told them we are here,"

"How long will we have to hold out?" Sebastian asked.

"It is under ninety miles by sea from here to Gibraltar, so it should take a day for the Hornfleur to make the round trip, weather permitting," Paul replied.

Sebastian thought for a moment or two.

"I think we can get to Gibraltar overland if things get too hot. We can cover the fifty miles in a couple of days given the terrain. We will burn or blow up all the supplies we can't carry."

"Alright, that's what we will do. If the French attack in force before we can pick you up, melt back into the hills in a fighting retreat and make your way to Gibraltar."

The first load of marines was taken aboard the Hornfleur and she set to sea. Sebastian and the remaining fifty marines prepared for sudden departure and he sent out scouts to keep an eye on the French scouting parties.

He was very proud that Captain La Pierre trusted him to command the fifty marines that would be last off. What he didn't know was that Paul had carefully briefed his NCOs and Lieutenant George Fairbrother to support him and keep him from making any impactful bad decisions. This was a test to see if he could apply what he had learnt.

Two hours after the Hornfleur left, a scout came running into camp and went straight to Sebastian.

"Sir, a platoon strength patrol has left Cadiz and is heading this way and our observation party reports that there are signs that a larger force is preparing to follow them."

"How long before they get to the perimeter?" Sebastian asked.

"No more than an hour," the scout replied.

"Mr. Fairbrother, get the men ready to leave. If we get word that the larger force makes a move, we will retreat back into the hills to the East."

The men quickly and efficiently broke camp, prepared their weapons, and got ready for a fight. Charges were set in the piles of supplies they would leave behind, or oil poured over them in preparation to burning them.

Shots were heard from the West; the leading elements of the French scouting force had reached the perimeter. The scout returned.

"Sir! A Brigade of infantry is heading this way behind the scouts. The observers are making their way to the first rendezvous."

"Lieutenant set the fuses and get the men moving. I will be with the rear guard," Sebastian ordered. "You come with me," he ordered the scout.

He ran to a platoon strength group of men and shouted,

"You are with me; we need to slow the French down."

He led them to the perimeter and found the marines there exchanging fire with the French scouts.

"Move back! Join up with the men moving into the hills," he ordered them.

"Set up skirmish lines in two ranks. We will retreat by rank."

This was a manoeuvre the marines were familiar with and one they practiced regularly as they were often in situations where they were outnumbered and needed to retreat to their boats. In this case, they needed to get back into the hills where the French couldn't mount a focused attack because of the terrain.

The first rank fired a volley at the advancing French troops then retreated behind the second rank that was some ten yards or so behind them. The second rank became the front rank and as soon they had a clear field of fire, picked targets and fired.

After four volleys, the relays became more ragged as each rank covered the retreat of the other, the men moving from cover to cover as the rifles would do in front of a line of battle.

This frustrated the French, who wanted to advance in force but faced a continuous storm of shot and an enemy that stayed just out of reach. To make things worse, the marines left them little presents of a new innovation from the tool shed. Pipe bombs detonated by a flintlock triggered by a tripwire. These delightful surprises were left attached to trees or across trails, the wires strung at ankle height, when tripped the little darlin's sent a hail of shrapnel scything outwards.

The French advance slowed as they started probing every gap and behind every rock, looking for boobytraps, allowing Sebastian and his men to slip back into the hills.

Sebastian stopped behind a large boulder and looked back down the trail to where the French were cautiously advancing. He spotted an officer waving his sword and extolling his men to move faster. He licked his thumb and cleaned the foresight of his Baker rifle then used the same thumb to test the wind direction.

He raised the heavy rifle to his shoulder then, as his instructors had taught him, breathed out slowly as he lay the sight on the officer's chest. He raised his aim to the top of the man's head to allow for the drop and squeezed the trigger. He knew his shot was good and saw the man fall to the ground, a large hole in his chest just below his chin.

The French spotted his smoke and returned fire, balls whined off the rock and he had to duck before scuttling up the trail where he was met by Fairbrother just around a bend in the trail.

"Nice shot," he complimented him.

"Thank you. How are we proceeding?" Sebastian replied.

"The main force is a half mile back into the hills and the rear guard is set to make life uncomfortable for the French if they decide to pursue us." Fairbrother grinned.

Sebastian stuck his head around the corner and ducked back as a ball ricocheted off the rock.

"Persistent bastards," he grinned and followed Fairbrother up the track to the waiting men.

The French kept up the chase for the rest of the day until they got into the Alcornocales Forest as night closed in. Not willing to advance into the trees in the dark, they retreated a mile or so and set up camp.

Sabastian didn't let his men stop. He wanted as much distance between him and the French as possible by morning. He gathered the men together and did a head count. They were missing the observation team who hadn't caught up yet but apart from that, he still had all of his men.

Now they turned Southeast, guided by a hand compass that Fairbrother carried, towards Gibraltar and made their way slowly through the forest for about five miles before they made camp. The men needed rest and something to eat but it would be a cold camp with no fires.

Dawn saw the British already on the move again. Sebastian had scouts ahead as trail breakers and behind to check on their pursuers. The trail breakers had to find a way through the hills and gullies that led in the general direction of Gibraltar, which wasn't always easy, and they made slow progress.

They didn't manage to shake off the pursuit and were constantly harassed by French scouts. The rear guard constantly engaged them to let the others get away, and casualties were mounting.

"We need to get some distance between us and the French," Sebastian told Fairbrother as they were about to enter a ravine that was their only way forward, "I will take five men and make a stand here and hold them for as long as I can. Leave me all the bombs, pistols, and the wounded men's rifles.

"You are sure, Sebastian?" Fairbrother asked. This definitely wasn't in the plan Captain la Pierre had outlined.

"Yes, it is my duty." Was all the reply he got.

The main force entered the ravine and Sebastian and his five men started piling rocks up at the entrance to form a low bulwark. They had about five more minutes before the rear-guard arrived.

"Sir," one of the men asked as he piled another boulder on, "I'm a bit worried about that big rock up there." He pointed up the slope to their right at a large boulder perched on a ledge.

"It looks like a strong breeze could knock it off there and we would be right under it."

Sebastian looked up, he was right but maybe…

The rear guard scurried back towards them working in pairs and Sabastian's team laid down cover fire to help them get over the bulwark to safety.

"We can hold off the scouts for as long as we have ammunition but when the main force arrives, we will be easily overwhelmed," Sabastian said between taking pot shots at any Frenchman stupid enough to show himself.

"Rogers, take the bag of bombs and climb up to that rock and pack them in behind it. Make sure you get them right under it even if you have to dig a hole. Prime one of the bombs and run the trip line down to that boulder over there," he ordered, pointing to a large rock twenty feet behind them.

"Ready?" he asked the marine once he collected all the bombs.

"Aye, aye, sir," Rogers replied.

"Covering fire!" he called, and Rogers set off.

The French must have had reinforcements arrive as the return fire was more intense than it had been and getting heavier. Several individuals were seen moving forward, braving the accurate fire from the marines.

Sebastian looked up and saw Rogers dive behind the big rock as bullets kicked up the dust and whined off the rocks around him. *The man must be part spider!* he thought as the rock face was all but vertical!

"Shit!" the marine beside him swore and fell back, blood coming from a bullet wound in his shoulder. Sebastian popped up and snapped off a shot. They couldn't hold out much longer. A stone bounced off his head and he looked up to see Rogers part sliding, part falling in a barely controlled fashion back down into the ravine.

"Move back in ranks!" he called, and half the men left the bulwark and ran into the ravine. He let the rest follow before taking one last shot and retreating to the boulder.

The string was hanging with a rag tied to the end so he wouldn't miss it. *Well done that man,* he smiled.

There was a shout and a French scout appeared at the wall. It was now or never. He grabbed the string and tugged. Nothing happened and he saw four more French climb up the rocks.

Shit, I'm done, he thought and raised his remaining loaded pistol. Then there was a loud bang.

He looked up; there was a cloud of smoke and dust drifting away on the breeze, but the rock was still in its place. He looked back and shot the first man over the wall, threw his pistol at the second, and drew his sword.

The three French scouts grinned evilly and raised their rifles. He was a sitting duck. It would be like shooting a fish in a barrel.

A rock bounced down and hit one of the Frenchmen on the shoulder. He looked up and his mouth opened in a scream just before the giant rock crushed the life out of the three of them as it crashed down followed by a torrent of dirt and rubble.

Sebastian staggered down the path pushed along by a rolling cloud of dust.

It took the whole day to cover the twenty-five miles until they sighted Gibraltar from the top of the last pass they had negotiated. They circled around to the East side of the main town of San Roque and crept down towards the Spanish side of the border. The Spanish there were generally sympathetic to the British as they traded with the Rock despite the French presence in the area.

"What do you think, Lieutenant? Make a dash for it?" one of the sergeants asked.

"One second," Fairbrother replied, dug in his pack, and pulled a folded cloth from it.

"Sergeant find a pole to tie this to please," he asked the NCO and handed him the union flag.

"Don't want our fellows shooting at us thinking we are an attacking French force, now do we?" he grinned, then asked,

"Any sign of Lieutenant Ashley-Cooper?"

Chapter 10: A Woman's Place

The Formidiable sailed with the Eagle tagging along under the command of Trevor Archer, who was made acting lieutenant in Ryan's absence. Antton and Matai were passengers on the Eagle which, when they got to the Bay of Biscay, peeled off and headed for Bilbao.

Marty was pleased that his marines were home and Sebastian had shown he really did have what it took to be a leader. He sent him back to Arthur with a glowing report. He had walked back over the border with his rear-guard two hours behind the rest of the men. They were carrying two wounded, were completely out of ammunition, and were exhausted.

A week's sailing saw them dock at Chatham and Marty, Sam, John Smith, Wilson, Chin, and Troy took a carriage to London. A fast courier preceded them with messages for Caroline and Hood warning they were on their way as he didn't trust the security of the semaphore towers. Wolfgang stayed with the ship and went shopping for spares with Fletcher.

The carriage pulled up in front of the London house and suddenly Troy sat bolt upright, his ears pricked forward and whined. The front door opened at about the same time as the carriage door and two blurs of brown met halfway, yipping, and cavorting in excitement.

A laughing James came down the steps followed by Caroline and Beth. Marty swept them up in his arms in a huge hug. He looked to the door where Mary, the family nurse, stood holding the twins by their hands. They had grown so much and looked at him wondering who the strange man was.

By the time the dogs calmed down enough to get to the sniffing bums stage, everybody was inside. Wilson went off with Mary, his wife, leaving the twins in the care of Tabetha, one of their West Indian servants. She was disappointed that her beau, Matai, wasn't with them.

The whole family gathered in the drawing room, and Marty reacquainted himself with his children. Beth insisted on showing him her sword skills and Marty was surprised. The child had some genuinely good moves. Caroline looked on proudly.

James sat by his father. He had obviously decided that at eight years old he was too grown up to sit on his lap and eventually, and quite artfully, looked to his father and said,

"It will be my birthday soon. Will you be here for it?"

"I will certainly try to be, but I have to help uncle Arthur with his war."

"I know what I would like for a present."

"Oh really? What is that?" Marty smiled.

"A bird gun so I can go hunting with Uncle Tom."

Marty wasn't surprised as his letter had forewarned him. He looked across at Caroline, who just gave him a, "this one is your problem," look.

Marty was feeling indulgent.

"I tell you what we will do: once I have finished my business with Admiral Hood and the government people, I will take you to Mr. Manton and we will see what he says."

James leapt into his lap, gave him a huge hug, and Marty soon had him in fits of giggles as he tickled him. Caroline raised her eyes to the heavens and sighed.

A note from Hood was waiting for Marty on the breakfast table the next morning. He was to report to his office at three o'clock this very afternoon. That was good because his welcome home by Caroline had been very energetic and he needed the morning to recover.

The waiting room at the Admiralty was as crowded as ever and a familiar face greeted him,

"Sir Martin, hello!" Captain Turner greeted him.

"James! How are you?" Marty replied, delighted to see his old mentor and friend, "and how is Juliet?"

"She is very well and will give birth to our first in a month's time," Turner replied with pride. He had a much younger wife than him and had started a family late in his life.

"Will you be at home for that?" Marty asked, having been at sea for the birth of his first two.

"Yes, I am sailing a desk these days," he admitted with an amused look.

Marty was about to ask what he was doing when a messenger came and whispered something to Turner.

"Come on, you can walk with me," he told Marty.

They made their way along the familiar route to Hood's office and Turner entered without knocking. Hood was sat behind his usual desk, but Marty immediately saw there was a second desk set to one side.

Hood stood and came around to shake Marty's hand.

"Good day to you, m'boy. You're looking well."

"Admiral, as are you," Marty responded and watched Turner out of the corner of his eye as he went to the second desk and picked up a folder.

Hood chuckled,

"You have noticed that Captain Turner has his own desk. I think we should explain."

The three of them sat at the conference table that took up a good third of the room.

"I have recruited James to be my successor. He is nearing the top of the list and will be made Admiral soon and has a much better grasp of current politics than I do."

Marty congratulated his friend and soon to be new boss.

"I didn't know you had an interest in our side of the Navy's business," he admitted.

"Oh, you can blame yourself for that," Turner laughed, "I have been following your escapades over the years and must admit to becoming quite intrigued by the intelligence world."

"I didn't think a tenth of it got into the Gazette," Marty replied, somewhat confused.

"I was keeping James informed of your adventures. It was part of the agreement we came to when I first recruited you," Hood confessed.

Marty looked from one to the other and was grateful to have such men on his side. Then he was hit by a thought, "So when we were at Miss Katie's and you were talking about the time the deal boys were arrested by that revenue cutter,"

"and Armand had to rescue them," Turner finished for him.

"You knew all about it!" Marty laughed.

Turner just winked.

"Now, tell us about the situation on the peninsula," Hood said chuckling at the look on Marty's face.

Marty gave a complete but succinct report and evaluation, leaving nothing out, but at the same time, keeping it short.

"Wellesley is correct. The Government is nearly broke; this war is bleeding us dry. But at the same time, Napoleon is in the same boat."

"The Flotilla doesn't need any funding to continue its work. There are ample funds from what we salvaged when they evacuated Lisbon to cover that."

Turner raised an eyebrow in question, and Hood nodded to Marty to enlighten him.

"They left in such a hurry they left a couple of carts full of valuables on the dock. We didn't want the French to get their hands on it, so we sequestered it in Gibraltar. We use it to fund the intelligence gathering and guerrilla activities on the peninsula. If there is any left when the royal family return, we intend to give it back to them."

"And they will be grateful for what you give them," Hood concluded, closing the subject, then asked,

"Do we have anyone in Madrid at the moment?"

"No, that is an area of concern. Enrique's cover was well and truly blown when we stole the copy of the Fontainebleau treaty and we haven't found anyone to replace him yet," Marty confessed.

"Canning will join us later. We can ask if he has anybody," Hood replied and added,

"We are having a problem in general in parliament as the house is split almost evenly over the war in the

Peninsula. Many politicians think it's irrelevant and should be left for the Spanish to sort out."

"They will never kick Napoleon out on their own," Marty said in a thoughtful tone. "Is it a split on party lines?"

"Not entirely. There are a few from the Government benches who are vocal in opposition as well as quite a few who abstain. Add to that we have a deeply unpopular Prime Minister, and you can see the problem. This is where you, or rather your good lady wife, can help," Turner added, looking intent.

"Caroline? What can she do?" Marty exclaimed before remembering what Admiral Cotton had said.

"Her influence would swing the balance. At the last count, she has some five votes in her pocket with another three she can influence," Hood smiled indulgently as if he were breaking good news to an expectant father.

"Has she b'damned!" Marty swore.

"She has a hold on most of the wine market as well as spices and precious stones. Her father is a major importer of sugar and coffee from the Caribbean and can influence the price of those by his position in the guild of merchants. The two of them have recently been actively trading coffee, tea, and tobacco. You are rich enough to be able to influence those prices as well. Quite frankly, the government is wary of your collective influence," Hood summarised, "but as long she is circumspect and doesn't present a direct challenge, they will ignore her."

This was all news to Marty, and he realised that he needed to be more aware of what his entrepreneurial wife was up to. Most men would have seriously limited or outright forbidden their women to dabble in trade and his was out there dominating it. In the end, it would be him that had to face the Government or whatever trade body she offended.

A knock at the door and the secretary announced Mr. Canning. After a round of greetings, he took a place at the table opposite Martin.

Spencer Perceval was Prime Minister and Canning was ostensibly his man although Marty knew Canning was more centralist in his politics than Perceval. They were both Pittites and Tory to their core but Perceval wasn't the most popular of Prime Ministers.

"Sir Martin," he said by way of greeting, "I hope you had a good voyage?"

"Not as fast as one would hope - contrary winds and all that," Marty responded, knowing Canning hadn't a clue about sailing.

"Yes, well you are here and can report on the situation in the Peninsula."

One more time Marty, he told himself as he went through the report as he had before. As he concluded, Canning looked thoughtful.

"If I understand correctly, you have the required resources and agents in place, or are recruiting them, in Portugal and Southwestern Spain but are lacking a source of information in the capital, Madrid."

The three Navy men all nodded in confirmation and Canning looked directly at Martin as he took a paper out of his pocket and handed it to him. Marty unfolded it and looked at a portrait of himself. He blinked and looked again. There were differences: the hairstyle, a moustache, but the shape of the face, eyes, and nose were almost identical.

"Who is this?" he asked as he laid the sheet on the table for Hood and Turner to see.

"That is Maurice Chastain, a senior clerk in the Ministry of Finance who is on his way to Madrid to take up a position with the French administration. He also happens to be one of our agents. It is a marked resemblance isn't it. He will embed himself in the bureaucracy in Madrid and gain access to or identify the location of information useful to our war effort. But that is all he is, a clerk, and if we need to do anything more proactive than reading meeting minutes and letters, then we would need to supplement his skills."

Marty knew what he was saying but it would be risky to take Chastain's place for any longer than a day or two as he would be bound to slip up and give himself away. He refocused as Hood continued,

"The other thing is we know that the French have changed the code for the signal towers, and it would be rather good if we could get our hands on it or a copy at least."

Turner chipped in,

"We also know they are going to try and insert a new agent into Lisbon. Another of our men has warned us of this. We think he will come in by sea rather than try overland as the roads are heavily patrolled and checked by the military."

Marty thought that through.

"If that were me, I would land somewhere on the small peninsula South of Lisbon and make my way up to the Tagus where I could get a fishing boat across the river to the city."

"Well, we will leave you to deal with that… and the towers." Turner smiled.

Marty knew when he was dismissed, rose, recovered the picture of Chastain, and bowed to his superiors.

"You should spend a few days with your wife before you return to Portugal," Canning said in, what Marty took to be, a significant way.

Marty made his respects and left them to whatever other business they had to cover, made his way through the corridors back to the reception, and wondered what Canning had meant.

He called a hackney to take him home as the weather was particularly foul with a persistent heavy drizzle, which forced the smog down to ground level. The air stank of coal smoke and the visibility was measured in feet.

Suddenly, the carriage stopped with a jerk and the horse gave an annoyed neigh. Marty immediately palmed a barker pistol, alert and on edge.

A vaguely familiar face appeared in the window, looked at him, then disappeared. The door started to open, and Marty sat more upright, reaching for his other pistol.

"Sir Martin?" a familiar voice asked.

"Mullins?" he responded.

"Yes sir, can I come in, sir?"

"Certainly!" Marty cried and put away his pistols.

The Lawyer, who he had saved from a particularly vicious money lender a few years before, climbed up into the cab and sat beside him.

"Are you in trouble again?" he asked.

"Oh no, sir," Mullins replied, flushing at the memory, "let me explain. I came to the Admiralty to find you as I have come upon some information about a move to be made on your wife's business interests. I saw you take the cab and made haste to intercept it before you got away."

"My wife?" Marty asked with an impending sense of doom, first Canning and now Mullins.

"Yes, there is a movement by some, let me say, disgruntled individuals who have been discomforted by your wife's political and business acumen. These people are going to make a move to discredit your wife by accusing her of misconduct in the stock market and trading of illegal goods."

"Well, the time is ripe for that. The papers are full of rumours, but are there any grounds for accusations against Caroline?" Marty asked, knowing the illegal goods accusation was probably true in the case of wine.

"None at all but the stock market is all about trust and if they throw mud, it will stick, and she is a woman, so the members will believe them much easier than if she were a man. It might take her years to recover her reputation. They also think as a woman she will be unable to respond in any significant way. They do not know you have returned. I found out because I have a cousin at Chatham who I asked to keep a look out for your ship."

"When and where is this supposed to happen?" Marty asked.

"Tomorrow, at the stock market. They plan to start a rumour led by a Mingus Colville Esquire who has been particularly hurt by her ventures in spices. It opens at ten AM."

The cab arrived at Marty's house and pulled up to the curb. Marty shook the man's hand and bade him take the cab home. He tossed the driver a crown and said,

"Thank you. Driver be so kind as to convey my friend to his residence. That should cover it."

Once inside, he went to Caroline and told her what he knew. She was furious.

"How dare they!" she fumed, "I have never resorted to such low tactics."

"They are not expecting you or me to be there. They will make the accusations then go into hiding to avoid any repercussions. There will be several members of the gutter press there as well. Completely by coincidence, of course."

Caroline became thoughtful.

"Do you trust me to follow my lead?" she asked.

"Of course I do." Marty smiled back while wondering what he was letting himself in for.

The next morning, they entered the stock exchange quietly through a private side entrance and made their way to the trading floor. They were met by one of Caroline's traders, who took them to where Colville and his cronies were gathered.

Caroline wore a man's overcoat and hat that hid her hair and Marty was dressed in a civilian suit, overcoat, and wide brimmed hat. They approached unnoticed from behind the group.

"Of course, that Candor woman is manipulating the markets to shut out her competitors and fixing the price of commodities," Colville was stating in a loud voice in reply to a question from another man who was scribbling furiously in a note pad.

"How is she doing it?" an anonymous voice asked.

"By using her wealth to buy up stocks and force the price up, thereby cornering the market, and she uses her tame politicians to influence policy and taxes. She is abusing her position and power."

Caroline had heard enough.

"Oh, what rubbish you do talk," she snapped, "If I forced the purchase price up, how would I make any profit either? It would be useful to know how to do that and make a profit if ever I was stupid enough to want to try," she added as she removed the hat and coat. "If I wanted to affect the price of commodities, I would need to know, in advance, how good the crops would be before they were even planted, and no one can foretell that."

Colville looked like he had sucked a lemon. His mouth actually puckered as he realised she stood right behind him, and worse, her husband stood right behind her. The hacks' faces lit up; this was wonderful.

"If I were a man, I would challenge you to a duel for this slur on my honour, but I am but a frail woman," she sighed, looking helplessly at the gathered hacks, who were looking at her in anticipation. She paused dramatically, gauging the mood of her audience, then said angrily, "what the hell…" and punched him in the nose.

"If you think that you can pick on me because I am a mere woman, you had better think again. You are a coward, sir!" She struck a pose of absolute disdain and looked down her nose at him as he sat on the floor trying to staunch the blood.

"My seconds will call on you this afternoon if you have the balls to face me," she said coldly, then tossed her head, turned, and walking away.

The hacks who were brought in to write up the revelations that were supposed to come from Colville and his friends were now furiously scribbling notes as they ran from the building to make the afternoon editions. This was a much more sensational story.

Marty sat in the drawing room that afternoon and read through the small stack of single page scandal sheets that were already shouting the news that Lady Candor would fight a duel with Mingus Colville Esq. and described the encounter at the exchange in livid and exaggerated detail.

One or two of the rags decried the fact that a woman would dare fight a duel, but they were in the minority probably because most of the commentators were women and were grabbing the chance to support their own 'Joan of Arc.' Many speculated the wretched man would run a mile.

"No chance of that now," Marty frowned, "there is no way he can back down without being labelled craven and no way he can come out of it with any honour at all."

"Just as I planned it," smirked Caroline. "Fight a woman and be ridiculed if he loses and face the same fate if he wins for fighting a woman in the first place. On the other hand, I will be lauded by the progressives and scandal sheets and criticised by the Times, if the government even let them comment."

Marty wasn't surprised that Caroline was aware that the government needed to keep her 'on-side.' He changed the subject,

"You think he will choose swords?"

"I have had people spread a rumour that I am crack shot and he will be afraid that you will try and affect the duel if guns are involved," she replied.

"Aah, the old shooter in the bushes trick," Marty grinned.

"Yes, he won't take that risk and the duel is only to first blood with swords."

"You have set a neat trap!" Marty exclaimed as he realised the extent of what she had done.

Caroline just smiled.

Two mornings later on the green at Bethnal, a huge crowd gathered to witness the event that had filled the scandal sheets for two days now. Bully boys were employed to keep the crowd back from the area where the fight would be fought, and vendors sold food and drink. It was a circus and just what Caroline wanted.

She stepped from her carriage dressed in a riding skirt that came down to mid-calf, giving her freedom of movement while being modest. She wore long boots to avoid the accidental exposure of her ankles and a demure blouse that was buttoned to her throat. Her hair was piled on top of her head in a loose auburn bun. To finish the look, she wore long soft leather gloves. She looked stunning and made sure the dawn light struck her just so.

Marty sat on top of the carriage to get a good view and to be, very visibly, unable to interfere. Caldwell had chosen small swords as his preferred weapon, which were not unlike the sword Marty had given her for her birthday. The carriage rocked, and Shelby climbed up beside him. Marty had summoned him as soon as the challenge was made.

"She looks capable enough," he commented, "can she really fence?"

"You'll see," Marty replied with a grin.

They watched and waited.

The combatants chose their weapons to a roar from the crowd. Caroline made a show of looking at hers as if it was the first time she had seen a sword. Marty picked up various calls of 'cut his nuts orf!' or 'stick the bitch!' He looked down and saw a bookmaker taking bets and was surprised to hear that he had changed his odds from 3:2 to 4:1 on Lady Caroline and evens on Caldwell. Shelby called down and placed ten guineas on Caroline.

The contestants made their way with their seconds to the centre of the combat area and positioned themselves on the lines. The master of ceremonies raised his cane to the horizontal and the combatants went en-garde.

"Commence!" he cried and lifted the cane away.

Caldwell immediately launched an attack, obviously trying to finish it quickly, but Caroline moved like a dancer and easily parried and avoided every attempt he made with immense grace and style. The crowd started to jeer his attempts as she made him look clumsy. He became desperate and pressed harder, but Caroline was like a will o' the wisp, never where he thought she should be.

He had to stop and get his breath, so he stepped back and took en-garde, thinking that Caroline would welcome the break as well. Unfortunately for him, she hadn't yet broken sweat let alone run out of breath.

She raised her blade in a mock salute then launched a flashing attack from appel, causing him to parry in sixte. This allowed her to bind his blade, then with a twist of her wrist that set his blade aside, the tip of her sword flashed across his eyes, narrowly missing scoring.

Caroline pressed her attack, and Caldwell backed up, desperately trying to avoid or parry her flashing blade. The speed of her arm, suppleness of wrist, and inherent grace and agility were dazzling. She beguiled the crowd, who cheered and crowed every time her blade snaked out and slashed the material of his shirt until he looked like he was wearing a rag, but she never drew blood.

The crowd loved it! Marty shook his head and grinned to himself. His beloved was playing them like a harp.

Caroline suddenly stepped back and went to en-garde, looking at him like a cat sizing up her prey for the kill, then she deliberately and disdainfully turned her back to him.

"What the hell?" Marty exclaimed and lurched to his feet, nearly falling from the roof as the coach rocked and causing Shelby to swear in agitation.

Caldwell, in desperation, lunged forward, trying to score on her unprotected back, a perfectly legitimate move if you were fighting a man in the privacy of a normal duel. The crowd, however, didn't like it at all and roared a warning.

Caroline spun, she had invited this and was ready. The Lady executed a perfect direct riposte that left her blade in line with his face. His lunge, which was parried past her shoulder, carried him straight onto the tip of her sword, which sliced through his right cheek to the bone, leaving a large flap hanging down and bleeding profusely.

It was over, the crowd surged forward, and the bully boys had their work cut out to hold them back until a large number of soldiers made their way to the front to help them. Marty looked down and recognised Captain Arthur Simmons, the husband of his first love Contessa Evelyn de Marchets. He grinned and waved.

Caroline was escorted by her seconds to their carriage, cheers of the crowd roaring behind them. She stepped up into the door, turned, and waved. The victorious heroine of the hour was greeted by her gallant husband, who took her in his arms and kissed her soundly.

Shelby collected his winnings and went to attend to the wounded loser.

Canning and Turner watched the duel from the comfort of a coach in a long line of coaches that rolled up on the green at dawn.

"Caroline seems to have been practicing," Canning remarked dryly.

James Turner grinned and held out his hand to receive the twenty guineas he had just won.

"Wouldn't want to face her m'self! The damn woman fights like a demon," Canning conceded as he passed the pouch of coins over.

Caroline wasn't finished with Caldwell or his associates. She launched an action for slander against him and employed Mullins as her solicitor. He, in turn, engaged William David Evans, an eminent lawyer, to handle the case.

As soon as Caldwell could, he ran, taking ship to Australia, according to the gossip columns, which were pouring scorn on him. The rest of his associates ended up in court, lost the case and were, in the main, bankrupted by the punitive damages Caroline was awarded. She now really could dominate the market.

Marty kept his promise to James and took him to Manton's. As they entered, they were greeted by none other than Joseph Manton himself.

"Sir Martin! Welcome and what can we do for you here today?"

"Joseph, allow me to present my son, James. It is a gun for him that we are here for."

Joseph held out his hand and bowed as James shook it.

"Milord James, what can I do for you?" he asked, using his title.

"I would like a gun for shooting birds in the rough, please," James replied, on his best behaviour.

Joseph looked at him and replied seriously,

"A four-ten bore shotgun would be best I think. Light enough to be carried, low recoil, and easy to load. May I take some measurements, sir?"

"Oh yes," beamed James and the two of them were soon in deep discussion.

Marty smiled. He had chosen Joseph over Durs Egg because he knew he would treat James like an adult. Durs was a nice enough chap but very stiff and formal, probably due to his Swiss upbringing, he thought.

He had time on his hands and took the opportunity to look around and spotted a fabulous pair of Manton's duelling pistols.

Marty picked one up. They were magnificent! The .51 calibre, ten-inch octagon barrels were scratch rifled and signed with "MANTON LONDON" in gold on the top flat, with gold breech bands, and touch holes. There were gold front sights with iron rear fixed notch sights, and the tangs were engraved with floral and military motifs. The full-length stocks were figured English walnut with checked grips, the ramrods made of mahogany with horn tips. The silver furniture was exquisite, made and signed by Michael Barnett, the best weapons silversmith in London. A nice touch was a devil's head engraved on the butt cap so that it would be seen by one's opponent when the pistol was used in a duel.

He hefted the piece; the balance was perfect; he could knock the eye from a fly at twenty paces with these. He was so entranced with them he didn't hear Joseph come up behind him.

"Some of my best work," he said with pride.

Marty started in surprise, jerked out of his reverie.

"They are truly beautiful," Marty smiled, "have you sorted out what you need for James?"

"Yes, I will make him a double barrelled .41 calibre bird gun. I have an idea to incorporate an adjustable stock so it can be extended as he grows. It will be ready in three weeks."

"Perfect," Martin agreed, "you will bill me directly for that and for these."

"Certainly, Sir Martin. Will you take the pistols with you?"

"Yes," he said, replaced the pistol in its case, and handed it to Joseph. He knew he would want to 'prepare them.' "I will return in an hour if that's alright with you?"

Joseph agreed and saw him and James to the door.

"Daddy?" James asked.

"Yes, what is it?" Marty replied as they walked towards a chop house for dinner.

"Will we have to eat everything I shoot?"

Marty stopped and looked down at him. "What is the point of shooting something that you aren't going to eat?"

"Well, for sport," James replied.

"And who told you that?" Marty asked.

"I read that gentlemen shoot and hunt for sport."

Marty knew where that had come from. He had seen copies of a magazine in the library that was purported to be for gentlemen and ladies of property. He thought it was a bunch of snobbish rubbish, but his young impressionable son was taken in by it.

"Gentlemen with nothing better to do than shoot birds or game for sport would be better off joining the Army or Navy, but then their prey would be shooting back, and they wouldn't find that sporting," Marty replied and started walking again.

James thought about that.

"So are men that hunt for sport cowards?" he asked.

"Not necessarily," Marty replied, "but if sport is chasing something that cannot defend itself just for the sake of killing it, I question their motivation."

"So, you never kill something just for the fun of it?"

He stopped and took a knee so that he was eye to eye with his son.

"I never kill without a reason, whether it's an animal or a man."

James looked him in the eyes for a long moment.

"I will only shoot for the pot. That is enough fun," he promised.

Marty nodded, gave him a hug, and they resumed their walk.

They got home in time for supper. Beth and James were old enough now to dine with their parents. Marty had found this odd to start with as he had always eaten with his parents and the rest of the family, but Caroline was adamant that the children should eat in the nursery until they were old enough to use a knife and fork.

Beth was telling a story of how she and Mary searched for the twins, who had conspired to escape the nursery and made their way to the stables. How they got out of the house, nobody knew. Blaez and Troy had joined in the hunt for them and the dogs tracked the five-year olds to the stables where they were found jumping out of the hayloft into a pile of hay and having a great time.

James told everyone about his visit to Manton's and how he was measured for his gun. Luckily, Marty had shown Caroline his new pistols already as James happily told everyone about them too.

"You will be leaving them here?" Caroline asked.

"Yes, I don't think I will need them in Portugal, and they are too fine to be stored on ship," Marty agreed.

"Part of the collection then," she smiled.

"What collection?" Marty started to say then realised he had been rumbled. He had recently made several purchases of especially fine examples of the gunsmith's art including, a pair of Nock duelling pistols, and a beautiful pair of pistols he had found in Lisbon by the French gunmaker Nicholas Boutet.

Caroline smiled; his last trip home, he'd installed a display cabinet in his study where the guns were proudly displayed along with the Nock pepper pots that Evelyn had gifted him all those years ago and there was ample room for many more.

"I suppose you will eventually add those double-barrelled Manton's you carry every day," she suggested.

"When I find something better to replace them, they have given good service."

"Can I have them when you have finished with them, Daddy?" James asked.

"When you are old enough to look after them, but by then you will probably want the latest and best that's available," Marty answered.

James looked thoughtful as he ate his pudding.

"I would still like them. They have been yours for a long time and should be looked after," he stated firmly, giving his mother a look that said, 'disagree with that!'"

"They are growing up so fast!" Caroline exclaimed as they got ready for bed that evening. "James almost sounded adult over supper. He thought out his argument before he asked."

"He will go to school at the start of the summer term. I would check his luggage for weapons before he leaves." Marty laughed.

"You joke, but he is a boy in his father's mould, and I wouldn't put it past him to take a few for 'personal protection.' I saw him looking at boot pistols when we were shopping the other day."

"Small enough for him to handle and pack a surprising punch," Marty summarised, "he didn't get one, did he?"

"Not that I saw, and I checked his things when we got home," Caroline replied with a worried frown. "Maybe I should take away his money."

"He has money?" Marty asked, surprised.

"Well yes, I gave him an allowance so he could learn the value of money and how to manage it."

"Very laudable and modern. Hope it don't bite you on the arse," Marty laughed and lunged for her pert backside.

In the morning over breakfast, Marty told them he would be leaving for Chatham the next day. He asked Caroline to use her influence in key votes as advised by James Turner and she agreed. She was grateful for the guidance as she wouldn't want to do anything to hurt Marty inadvertently.

He had a word with his precocious son and asked him not to take any weapons to school with him outside of a small quill cutter folding knife with a mother of pearl handle he gifted him.

James promised he wouldn't and boasted that he was getting boxing lessons from Arthur Standish, one of their footmen who had been a bare-knuckle fighter for the Army, so he wouldn't need any.

Chapter 11: An enemy re-found

The Formidiable was as clean and shiny as a new pin after her stay in Chatham. Marty stood on the dock and admired her from afar as she was moored in the Medway, yards crossed. Sam gave a piercing whistle, and a boat pulled away from the frigate heading towards them. It was his barge and the men were dressed smartly in their matching uniforms with Stanley Hart in the stern directing the oars and manning the tiller.

"Welcome back, sir!" he cried happily as the bowman hooked on and the barge swung neatly up against the steps.

"Thank you, Mr. Hart. All well with the ship?"

"Yes sir! Fully provisioned and ready to go at your command."

The Shadows were busily getting the dunnage aboard and getting themselves distributed along the centre line, he was last in of course. Sam relieved Stanley of the tiller, as was his right as Marty's cox, and Stanley moved over to the larboard side of the stern where he could stand and command the oars. Marty sat in the centre of the thwart ahead of them in his regular place.

"Back oars starboard!" Stanley called as the bowman pushed them away from the steps, and as soon as the larboard side was clear,

"Give way both!"

The barge fairly shot across the river towards the Formidiable and soon they were hailed.

"Ahoy the boat!"

"Formidiable!" was the reply.

Then before he knew it, he was running up the batons and being greeted by the song of the Spithead nightingales and the crash of Marine rifles hitting the deck. Clouds of pipeclay drifted away on the breeze.

"Welcome back, sir!" Wolfgang grinned as he shook his hand. "That was an entertaining time in London. The hands have all read the accounts in the press or had them read to them."

"Yes, Caroline was amusing herself," Marty grinned back then added, "I would like to meet all the officers in my cabin in twenty minutes."

"We will leave on the evening tide and follow the French coast down to Bilbao where we will collect our men. The Eagle has been redirected to patrol the coast around Arridada as we have intelligence that the French will try and sneak in a new spymaster.

I want careful watch kept for enemy ships. I intend to take or burn any we see; the crew haven't had much sea time and are getting rusty so we will take every opportunity to sharpen them up. We will also keep a look out for semaphore towers." He looked around; all his men were listening intently, expecting something more.

"We will burn a couple, but what I want is a copy of their code book. Like we did before, we will leave the original in the ashes to hide that we have the codes. We don't want to go to all that trouble just for them to change them do we."

The men dutifully laughed, and drinks were brought in by Adam and his new under steward, a youth sent up by his brother Alf from Dorset. He was the youngest son of the vicar of East Knowle who had expressed a yearning to go to sea. Eli Dyer was twelve years old and as keen as mustard.

"A toast, gentleman," Marty proposed as soon as they all had a glass, "Confusion to the French!"

They set sail on the evening tide and slipped out of the Medway with little fuss and no fanfare. Wolfgang commanded her; Marty was ensconced in his cabin catching up on all the paperwork.

The ship had been drydocked; any thin copper replaced, her rudder pintails renewed, as one had shown an excess amount of corrosion, and a couple of soft planks replaced. Enormous bribes had been paid to jump them ahead of the other ships waiting for the dry dock.

They stocked up on spare spars and anything else that was scarce in Gibraltar, including a new foremast for the Hornfleur which had a split in her old one. This was stowed on the main deck where it was lashed firmly in place.

Fletcher had been particularly busy and ensured that Marty had plenty of private stores and wine in stock, which Roland could turn into sumptuous meals.

He felt the ship's motion change as she left the estuary and smiled as he remembered his first trip to sea as the old Falcon had left Poole and passed Sandbanks out into the Atlantic. He was twelve years old then and had no idea how going to sea would change his life. He wondered if Eli's life would change as much.

He sighed and got back to checking the muster list. There were a few new names and no runners; that made him smile again as few Navy captains could say that. The new names were almost all men that were recommended by existing crew members or sent by Hood's office. They were a tight knit group and didn't trust people they didn't know.

They crossed the Channel and cruised down the French coast, staying a couple of miles offshore, practically inviting shore batteries to take a shot at them. However, the French were used to British Frigates doing this and saved their powder, not giving away the number and size of their guns.

They spotted a semaphore tower about twelve miles South of le Touquet that was in a remote spot on a headland. Unfortunately for the French, it was the only high place they could site it to complete the chain along that stretch of the coast. Its tall mast and three signalling arms were mounted on what looked like an old stone chapel that had a stunted tower at one end. The arms signalled furiously as soon as they came in sight.

Marty cruised right past it and kept going until they saw the next in the line, which was on hill outside of Le Tréport. By then, it was getting dark and they eased out to sea before turning back North to slip up the coast back to the first tower.

Now all the training of his marines came into play. As soon as they were positioned a half mile off the beach just North of the tower, their lone whale boat and the cutter were brought alongside. The marines, dressed in dark clothes with no white belts, boarded quickly and quietly, and were rowed in. Once ashore, they disappeared into the dunes and all the boats could do was wait.

Paul la Pierre was leading the raid himself, dressed in dark clothes like his men and face blackened with burnt cork. He ran in a half-crouch at the head of the thirty-five marines and NCO's under his command. On his shoulder was Sergeant Bright and in charge of the two fifteen-man squads were corporals Stokes and Everett. Out in front were two specialist scouts.

All the men were armed to the teeth with pistols, musket, bayonet, second knives, swords, and coshes. The scouts carried crossbows to deal silently with sentries. They moved quickly and silently through the dunes and up the rise towards the tower.

A scout appeared, and the group halted at a signal from Paul.

"Yes Collins?" Paul asked in a whisper.

"Like to report, sir, that there is a reinforced platoon of French infantry guarding the tower. Sentries are patrolling the perimeter seventy-five yards ahead."

"How are they camped?" Paul asked.

"Tents in a paddock behind the building for the ranks. We saw an officer heading into the building."

"Do they look like they are expecting us?"

"They are vigilant, but I don't think they know we are about," Collins concluded.

"Sergeant Bright, I want the sentries dealt with silently if you please, three men and the scouts should be enough. I want two men with me to take on the building and the rest to neutralise the camp."

"Aye aye, sir," Bright replied and stepped away to organise the men.

Paul knew he could trust his non-commissioned officers to solve their own problems as they found them, so he didn't feel the need to over direct them. The good thing about a force trained as well as his was you could wind them up, point them in the right direction, and let them get on with it.

"All set, sah," Bright reported a minute or so later.

"Right, let's get on with it, give the order, Sergeant."

"Sah!" Bright responded in as close to a whisper as he could get.

Men streamed past him with deadly purpose. He almost felt sorry for the French, but *then again*, he thought, *what the hell.*

Soft twangs told him the crossbows had been put into use and he moved forward, Sergeant Bright and marine Cosgrove close behind him. Both Bright and Cosgrove were close combat specialists and were perfect for this part of the mission.

He almost tripped over the prone body of a French sentry just before he reached the door. The man would never wake again if the gaping wound in his throat was anything to go by.

They reached the door and Bright put his ear to it.

"Nothing but snoring. Sounds like three people."

That made sense as the system needed two people to operate it - one to operate the signal arms and one to write down the messages, plus the officer.

He eased the handle and as the latch gave, with a click, counted to three in a whisper. He hauled the door open on three and they piled in. Inside was the kitchen and eating area and off of that, screened by blankets, were three sleeping booths.

Just then, there was shouting and shots from outside, the alarm had been given in the camp. Paul stepped up to the closest booth and wrenched back the blanket. A man sat on the side of the bed pulling on his boots. He didn't hesitate and shot him at almost point-blank range. The sounds of a struggle came from the next booth then the curtain wall exploded into the booth followed by Bright, who jumped on top of the heap and repeatedly stabbed his fighting knife through the blanket into the body beneath.

"I think he's probably dead now," Paul drawled as he swapped his empty pistol for its unfired brother. "How's Cosgrove doing?"

"All done, sir," called Cosgrove from the other end of the room.

"Excellent, be so kind as to run the code book down to the beach so they can copy it."

"Sah!" Cosgrove saluted and took both the code and message books with him as he left.

"Now, Sergeant, let's get this place ready to burn."

Marty was happy as they resumed their journey South. He had a copy of the code book and they had copied the last weeks messages from the message book as well. Now they needed to attack another tower or two to make it look like just an attempt to disrupt communications.

Paul was happy as well. He had only two slightly wounded marines and his men had performed well. They eliminated the French infantry after a short but brutal fight, killing them all. Then they chopped down the tower and burnt the house, the code and message books were partly burnt in the hearth before they torched the house proper.

Their next target was the tower at le Tréport. It was close to the town but was atop sheer cliffs and protected by a fortified position. The town, being a port, was also garrisoned. So, this was a job for the guns.

"A guinea for the gun that topples that tower!" Marty challenged them.

"No broadsides for this job," Wolfgang grinned as they watched the guns being loaded and trained by the gun captains.

"Their level of concentration is amazing," Marty commented as he noticed the ship was almost completely silent apart from the orders of the gun captains to their training crew.

Number four was the first to fire, and they knocked a large hole in the roof of the building the tower was built on top off. There were jeers and cheers from the watching men. Number two was next, and the shot flew with the odd whistle made by bar shot.

"That's a bright move," Marty commented as the bar tore a large chunk out of the central mast of the tower.

"GOOD SHOT!" he congratulated the crew.

Number one followed then number three then the other guns fired one by one. Around half had loaded bar, the rest ball, hoping for a killer hit.

It took a second round of shots to bring it down and the 'kill' was credited to the number three gun. In fairness, Marty awarded all the guns that had scored a hit on the tower half a guinea each.

They sailed on, practiced their gunnery on more towers, then rounded Ushant into the Bay of Biscay.

Marty flew a French flag and decided that he would take the direct route to Bilbao and stay off the lee shore.

"Sail ho!" the voice of the foremast lookout drifted down the deck.

"Two points of the larboard bow!" yelled the mainmast lookout, not to be outdone.

"Steer towards it," Wolfgang ordered, "Mr. Hart, I would be pleased if you would oblige me by taking a glass into the tops and telling me what it is."

Aye, aye, sir," Stanley responded smartly, grabbed a telescope from the rack by the binnacle, and shot up the ratlines.

"Ahoy the deck! It's a Fluyt sir!"

"Mr. Williams, give the captain my compliments and tell him we have Fluyt in sight, probably a Dutchman."

The Dutch, at the time, were still occupied by the French and considered enemies of the British so a Fluyt would be a legitimate prize.

"She's seen us and is turning to pass us at a distance," Stanley called down as Marty came on deck, pulling his coat on as he did.

"She's well out of her normal waters," Marty commented as he took a look with his most powerful telescope. Fluyts were an old design of ship and, while capable of crossing the Atlantic, could only carry three hundred tons or so of cargo, so they were more often used for coastal work nowadays. This made Marty curious and he decided it was worth giving his curiosity some rein.

"Intercept him. Let's see what he is up to," he ordered.

The chase was short and ended as soon as they showed their colours. They didn't need to fire a gun.

"M'thinks he gave up a mite easily," Marty mused as they put the fluyt under their lee.

Third lieutenant Stamp got the job of taking a prize crew across and was only onboard for five minutes when he was back in the boat with a civilian and heading back to the Formidiable.

Marty had the side manned and stood back while his number three brought the man aboard. The plain black suit he wore was definitely Dutch as was the style of hat that rose over the side as he climbed the batons. He had a sense of familiarity when he saw his face and racked his brain trying to dredge up who it was. He need not have bothered. As soon as the man's feet hit the deck and he looked across at Marty, his face split in a huge grin.

"Martin Stockley? It is me Martyn van Boekel!" he cried and waved his arm.

Martyn van Boekel? That was a name from his past he had all but forgotten.

"My God! It can't be, what the hell are you doing here?" Marty cried as he recognized the man he had rescued from occupied Holland all those years ago. "Please come and join me in my cabin."

Martyn followed Marty down into his day cabin and was made comfortable in one of the two new club chairs Marty procured while in London.

"What are you doing in Biscay?" Marty asked.

"We, the Dutch in exile, are supporting the Spanish rebellion against Napoleon. We believe if they are successful, there will be a knock-on effect as the other countries see he can be beaten."

Marty considered that then replied,

"We should coordinate our efforts then as I am working with Viscount Wellesley to achieve the same goal."

Adam came in and asked,

"Can I bring some coffee m'lord?"

Martyn blushed when he heard that. He had forgotten that Marty was a Baron and a Knight.

Marty nodded and Adam left to brew a fresh pot.

"Lord Martin," he stuttered, and Marty held up his hand.

"Please, just Martin on ship or Captain if you must," he smiled, "my steward has an overdeveloped sense of the proper at times. Now as I was saying, I am acting as Viscount Wellington's intelligence officer and am working to disrupt the French occupying forces in advance of our moving to kick them out. Can you tell me what aid you are giving the Spanish?"

"We have just delivered funds and arms to our contact in Bilbao to be used to help the guerrillas take the fight to the French," Martyn answered proudly.

"Oh, that is excellent and just what we are trying to set up as well. Can you share the name of this worthy as I am looking to aid the guerrillas as well and do not have a contact in the North?"

Martyn looked troubled for a moment then seemed to come to a decision.

"We are supposed to keep his identity secret so the French do not find out who he is but if you can give me your word you will not share it with another living soul, then I will."

"You have my word that I will only share it with my own men," Marty solemnly promised.

Martyn nodded. That would be good enough.

"His name is Father Frances Domingo; he is a monk of the order of St Francis and can be found at the church of San Nicolas in Bilbao."

"I will contact him personally," Marty promised him.

The rest of the meeting was taken up with catching up on what happened since last they met. Martyn was incandescent with rage at the death of Jeroen, and the perfidy that almost found Marty in French hands whilst on a diplomatic mission to Amsterdam.

They parted with a handshake at the entry port, Marty gifting Martyn a half case of excellent Burgundy to help him home. As soon as the Dutch were safely under sail, Marty ordered,

"Get us to Bilbao please, Wolfgang. I want to talk to the boys, and I have a priest to track down."

The city had finally fallen to the French the year before, but the Basques didn't take the occupation lying down and there was a very active resistance who Antton and Matai had been sent to connect with.

Marty left the ship by boat after dark, was put ashore on the estuary and walked for two and a half hours to the Taverna that the boys should be staying at.

He arrived as the last of the evening's drinkers were leaving and asked the owner for a room.

"Senior, I have just one room left, and it is my best," the moustachioed man replied as he leant on the bar, picking his teeth with a stick.

"That is perfect. I have friends who are staying here, and I would like to surprise them in the morning."

The landlord looked at him suspiciously but called a girl over and told her to show him up to his room.

"If you could send up some food, I would be most grateful," Marty asked and dropped a silver eight-Real on the counter. This famous coin was also known as a 'Piece of Eight' or a Spanish dollar.

"We still have some paella left. I will send it up," the coin disappeared and the girl, who was a typical Spanish beauty, led Marty to his room. She fluttered her long dark eyelashes and turned down the cover on the big double bed, making it abundantly clear that he didn't need to sleep alone.

Marty politely, but firmly, showed her out and sat to take off his boots. He was just wiggling his toes in bliss, it had been a long walk for a sailor, when there was a knock on the door and the landlord's voice called,

"Senior, your meal is here. Can I come in?"

Marty sat upright and reached for his pistols. Why would the landlord bring his food and not the wench who showed him to his room?

He moved silently to a shadowed corner, stood with his back to the wall, and cocked his pistols.

"Yes, bring it in," he called.

The door opened and a man, not the landlord, stepped through carrying a tray. He left the door open behind him, and Marty saw a shadow in the flickering candlelight in the hall. There was at least one more outside.

The tray was placed on the table, and the man turned, a pistol in his hand.

"Hello Antton," Marty greeted him as he stepped out of the shadows, "come in Matai, you need to watch your shadow more carefully."

Antton grinned and put his pistol back on his belt as Matai stepped through the door after telling the landlord all was well.

"I hope you brought enough wine for three. We have some things to talk about."

"Tabetha sends her love," Marty told Matai as they settled down.

"Thank you," he grinned, then reported. "The French only have a loose hold on the region. The governor is Pierre Thouvenot and he is basically a royalist who now works for Napoleon and is universally loathed. The Basques don't have the organization or the military strength to kick them out, but they have set up an active resistance which is set up in cells."

"That's very modern of them," Marty commented.

"Yes, the cells have six to eight members known only to them. Their leaders get their instructions from a central committee, it's all done with drop off points and codes," Antton added. "We have made contact with the central committee, and they have agreed to feed us all the information they gather."

"That's excellent, and you agreed to fund them?" Marty asked.

"Yes, they are starved of funds and weapons and welcomed our offer." Matai grinned.

Alarm bells went off in Marty's brain and he asked,

"Do you know of a Franciscan monk called Father Frances Domingo? He is from the church of San Nicolas."

Antton and Matai looked at each other blankly.

"We haven't heard that name or met any priest or monk," Matai replied frowning. "Is he someone relevant?"

"He might be. Check him out with your contacts tomorrow. I will go to the church and see if I can find him."

They broke up and went to bed after that. Marty locked the door and put a chair in front of it, and another by the window, just to be safe.

The next morning, he got directions to the plaza de San Nicolas and after a breakfast of churros and coffee, set off at a stroll. The weather was beautiful this early in the summer, the scent of wisteria heavy in the air. To the casual observer, he looked like any other Spanish gentleman and sauntered along, looking in the occasional shop and chatting to the shopkeepers.

What he was actually doing was checking his back trail for anybody following him and making it look as if he was wandering for the pleasure of it. He spotted a seedy looking individual who was tailing him about thirty meters behind. He wasn't very good at it and jumped behind walls and pillars whenever Marty obviously looked in his direction.

He finally arrived at the church and made a show of admiring the baroque façade and its strange octagonal tower. He entered through the central door and found himself in an octagonal interior, which was surprisingly plain. He approached the dark wood altar with its large ornate wooden screen above it. In the centre was a golden statue of the Virgin Mary haloed by a golden sun, dressed in an ornate white skirt or robe with golden embroidery, all set in a blue arch.

He knelt, crossed himself, and muttered an appropriate phrase. He maintained that pose until a priest dressed in the robe of a Franciscan appeared and asked,

"Do you want to be confessed, my son?"

"Thank you, Father, but I already confessed this week and I haven't built up enough sin to warrant another one." He smiled at the old man, who smiled back and replied,

"Too much confession takes all the fun out of life. We must all keep a balance."

"You have an unusual church here, but it is quite beautiful," Marty flattered him. It worked the old man preened up a bit and looked proudly around his domain.

"Yes, it is unique to the Basque country and represents our independent nature."

"I am sorry, Father, I should introduce myself. I am Martin del Carpio, traveller and lover of art."

"I am Father Pedro. You are interested in art?"

"Yes, Father."

"Come, I can show you something rather interesting."

He led Marty to an anteroom and to a small wooden cabinet mounted on a wall. He opened it and inside was a beautifully painted Icon depicting St. Christopher carrying Jesus across a river.

Marty truly appreciated the piece as a work of art and made all the right noises.

"This is quite a church for one man to care for," Marty enthused.

"Oh, I am not the only one here. I have my novice father Cristobel to assist me and the good mothers of the parish who clean and cook for us," Father Pedro replied modestly.

"Even so, it is an admirable feat. Especially if no other priests come in to assist and give you some time off," Marty continued.

"We have been on our own for ten years now and have no need of holidays. The service is a reward in itself," the old man replied piously.

Marty had heard enough and excused himself, saying he wanted to visit at least one other church in the neighbourhood.

"The inglesia de Santos Juanes is nearby. You will enjoy that. Father Rodrigues is the priest there and a fountain of knowledge about local art. If he isn't available, then talk to Father Simon. Now go with god, my son," the old man said in parting.

As he left, Marty saw his tail sitting on a bench across the square and decided he would lead him around by the nose for a while. The father was right, Bilbao had some beautiful churches.

It was almost dusk by the time Marty got back to the taverna. He had visited five churches, had dinner at a lovely restaurant overlooking the river, which served some of the best fish he had ever eaten washed down with a delightful local red wine. He made a mental note to tell Caroline about that when he next wrote to her.

His tail had doggedly followed wherever he went and as he passed Matai, who sat on the terrace, he signed for him to follow the man who he knew Matai would have spotted.

He went to his room and changed into a fresh set of clothes for the evening meal and thought about what he now knew. It was a safe assumption that the Dutch had been duped. There was no father Francisco in Bilbao. So, who had they given the money and guns to and how did whoever that was make contact with the Dutch in the first place? He would write to Hood and Turner once he got to Lisbon and get them to check that out or ask Canning to.

There was a knock on his door. He palmed a pistol before answering it. It was Antton, who came to report on what he had found out from his contacts.

"None of my contacts know of a priest called Father Francisco and they were not aware of any aid been given by the Free Dutch. They were actually very angry that someone had diverted what should have been theirs."

"Hardly surprising. Any ideas who might have stolen it?" Marty asked.

"They say there have been rumours of a French agent operating in Bilbao, but nobody knows who he is or where he operates from."

"Wonderful, we are just as much in the dark as we were this morning," Marty grumped.

Matai didn't show up that evening nor was he seen at breakfast the next day. Marty was beginning to worry when a child walked up to him as he sat on the terrace drinking coffee and handed him a note. The urchin stood waiting until Marty flipped him a coin then ran away.

The note was short and succinct,

Captain Stockley

If you wish to see your man alive, please present yourself, unarmed and alone, at the Plaza Barria at noon tomorrow. Stand in the centre with your arms outstretched to the side. You will be contacted.

It was signed D.

Who the hell is D? Marty thought. Whoever it was knew that Matai was his man and knew him well enough to know he wouldn't abandon him.

He prepared carefully, knowing that Matai's life could depend on what he did next. He assumed that he was walking into a trap, and he did so with his eyes wide open. To be safe he sent Antton back to the ship, telling him to be careful and not to get taken as well.

The next morning, he walked briskly to the Plaza Biarra. He pulled his hair back in a simple loose ponytail, dressed simply in a long-tailed coat over white breaches and shirt. and hessian boots as he had the feeling his opponent probably knew all about his trick boots.

He arrived at the Plaza on the stroke of noon, walked to the centre, and stood with his arms out from his sides. It was unusually empty, even for this time of day in Spain, and extremely hot with the sun beating down from almost straight above. It was an unusual enclosed square with buildings on all sides, the ground levels of which were supported by pillars to form covered, shaded walkways.   There were two entrances through tunnels under the buildings in the North and South terraces.

   Then he understood, soldiers appeared at the exits, sealing the square off. The seedy-looking individual who followed him yesterday walked out from under one of the walkways.

He approached Marty with a lopsided grin and indicated he should keep his arms up. He thoroughly searched him, patting down every part of his body and even running his fingers through his hair. He got so close Marty got a whiff of rotting teeth and garlic from his breath.

"You really should do something about that," he quipped as he recoiled at the smell.

Once 'stink breath', as he named him, finished, he made a signal, and a man dressed in a dark suit with lank brown hair approached from the Northern exit.

Marty squinted through the heat haze as the man approached then grinned.

"Dupreeh as I live and breathe! When did you escape from the Isle de France?" he called.

The French agent from the Ministry of Internal Affairs, their secret service, strolled up and waved his hand for Marty to lower his arms.

"Bonjour, Captain, I must say it is a pleasure to see you again."

"How's your head? I really tried not to hit it too hard last time we saw each other."

"I thank you for that. I was convinced you would kill me."

"What? And waste all that talent?" Marty grinned.

"This time I have taken extra precautions. Will you walk with me?"

He walked towards the left-hand exit on the South side of the square, Marty falling into step beside him. The soldiers from the other exit moved in and formed up around them.

"Yes, I see," Marty observed wryly.

"I knew you wouldn't abandon your man as I knew you would send one to follow mine," Dupreeh stated matter-of-factly.

"Is he really that bad or was it an act?" Marty asked, referring to his inept tailing of him.

"He really is that bad, which is why I chose him. You had to believe it."

"Well you got me there, I have to admit," Marty confessed then asked, "It was you who contacted the Dutch?"

"Actually, no that wasn't me. I knew they delivered a consignment to someone in Bilbao, but I don't know who it is. I thought it might be you."

Marty was surprised. He had been convinced it had been the French now he had to start all over again. Once he had gotten out of this pickle that is.

They marched to the French embassy, which was in a grand building overlooking the river with a magnificently decorated interior.

"Nice place you have here," Marty noted.

"We like to keep up standards," Dupreeh answered straight-faced. "I expect you want to see your man?"

"If I may," Marty replied as calmly as he could.

They crossed the ornate foyer and entered a corridor decorated with paintings of past Spanish heroes. At the end, they took a stair down into the cellar where two guards were stood outside of a heavy door.

"Open it please," Dupreeh said in the first French he had used since they had met.

One of the guards produced a large ring with several keys and proceeded to unlock the two mortice locks and a padlock. Marty raised an eyebrow as if to say 'really?'

The door opened and Dupreeh bowed Marty through. Marty stepped inside to find Matai sitting comfortably on a cot, his wrist manacled to a ring bolt in the wall.

"Hello boss," he smiled, "I found out who the fellow that was following you worked for."

"Good work that," Marty replied, flicking his fingers in their sign language.

"Didn't see the ambush coming though. Very nicely set up if I may say so."

"You are unhurt?" Marty asked as he moved to shield Matai's reply from the French stood behind him.

"Treated unusually well and the food's not bad either," Matai replied.

"That's enough. You can see he is unharmed. Unfortunately, he is a deserter from the French Navy, so he will be handed over to them to deal with," Dupreeh announced.

Marty noted that and interpreted it that a Navy warship would be arriving or was nearby to take Matai.

Marty was led to another room and stripped, every stitch of clothing and his boots were minutely examined for hidden weapons or picks. His hair was released from the ponytail and combed through. At the end, he was given another set of clothes and a pair of shoes to wear just in case they missed something.

Once dressed, he was escorted to the second floor and into a room where there was a dining table with two places set. The guards said nothing but the three positioned themselves at the two doors and the window.

Dupreeh entered, sat at one of the places and invited Marty to sit at the other.

"Please sit, Captain. You have made me a wealthy man and the least I can do is offer you a good meal before I hand you over to be transported to Paris."

"Of course! You will get the, what is it, ten thousand Louis reward," Marty exclaimed.

"Twenty thousand, actually," Dupreeh replied as the door opened and servants started to serve the first course.

As they ate, Dupreeh tried to extract information from Marty by injecting questions into an otherwise innocent conversation. Marty either deflected them by changing the subject or by telling outrageous lies and countering with questions of his own. By the second course, Dupreeh had given up and the conversation centred around art and music.

The desert was a delight of fresh fruit and cream with little pastries filled with baked custard or honey and nuts.

At the end, sated and a little tipsy from the wine and brandy, he was led back to his cell with the news that a French line of battleship was arriving tomorrow or the day after to take them both to Paris.

Marty lay on the bed and waited until it was completely quiet then stripped off his trousers and squatted over the pot. An uncomfortable minute later there was a dull clink as a pig's bladder condom full of tools carefully wrapped to make a smooth sausage shape was deposited.

He split open the condom and hid it in a crack in the wall then unwrapped the tools; a pair of lockpicks a folded slim-jim and the blade of a cutthroat razor, the edge of which was encased in resin.

He platted his pigtail into what was a decent approximation of a sailor's queue into the middle of which went the lockpicks. The slim-jim went into one shoe and the blade the other. This made the shoes uncomfortable but as long as he didn't have to walk miles, he would be fine. Now as ready as he could hope to be, he waited.

Nothing happened the following day. He was fed and allowed to empty his pot into a nearby midden. The day after that, guards arrived in force and he and Matai were escorted up to the ground floor and out to the front of the building.

Sitting right outside, moored against the river wall was a ship's barge. Sixteen sailors, ten marines, and a naval officer were waiting for them to board. Behind that was a cutter with a swivel mounted in the bow and another squad of marines. The French, it seemed, weren't taking any chances.

They could only sit while the oarsmen manoeuvred the barge into the centre of the river and headed downstream. Marty was surprised when squads of cavalry appeared on each bank and paced the boats as they rowed.

"I'm going to get a persecution complex if they keep this up," Marty quipped, trying to put a brave face on it.

"You should have killed him when you had the chance," Matai reproved him, "you always said 'never leave a live enemy behind you' now look where it's got us," he snapped grumpily.

Marty knew this was an act. He had told Matai that he had weapons during their brief exchange of sign but how they could turn that to their advantage? Neither had a clue.

Chapter 12: Out of the frying pan

Antton got a boat to take him to the ship and went straight to Wolfgang,

"The boss has been captured by the Department and they are shipping him down river by boat under heavy guard to a man of war to be sent back to France," he announced as soon as he arrived and then had to explain.

"He ordered me straight back here, but I hung around to see what was going to happen and found out from a Spanish servant at the Embassy that they would be moving him by boat."

"There is a seventy-four in the estuary, which is the only ship they could use," Wolfgang stated, "everything else is too small to be secure.' He looked to his signal midshipman,

"Mr. Williams please be so kind as to signal the Alouette for the captain to report aboard."

"James is here?" Antton smiled with a sudden ray of hope.

"Yes, sailed in yesterday," Wolfgang replied.

James listened to the tale and asked Wolfgang what he knew about the seventy-four.

"Well its simple. Step one is to stop that ship leaving the estuary, preferably by burning it or rendering it un sailable. Then they will have to move the captain by land where we can use our resources to get him back. Antton get back ashore and contact the gypsies. If Ryan's reports were accurate, there are a significant force of them out there, but they are scattered." He looked at the map. "The French will either have to follow the coast road or head down to Durango and Elbar and then back up to Itziar to follow the road to the border."

"Either way, they have to pass through Itziar," Phillip Trenchard, the second lieutenant, concluded, looking over James's shoulder.

James nodded thoughtfully. "And by the time they get there they will think they have gotten him away. Now what to do about this seventy-four?"

"He was anchored bow on to the down current last time we had a look," Arnold Grey the sailing master added.

"Well we can bet they will have him facing downstream and ready to go as soon as the boats arrive, what is the state of the tide?" James asked.

"Will be on the rise in the next forty minutes," replied Arnold.

James grinned at Wolfgang.

"Then I suggest we get to quarters and get ready to sail."

Captain Robert St Luke of the Bonne Marche, seventy-four-gun, third rate of the French Navy, read the letter from the local head of the Department of Internal Affairs again. It was quite specific; he was to take aboard a British Naval officer and his man and transport them with all haste to Saint Nazaire where he would be collected by a squadron of cavalry and taken to Paris via Nantes, le Man and Chartres. He was to be kept chained at the ankles and wrists at all times and constantly under watch.

Who the hell was it who warranted this level of security? he thought and looked at his watch. It was three in the afternoon and the tide was coming in. Even if the prisoners arrived in the next ten minutes, they would not be able to leave until it started to ebb. When the tide reached its peak, he would order the ship warped around to face down stream.

There was a hail from the lookout, and he heard that a French Corvette was coming into the Anchorage followed by a Spanish Frigate which it had as a prize.

That was good timing. The tide was just reaching its peak and this should be worth looking at, he thought and stood to take a look out of his transom windows. There was a very pretty older style twenty-eight-gun Corvette dropping its bow anchor no more than fifty meters directly behind him.

"Blanchet! Tell that fool he needs to anchor further up, he will be in our way when we leave," he called to his first through the skylight. Then he looked again and caught a glimpse of the frigate slipping past them and the Corvette swinging around using the incoming tide and their spanker to push her stern around her anchor. Something suddenly felt very wrong, and he grabbed his hat to go in deck.

"Drop the stern anchor as soon as we bear!" James ordered, "run out and prepare to fire!" They had gotten thus far unscathed as they had a copy of the latest signal book taken from a French cutter they captured on his way to rendezvous with the Formidiable. But as soon as they opened fire, they knew it wouldn't be long before the shore batteries opened up against them.

He looked across at the Formidiable, she was anchoring just fifty feet off the Bonne Marche's starboard quarter and smiled as their gun ports opened and the dark shapes of the eighteen pounders appeared through the gaping holes. They were fully depressed.

A rumble announced his carronades were running out, the big smashers would be devastating at this range. He spotted movement on the quarterdeck of the Bonne Marche and a tall man in the uniform of a Capitaine de Vaisseaux appeared at the rail waving his hand at him and shouting something. James smiled and waved as he called, "show them our colours!" and as the flag broke free cried, "FIRE!"

The nine stubby thirty-six-pound carronades in their main battery plus the two twenty-four pounders on the quarterdeck threw three-hundred and seventy-two pounds of iron, which, when added to the almost six hundred from the Formidiable, had a devastating effect on the French ship. The Alouette's broadside hit her stern and raked the gundecks from end to end, sending splinters and shards of shattered balls scything through the hull. The Formidiable's eighteen pounders were directed at her waterline, her gunners aiming to punch three large holes through her hull to fill her up with water as fast as possible. Her big sixty-eight-pound carronades would take down rigging and the aft thirty-six pounders targeted the big ships quarterdeck.

James had concluded they needed to cripple her, not destroy her, to render her useless for transporting Marty, so their tactics were set accordingly. It was hit and run to get away before they were sunk by the shore batteries.

The French ship was obviously being called to action and it wouldn't be long before they were able to answer, but before then he could serve her at least twice more.

The shore guns were silent and a quick scan with his telescope showed that they were manned but not firing. They were so close to the French ship, they must be frightened they would hit her as well.

The carronades spoke again just over one minute after the first broadside. The transom dissolved as shards of glass and frames tumbled into the sea revealing the interior of the ship. It looked like hell, the balls had smashed their way down the deck clearing the partition walls out of the way, allowing them to see their full effect. Her rudder was hanging awry held only by the lower pintails. The stern chasers and after guns were scattered in disarray with some on their sides. Men were trying to move them back into position but the Alouette's marines were sending a hail of musket fire through the opening to disrupt them between broadsides.

"Round shot next salvo, if you please," James called, asking for the guns to be loaded with nine, four-pound balls each to turn them into enormous shotguns. The first shore gun fired and splashed down the other side of the Alouette. Yes, they were afraid of hitting the Bonne Marche but as soon as they disengaged, they would get their full attention.

The Formidiables were keeping up a steady broadside every minute and a half, and after the third, a few of the mid-upperdeck guns on the Bonne Marche started to fire in reply. Nothing aft of their centreline could be trained around far enough to bear, so they were relatively unscathed.

The French were in a chaotic state. The captain and first had been killed in the first salvo from the frigate's aft carronades, swept from existence in a hail of cannister. The other officers were trying to make some order but they were faced with a panicked, unprepared crew.

"My god! How do they fire so fast?" the young sixth lieutenant screamed as the fourth broadside came in from the Corvette in as many minutes. He had come on deck to report that all the after guns were out of action. It didn't matter to him for much longer as one of the marine sharpshooters in the tops of the frigate picked him out. The ball took him in the upper chest, angling down through his body, ripping his lungs to shreds.

A carpenter appeared on the deck and looked around frantically for someone to report to. He spotted the third leaning against the main mast, blood coming from a wound in his leg.

"Are we sinking?" the lieutenant asked as he approached.

"No sir," the carpenter shouted, *"we are aground on the mud. They have shot our bottom out."*

"Signal the Formidiable to disengage, Archie. The Frenchman is aground, her lower gun deck is barely above water," James ordered his midshipman. He was satisfied. That ship was going nowhere. In fact, he smelt a whiff of smoke and as he looked, he saw a flicker deep within her hull.

"Oh my! They had the galley fires lit!" he cried, "she's on fire!"

He ordered; 'cease fire' and 'secure the guns ready for making sail.' It was time to get the hell out of there as they could see a column of horse artillery moving up from the South and they, with the shore battery, would be able to make it very hot for them.

The crews of both the British ships knew they had to be quick. The tide had slackened and peaked during the engagement. Now they had to run for their lives through a gauntlet of hot iron with only the river current to help them.

Both crews simply cut their anchors and using a combination of sails and rudder, swung their ships around on the current to face down stream. As soon as they were clear of the Bonne Marche, the shore guns opened up and they were taking hits.

Ryan watched a shot hit one of his midship carronades, throwing it into the air and killing two of its crew. Damn it was getting hot!

The Formidiable's broadside roared out in reply, their longer guns able to reach the batteries, then James had an inspiration.

"Run out and fire blanks with wet wads!" he shouted to his men, the damp wad would cause smoke and help hide them. Soon, the guns were roaring, and the smoke was billowing down the sides, and with no shot the rate of fire was even faster than usual.

Marty, sitting in the boat, heard the roar of guns from a couple of miles ahead. The French crew was looking concerned, this obviously wasn't expected, and the sailors could tell that the guns were not French. He identified the boom-chuff of carronades and then the rolling thunder of eighteen pounders. Had James arrived? Were they the Formidiable's guns?

The officer in charge pointed his pistol at him and looked nervously downstream. He barked an order, and the oarsmen ceased rowing to let the boat drift on the current.

Marty grinned when the second broadsides echoed out. That had to be the Alouette. They were firing at a minute a round. The eighteen pounders went again about half a minute later. Now he was sure.

After about twenty minutes, during which he only heard the occasional French gun, it all went quiet. The officer ordered the men to start rowing again and they rounded the corner at Astrabadua. The shore batteries suddenly burst into life and Marty strained to see what was going on. He could see that there were clouds of smoke and two ships were making their way out of the estuary.

It was getting desperate. The Alouette had taken a lot of hits, the rigging was seriously damaged, and he had men manning the sweeps to push her along as fast as they could in the narrow channel. The Formidiable was in just as bad a way but her guns continued to roar defiantly. She had lost both her fore and main topmasts and staggered from hits to her hull.

James strained to look back through the smoke at the Bonne March and saw flames. If they had been sensible, they would have flooded the magazine or maybe it was already flooded as they had sunk. In either case, it didn't explode, which would have helped.

There was a stronger gust of wind and the smoke cleared momentarily to reveal they were out into the widening funnel of the estuary proper.

"Make all sail!" he shouted in relief as he realised, he had some sea room at last.

Marty stood on the shore and watched the big seventy-four burning. They looked like they would put it out, but she had taken enough damage that there wasn't any way she would be taking him anywhere.

"It will not help you, Captain," the French officer snarled, *"we will just take you over land to the border. Your ships cannot help you then, as we are in command of the roads between here and there."*

"I am sure you are!" Marty murmured with a frown. A large force would be hard for his men to overcome.

First thing the next morning, a full company of lancers formed up around the coach that had been requisitioned to carry Marty and Matai to Bayonne. It was old, landau style with leather strap suspension and was pulled by a pair of horses. Marty figured that if they travelled all day, they could probably do the trip in around ten hours if the coach and cavalry could get remounts around halfway.

However, the French set out at a pace that made it clear they were going to preserve the horses they had and progressed at a walk. The terrain was mountainous, and the coach horses weren't the youngest he had seen, so by lunchtime they had only reached Elbar. The Cavalry fed and watered their horses before settling down to lunch at a tavern. Feeding eighty horsemen plus officers and a coach driver would present a challenge to any landlord and it took around two hours to get them fed and back on the road. The Navy officer, who refused to introduce himself personally to Marty, ate with the Lancer Captain. Marty was left under the supervision of a Sergeant of the Lancers and ate with Matai. They were both still shackled hand and foot.

They continued at the same unhurried pace. It was hot and the sun was relentless, making everyone grumpy. Sweat ran down under the irons, causing them to chafe if they moved, so Marty sat back, tried to relax and enjoy the mountainous scenery.

Matai nudged him and nodded at a nearby peak. He casually looked in that direction and spotted, after a moment's scanning, a figure which was obviously watching the column. He checked the soldiers and couldn't see any reaction from them, so he was left wondering if anybody else had noticed.

A mile further on and a gypsy caravan was seen approaching from behind the column. It wasn't travelling particularly fast and was catching the column slowly, the soldiers saw it and ignored it.

The road dropped down into a valley and started to follow the Deba river, which twisted and turned as it made its way to the coast. The soldiers started to be more alert as this was one place that they thought the British Navy could try and effect a rescue. They would almost touch the coast at Deba before turning back inland.

"The land is too flat here," Marty whispered to Matai, "it gives the advantage to the cavalry."

Matai nodded. If their men were going to do a rescue, they would choose a spot that disadvantaged the escorts.

They passed through Deba without incident and turned back inland. Once they got away from the coast and into the hills, the guards visibly relaxed. The next village was Itziar and that would be their camp for the night.

There were some relatively flat fields on the edge of the village where the horses were picketed, and tents set up. Marty and Matai were given one of their own, right in the middle.

The gypsy caravan pulled up on the edge of the camp and a man got down and approached, a woman and a teenage girl sat on the steps at the back.

"Hey soldiers!" the man called in broken French, *"You want swords sharpened? Pots fixed?"*

"Damn gypsy scum," their Navy escort snarled.

"Don't be such a snob," reprimanded the Lancer Captain, *"they sharpen most of the swords in the army, and their woman will dance for a few coins and that entertains the men."*

"But they will steal anything that's not tied down!" Navy responded.

"We will search them and their caravan before they leave. That is standard procedure."

Marty was intrigued by this exchange; the French Army were obviously conditioned to seeing the gypsies around and had developed a few precautions when dealing with them.

Within minutes, the gypsy man had set up a grindstone and was busy sharpening swords and knives, his woman and the young girl, who Marty assumed was his daughter, wandered through the camp talking to the men. He noticed that the girl would talk to the men while the woman wandered around looking into their cookpots. She would tease them about the standard of their cooking and offer to sell them herbs.

After dark in front of the officer's tents, the man played a set of pipes, the woman and girl sang and danced. It was all very jolly and both Marty and Matai clapped along with the rest. However, the guards made sure the gypsies didn't get close to them.

The next morning, the caravan was gone. From what he overheard, they had had left at dawn and headed back the way they had come.

They broke camp and resumed their journey towards the rising sun into forest covered hills. After an hour, Marty noticed that the column was looking ragged. Some men were slumped in the saddle and weren't paying attention to their mounts who were just following the horse in front.

Then men started pulling out of the line, jumping from their horses and running into the trees. Judging from the smell that drifted out on the slight breeze, they were having a very bad reaction to something they ate.

The captain called a halt when it became obvious that almost half the men were affected. The smell from the trees was noxious. The Navy officer who sat opposite Marty was covering his nose and mouth with a handkerchief when his forehead suddenly spouted a crossbow bolt. Marty pushed his body upright with his foot as it slumped forward to try and hide his sudden demise, then reached behind his head and loosed his ponytail, retrieving his lock picks.

A few seconds saw his hands free and a few more his feet. Matai was free soon after. Marty gathered up the Navy officer's weapons. *Never did find out his name,* he thought and waited.

Screams suddenly erupted from the trees where the men had gone to relieve themselves. Horses started to rear and buck when grenades arced from the trees exploding in the middle of the escort.

"Now!" Marty hissed and the two of them slipped out of the carriage and ran for the trees. Someone noticed and they heard the sound of hooves behind them. Marty was about to spin and snap off a shot when the treeline erupted in smoke and fire as a volley of muskets went off along the length of the column. He looked over his shoulder to see his pursuer, the sergeant who had been their guard for the first day, rolling out of the back of his saddle, his chest covered in blood. His horse veered to the side and galloped back along the road.

Inside the treeline his arm was seized, and he was dragged behind a tree. James grinned at him then raised Marty's own Durs Egg Carbine and shot another soldier.

"Thought you might like to have this along," he winked and passed the gun over along with its powder horn and bullet pouch. Sam stood about ten feet away loading a musket, his white teeth dazzling in the gloom under the trees.

Marty reloaded the carbine and picked out a target. The man dropped off his horse and he automatically went into the routine to reload. It suddenly occurred to him that the French weren't running away.

"The Gypsies have the road blocked at either end with caravans," James informed him, "we don't want any of them to get away."

Marty was surprised at his lieutenant's ruthlessness and asked,

"Why?"

"We did a deal with the Gypsies; they get the horses and any loot, and they insisted there would be no witnesses to their involvement."

Marty decided not to think about the fact that eighty men were going to die so he and Matai could go free.

It got to the point where there were no French standing and the Gypsies moved in to finish off the wounded with knives. Their leader came to Marty and introduced himself.

"I am Danior, the leader of this band. You are Martin, the leader of Ryan?"

"I am," Marty replied and shook his hand.

"The horses and goods will pay for the rescue as none of my people have been hurt," Danior grinned, gap toothed.

That's generous, thought Marty sarcastically but answered,

"You have my thanks. They meant to take my head."

"You need to kill the man Dupreeh in Bilbao. He will come after you again. You have three days before he finds out you didn't get to the border."

Marty understood.

"Can you lend us some horses so we can get back to Bilbao quickly?" he asked.

"For you, I will give a special price for the hire of my horses, you will need two for each man." Danior smiled.

Marty sighed; he was sure the 'special price' would still be extortionate but he didn't have a choice and two horses each would enable them to get back to Bilbao that night.

Chapter 13: Tales in the Crypt

Marty, Chin, Matai, and James had ridden hard, changing horses every hour to get back to Bilbao by midnight. They didn't go back to the tavern Marty stayed at before but did pick up the weapons and tools he had hidden before his capture.

They were given an address of a 'friend' by Danior, who they roused, gently, by breaking into his house and Marty sitting on his bed to introduce himself. When the poor man got over the shock, he gave them rooms on the understanding that they would show him how they got in and how to stop anyone else from doing the same.

As James wasn't known, he carried out a reconnaissance the next morning to establish the whereabouts of Dupreeh and whether he lived at the embassy or somewhere else. While he was gone, Marty checked over his weapons and put together a shopping list of items he thought they might need. He would finalise it when James returned.

"He lives in the embassy. I talked to one of their Spanish servants, and she told me that he has rooms at the back on the second floor. She thought he was creepy and a cold fish," James reported that evening. He had made a drawing of the layout of the exterior of the embassy and the foyer.

"I went in pretending to be a French merchant wanting to set up trade with Bilbao and looking for support from the embassy. I got in as far as a clerk's office on the ground floor."

The Embassy was a large building facing onto a plaza by the river. It was different from other French Embassies they had seen before in that it didn't have a stable or courtyard and the back was right up against another street. Dupreeh lived in an apartment on the second floor at the back that had a flat roof or roof terrace inset into the building. It was built of red brick with ornamental stone corners and window frames.

"I can climb that," Chin pronounced as they debriefed later that afternoon.

"In the dark?" Marty asked surprised at his confidence.

"Yes, then I can let a rope down for you clumsy sailor boys to climb," Chin replied with a grin.

Marty raised an amused eyebrow at the tease and went on with the planning.

"Right then, Chin climbs the sheer wall of the building, drops a rope for the rest of us to climb, and when we get to the roof, we let ourselves in and extract our friend Dupreeh."

"Why not just kill him and leave him in his bed?" asked James.

"I want to have a long talk with him. He has information that would be very useful to us," Marty explained.

At one in the morning, four dark shapes made their way through the almost deserted streets to the back of the French embassy. Three positioned themselves so they could keep watch on the approaches and the fourth made his way to the building's rear wall.

Chin stood facing the wall. He wore completely black clothes and was hooded in the same material, which rendered him almost invisible. On his feet, he wore fine silk slippers with a sole made of rough chamois leather.

Focusing his chi, he reached up and felt the wall with his fingertips. He could feel the texture of the bricks and the mortar between them. He found a line where the pointing was slightly more depressed and pushing his fingertips into it started to climb. He took his time, making sure of every move before he made it. From where Marty stood, he looked like a spider. It took him fifteen minutes to reach the roof, which had a convenient flagpole to tie the rope to.

Marty was the first up and silently approached the window; it had a standard latch and a second's work with a slim jim unlocked it. The window had heavy curtains across it, and Marty checked James had him covered with a crossbow before he eased them aside. Keeping low, he stepped into the room and looked around. It was very dark, but he could just make out a curtained, fourposter bed in the starlight coming through the open window.

Taking extreme care, he worked his way across the room, checking every step to make sure he didn't tread on, or run into anything. The bed's drapes were down so he couldn't see who was inside. He stopped and listened; there were definitely two people from the sounds of breathing and gentle snores. James unclipped a shuttered lantern from his belt and opened it, allowing a weak beam of light to shine out.

Marty signalled Matai to go to the other side of the bed then gently pulled the drape aside. The faint light of the lantern revealed Dupreeh and the slender form of the governor's wife! Marty smiled; he wasn't such a cold fish after all. They knew the governor had been in Madrid for the last two weeks and wasn't due back for at least another week. He nodded to Matai, who took a pillow that was lying on the floor and placed it over her face. Marty simultaneously stepped up to Dupreeh's head, placed a pistol barrel in his mouth and clamped a hand around his throat

Dupreeh woke with a start and was immediately aware of the hard metal barrel and the hand around his throat. The governor's wife was struggling but Matai held her down while she slowly suffocated.

"Will you behave?" Marty asked, "if you do, we will let her live."

Dupreeh nodded, and Matai removed the pillow, allowing her to take one big breath before clamping a hand over her mouth.

"Shhh, if you want to live, do not make a sound," he whispered in her ear. She relaxed, but her eyes were wild and as round as saucers.

"Now, if you would be so kind as to get out of bed and move over to the window," Marty instructed Dupreeh, removing the pistol so that the man could swing his legs over and get out of bed. He stepped back and gestured for Dupreeh to move past him.

"Slowly now, any sudden moves will get you shot somewhere that hurts a lot but won't kill you by my friend with the crossbow." Once his back was turned, he followed him to the window then rapped him under the ear with a cosh he took from his pocket.

"Put her to sleep," he instructed Matai, who put the woman in a sleeper hold and squeezed. She struggled briefly then relaxed. He held it on for a few more seconds then gently laid her on the bed. On his way out, he collected Dupreeh's trousers shoes and shirt and stuffed them in a pouch.

Chin and James had, meantime, picked up the unconscious Dupreeh and moved him to the edge of the roof. James quickly and expertly tied him onto the end of a rope while Chin slid down the rope they used to climb up. Once they were ready, James and Matai lowered the naked body over the edge and down to street level.

Dupreeh came to stretched out on a cold stone surface and looked up at a vaulted stone ceiling about eight feet above. His head hurt and he felt sick. He was naked and cold. He tried to move his hands but found he was manacled to the stone.

He let his head roll to the side and took in his surroundings. He was in a crypt or a mausoleum lit by a number of oil lamps hanging by chains from the ceiling. There were two stone coffins to his left and another one to his right. He concluded that he was lying on a fourth.

"Ahh you are awake!" the cheery voice of Captain Stockley greeted him and his face appeared above him.

"Sorry about the bang on the head. That really is a habit I should break, but it was the easiest and quietest way to get you out of the embassy."

He said nothing. His mouth was dry anyway and he wasn't about to start a conversation.

"You must be thirsty. Would you like some water?" Marty asked.

Dupreeh squinted at him then nodded and suddenly a piece of wet sacking was clamped over his face and held so he couldn't turn his head. Someone poured water onto it so it ran up his nose and into his mouth, constricting his breathing. He was gasping for breath and trying not to drown by the time they stopped.

"Ingenious, isn't it?" Stockley asked him. "It was suggested by my Chinese friend. I call it the Chinese water torture. Doesn't leave a mark on the body but is unbelievably unpleasant. Now we are staying here until tonight when we will return to our ships and it's up to you how pleasant the stay will be. Will you answer some questions?" Dupreeh shook his head; he wasn't going to tell this asshole anything!

He could be proud he lasted three hours before he was telling them everything he knew.

Once Dupreeh started talking, Marty had him unchained and sat on an old wooden chair that someone had left in the crypt. He was not made comfortable, allowed to dress or dry off, and the chains were left in his line of sight along with the water bucket.

They were in a crypt in the church of San Nicolas, which conveniently had a well and was, to all intents and purposes, soundproof. According to the priest, the well was originally dug for when people were given sanctuary so they could stay for an extended period. It was now used by the resistance as a safe place.

Dupreeh didn't have much information about the military plans of the French in the area, apparently that wasn't why he had been brought here. He did have a wealth of information on French counter espionage activities and admitted that he had been brought in to counter the threat that Marty presented.

"I'm flattered," Marty told him, "I had no idea I was causing so much trouble to the French cause."

"I believed, correctly, that I could trap you after I studied your file. The Dutch presented a lead that could be exploited."

"So, you do not know who Father Frances Domingo is," Marty concluded and got a nod in confirmation.

"Or where the gold and guns ended up?"

"The guns we found in a warehouse in Duesto. No idea about the gold."

Marty smiled and turned to the subject of his agent network. Dupreeh had recovered his courage and refused to answer. They picked him up and dumped him back on the coffin lid, held him down, chained him up again and filled a bucket with water. One dose was enough to get him talking again but they ran out of time. It was time to leave for the ships and Marty wanted everything he knew before he decided on any action.

They passed on the location of the guns to the local resistance with a request that they look out for anyone who had suddenly come into a lot of money. They prepared to get back to their ships. Marty handed Dupreeh his clothes; the trousers, stockings, and shoes were fine, but the shirt turned out to be the governor's wife's blouse. He wore it anyway as it was all they had.

The gold would have to wait for another day as they had stirred up a hornet's nest and the town was full of soldiers looking for the missing agent. The church was separated from the river by a wooded park that was crawling with soldiers and the riverbanks and river were being constantly patrolled so they would have to leave overland.

The local resistance committee agreed to help them and sent a contact to the church. He was shown down to the cellar by Father Pedro who was enjoying 'thumbing his nose at the French.' The contact led them from the Casco Viejo to the Barrio Zurbaranbarri Auzoa, where they were passed from one resistance cell to another across the city to the forested hills to the West. Diversions pulled the soldiers away from their escape route, but it was still a very nervous time.

Dupreeh was amazed; he had no idea the resistance in Bilbao was so well organized, and he realized that with what he had seen, he would not be allowed free or maybe even to live. His agile mind constantly looked for ways to escape or attract the attention of one of the patrols but everywhere he looked, there was one of his escorts keeping him under his gimlet eye or a Spanish agent fingering the blade of a knife.

The other problem was, the water treatment he received had left him weak and it was as much as he could do to keep up with the strange band led by the young British captain.

Once they were in the hills, they were met by a group of Gypsies with horses and, once mounted, turned North to the coast. Dupreeh was not much of a horseman and as the group kept the horses at a fast trot, his backside and thighs were soon reduced to a painful mass of bruises.

Dawn saw them approaching a beach near the village of Gorliz where a pair of ships boats were pulled up. As it got lighter, he noticed that a couple of the horses had French cavalry brands and the Gypsies were carrying swords that probably used to belong to Lancers.

A big dog leapt out of one of the boats and ran up to the horse Stockley was riding, bouncing up as high as it could jump, yipping and whining in joy, a big doggy grin revealing its long white canines.

He found he couldn't move his legs to dismount, much to the amusement of the rest of the group. Stockley called to someone from the boat and the big black man he captured on the Isle de France approached and helped him down.

"Hello Sam," he groaned as his feet hit the ground and his knees buckled. Sam held him up. "Is that Troy?"

Sam gave a deep chuckle and replied,

"Sure is, Mr. Dupreeh, but don't worry about yo balls he is busy saying hello to his boss."

Troy was indeed busy. Once Marty dismounted, he had placed his paws on his chest and proceeded to give his face a thorough wash. Marty, in return, was rubbing his neck and making, 'good boy,' noises.

The greetings over Marty thanked the leader of the Gypsies and passed him a pouch of coins. It paid to keep the account current when dealing with mercenaries. As they galloped off, he turned to Dupreeh who was being held up by Sam.

"Can you walk?" he asked.

Dupreeh tried but his legs just gave way. Sam scooped him up like he was carrying a girl and strode to the Formidiable's barge where he handed him to the crew.

"Let's get out of here. We need to get back to Lisbon to see if the Eagle caught the new spy chief the French were sending in," Marty said to James as they shook hands in parting.

Chapter 14: An Uncomfortable Voyage

If Dupreeh thought his time in the crypt was bad, then the Formidiable was the seventh layer of hell. Marty wasn't set up to play clever mind games, so he took the direct approach; stress positions and sleep deprivation.

It didn't help that they sailed straight into a storm before they left Biscay, which threatened to drive them onto a lee shore, forcing Marty and James to find shelter behind the Punta Gaztelgatxeko Donia and giving Marty more time to work on him.

Dupreeh was supervised by one of the Shadows at all times. He was kept in a kneeling position with his hands tucked behind his bent knees, which caused pain in his knees and back. He was not allowed to sleep and had been awake now for thirty-six hours. He was hooded, so he could see nothing, and no one spoke to him.

Marty let him soak for twelve hours then had him brought to his cabin. Troy was laying on his blanket and watched curiously as he was brought in. Marty and Paul la Pierre were the interrogating team and started by asking his name, where he was from, his parent's names, and where he had been posted.

This confused him. He couldn't think why they were asking this and started answering truthfully. They kept questioning him for half an hour, repeating the same questions in different ways then returned him to the brig.

Four hours later, he was brought out again. They started with the same questions then Marty asked,

"What is the name of your superior?"

"What?"

"What is the name of your superior?"

"Stefan Janout."

"You're lying," shouted Paul, causing Troy to stand as he reacted to the tension in the room. He walked over and growled at Dupreeh.

"No, no. It's true. My superior is Stefan Janout," Dupreeh sobbed, terrified.

"What is your mother's name?"

"Marie, I told you already Marie."

"What are the names of your agents in Spain?"

Before he knew it, he had told them the names and where they lived. He wanted to please them. He didn't want to go back to the dark. He wanted to sleep.

They questioned him for two hours then he was returned to the brig, which now had a cot and some soup for him to eat.

The next morning, he was brought to Marty's cabin again. He was still exhausted. His legs and ass hurt from the ride and from being in the stress position for so long and he had a headache.

"Good morning, would you like some breakfast?" Marty asked him pleasantly and motioned him to a chair. Roland had prepared fresh croissants, bacon, eggs, Spanish sausage, and toast. A fresh pot of coffee was brought in, its aroma permeating the cabin.

"Thank you," Dupreeh said and sat where Marty pointed.

"I would advise you to eat a little to start with as you will make yourself sick if you eat too much too fast," Marty advised as he helped himself to three eggs and a pile of bacon.

"You speak from experience?" Dupreeh asked.

"Yes, I have been the guest of the French a couple of times and gone long periods without food," Marty replied.

"I am sorry for that," Dupreeh said around a mouthful of croissant, "these are wonderful! Where do you get them?"

"My cook is a Frenchman, a royalist who defected during the revolution and stayed with me when Napoleon took power."

There was a knock at the door, and Shelby came into the cabin.

"Aah, doctor. I was just telling Dupreeh here about Roland," Marty greeted him.

"That man is a genius in the kitchen," Shelby agreed, then to Dupreeh, "I would like to examine you to make sure there is nothing I need to treat."

Dupreeh made to stand up.

"No, finish your breakfast. I will eat as well. Is that coffee as fresh as it smells?"

Dupreeh was now totally confused. They had abused him and kept him awake for hours on end, questioned him until his head spun, and were now feeding him breakfast?

The sheer domesticity of the situation would have been comforting if there weren't the ever-present weapons his host had about him. The cabin was full of them and the fact they were so easily accessible told volumes about the confidence his captor had in overcoming him if he did make a lunge for one.

The doctor and Captain Stockley chatted about mundane things, a crewman with a broken arm, sustained in the storm, another with an abscess under a tooth that would require extraction. He gradually came to understand that the ruthless intelligence officer cared for his men but would not hesitate to use them in pursuit of his duty.

"All finished?" Shelby asked cheerfully. When Dupreeh nodded, he got him to stand and take off the blouse he was still wearing. He listened to his heart using a wooden device with trumpet bells on either end, took his pulse, tut tutted over an open sore.

"You are in surprising good health," he declared.

The door opened and two of the evil-looking Basques came in with the dog behind them.

"Escort Mr. Dupreeh to the deck pump and allow him to have a good wash then bring him back here," Marty instructed and handed Antton a bundle of clothes.

Dupreeh returned to the cabin dressed in a pair of nankeen trousers and a shirt from the purser's slops. His hair was still damp, but he had a healthy glow about him.

"Do all your men bathe under that pump?" he asked.

"Once a week. Cleanliness is important onboard a ship," Marty informed.

"Always in saltwater?"

"No, if we are in port, they get to wash themselves and their clothes in fresh."

"Interesting, that is something our sailors could learn from," Dupreeh said thoughtfully, then asked.

"What will happen to me now?"

"You will continue to be questioned then you will be incarcerated for the rest of the war."

"In a prison?"

"It depends what you call a prison, Cedric," Marty replied, using his Christian name for the first time. "I plan to have you taken back to England and kept under house arrest on my estate in Cheshire."

Dupreeh didn't notice. He was busy thinking about what Marty had said.

"I know you are a Knight and a Baron. Why do you do this?"

Marty laughed.

"I wasn't always a Knight or a Baron. My parents were clay miners. The Navy rescued me from that life and enabled me to improve my lot. I have been incredibly lucky in life. Now we have to get back to our conversation of before."

Dupreeh looked alarmed, which caused Marty to reassure him,

"Don't worry, no more water torture or sleep deprivation as long as you cooperate."

There was a knock at the door and the marine announced,

"Midshipman Hart, sah!"

"Come in," Marty called.

"Good morning, sir, and Mr. Ackermann's complements, but the storm is abating, and he feels we can get under way now."

"Please tell him I will be up directly and to prepare to get us under way. Please be so kind to signal the Alouette accordingly."

"Aye, aye, sir," Stanley replied and touched his forelock in salute.

After he left, Marty gathered up his coat and put it on, then noticed that Cedric didn't have one.

"Adam!"

"Yes, m'lord," Adam replied as he stuck his head through the door from the steward's pantry.

"Dig out one of my old coats for Mr. Dupreeh here. We can't have him freezing to death."

Suitably attired, Marty escorted him onto the quarterdeck. He wanted him to see the hopelessness of his situation and the absolute lack of any way he could escape.

The crew was busy; the men at the capstan stamped and heaved, the nippers ran back and forth securing the anchor hawse to the messenger, topmen ran up the shrouds to get ready to set the sails and landsmen positioned themselves to haul. It all looked efficient and well-organized.

Off their starboard beam, the Alouette was ahead of them as James had anticipated the command. Marty smiled; his friend was ever competitive.

"It's going to be a long, hard track to get to Lisbon with this wind," Arnold Grey said to Marty as they stood together beside the binnacle.

"I know, but we need to get back. We have things to do," Marty frowned as he looked at the sky.

The wind was coming from the South, which made getting out of the bay simple but as soon as they reached the Atlantic, they had to sail as close to the wind as they could, heading out to the West to enable them to make

Lisbon after a couple of long tacks. The sea was up and
from the South, forcing them to run at an angle across it
making the ship corkscrew nastily.

Dupreeh was surprisingly unaffected, taking the
motion in his stride. The interrogations continued in an
almost gentlemanly fashion. He had a salutary lesson
when Marty was forced to punish a man with the cat. He
was an old hand that had gotten drunk and picked a fight
with the carpenter, which was tantamount to striking an
officer. Punishment was called, and the men assembled,
the offending individual brought before the captain.

"Joseph Marler, charged with being drunk and
striking the carpenter," the master at arms announced as
the wretch was brought forward.

"Joe, this is out of character. What do you have to
say for yourself?" Marty asked.

"I am most 'umbly sorry, sir. I had too many sips o'
rum and can't say as I remember anything."

Marty was clearly not impressed and turned to the
carpenter.

"What do you have to say, Watkins?"

"I was working on a new rail to replace the damaged
one over on the port side when Marler staggered into my
shop and started picking up tools and dropping them on
the floor. He said he was looking for an awl to bore an
'ole. I told him to get out and to stop throwin' me tools
around. He got angry and started shouting. I tried to get
him to calm down and that's when he punched me."

The carpenter turned his head so Marty could see the
bruise on his left cheek.

"Anyone else have anything to add?"

Andrew Stamp, the third lieutenant, stepped forward.

"Marler is in my division and has, until now, behaved well and worked hard. I believe he is of good character and that this episode is an exception."

Marty considered, this was clearly in contravention of the 2nd article of war;

2. All flag officers, and all persons in or belonging to His Majesty's ships or vessels of war, being guilty of profane oaths, cursings, execrations, drunkenness, uncleanness, or other scandalous actions, in derogation of God's honour, and corruption of good manners, shall incur such punishment as a court martial shall think fit to impose, and as the nature and degree of their offence shall deserve.

He had the right, as captain, to impose punishment as he saw fit.

"Joseph Marler, you are clearly guilty of the offence as presented. Are you willing to accept punishment from me or go before a court martial?"

"From you, sir."

"Then you will receive a dozen lashes- six from Wilson and six from Sam."

Wilson was left-handed and Sam, right. This would make it easier on him as the cat wouldn't repeatedly hit the same spots and cut as deep.

"Thank you, sir," Marler stated, bobbing his head.

The grating was rigged and Marler tied up to it. Shelby tied a leather apron around him to protect his kidneys and the cat was brought up in its red baize bag.

Sam went first and laid on his strokes with force and precision, blood trickled down Marler's back. Wilson took up the cat and laid on his with equal dexterity. By the end, Marler was sobbing in pain.

"Mon dieu, I had heard about the famous cat with nine tails, but it is even more of a fearsome instrument of punishment than I imagined," Cedric gasped.

"Its' even worse if salt is rubbed into the tails," was all that Marty replied.

The interrogation resumed that afternoon and was expertly conducted with each answer confirmed by cross examination. By the time they got to Lisbon, he had been wrung dry.

The ship docked and a young officer came aboard immediately, reporting to Marty.

"Well, Mr. Archer, did you capture our spy?" Marty asked the serious young man stood before him.

"We did catch him landing a boat on the shore, sir, but we were unable to take him," Midshipman Archer, temporarily in command of the Eagle, replied with a blush. "He got ashore and ran for the dunes. Stan Rogers, the marine sharpshooter, shot him in the arse, and he fell to the ground, but before we could get to him, he pulled a pistol and shot himself in the head."

"Unfortunate, but not a bad result," Marty reassured him, "I trust you have made sure you have covered all the details in your written report?"

"Yes, sir," Archer replied, visibly relieved.

"Now, any word from Lieutenant Thompson?"

Archer passed a sealed packet of papers over.

"He also sent a verbal report that the French were pulling out of Cadiz."

"Hmm," Marty murmured as he read the report from Ryan and Linette. "That doesn't surprise me. After they sent ten thousand men to Masséna, they only had a token force left there."

The report from Ryan detailed the strength and makeup of the forces in Badojez, which had fallen after the first salvo from the French guns. The walls were so decrepit, they stood no chance. There had been a major action at Albuera where Beresford's combined Anglo Portuguese force had grappled with Soult's army as it moved North. Ryan's report detailed the fight that ended with a French retreat despite having mounted the biggest infantry assault of the war.

It also told him that they might have a lead on who took the Dutch gold. There was a new resistance group who not only wanted independence from the French but from Madrid and the royal family as well. It seemed the leader was styling himself as the champion of the middle and working classes and was rumoured to be a merchant. The regular resistance and guerrillas wanted nothing to do with them, but he was building a significant following South of the Basque region.

Marty decided after some thought he was a problem the Spanish would have to solve after the French were kicked out. In all probability, it would just go away on its own after they were liberated, and life returned to normal.

Chapter 15: Face to Face

A message arrived from their man in Madrid, Maurice Chastain. He was being directed to visit Ciudad Rodrigo and Salamanca to audit the army accounts there. It seemed that bureaucracy didn't stop even for war. He suggested it might be a good time for the two of them to switch places as he would be gaining access to Soult's headquarters.

Only problem with that is Soult knows me by sight, Marty thought.

He would be leaving Madrid mid-June, had provided them with his itinerary, and suggested that they should rendezvous at Ávila where he would overnight. He would also provide a suit of the clothes like those he would wear and said he would brief Marty on the rest when they met.

Marty had a good hard think. He doubted he could fake the audit of finances in any way, shape, or form. The idea that he could just replace Maurice outright looked not to be as good as those, over clever men, in London had thought. That made him think a double blind might be in order.

"Sam, can you ask Matai, Antton, and John Smith, to attend me," he said, without looking around.

Sam, who had been playing tug with Troy, grunted and left for the main deck. Troy, deprived of his playmate, came over and plonked his head down on Marty's lap for an ear scratch.

"It would be better if James was still here, old son, but he won't be back for at least four weeks now, will he," he told the ever-attentive dog. James had left two days before to take Dupreeh to England and would sail directly to Liverpool.

Troy agreed with him and bumped his hand with his nose for an extra rub as he could hear the others coming down the steps from the deck.

"We have an opportunity," Marty announced when they were all in and comfortable, causing hearty grins all around as they saw the opportunity for some fun coming over the horizon.

"We have an agent in Madrid in the Ministry of Finance who bears an uncanny resemblance to me and is on his way to Ciudad Rodrigo and Salamanca. The idea of Messrs Canning and Hood is for me to switch places with him at some point before he gets there so that I can use my skills to break into Soult's headquarters and gain access to his plans. There is only one tiny flaw with that and that is I know nothing about accounting or finance and my cover would be blown in minutes as soon as anyone asked me anything."

John Smith barked a laugh.

"So, what we goin' to do then?" he asked.

"That's what we need to talk about, the headquarters is in Salamanca and it's going to be risky as that place is crawling with military and intelligence. We need to protect our agent as well, so anything we do cannot be traced back to him either."

"What would hurt the French most?" Adam, Marty's steward, asked as he placed a tray of coffee on the table.

Marty looked at him in surprise. He hadn't thought that Adam would want to contribute anything to their operations and before he could answer John replied,

"That's easy, Soult needs to supply his men and horses. They can only get so much locally, so he either has to buy local like or ship it in from France. He has to pay 'em as well, so he needs cash."

Adam nodded.

"So, if we could stop the supplies and gold, then Soult would have problems?"

Marty gestured for him to take a seat and replied,

"Yes, if he doesn't get what he needs from France, he will have to send out foraging parties to make up the difference and they will have to travel further every day to find food for the men and horses. The downside of that is it really hurts the locals as the French are absolutely ruthless when it comes to foraging."

"But it does open up all sorts of possibilities for the guerrillas to ambush those parties," Antton pointed out.

"Which will just force him to dedicate more and more troops to the foraging parties. It helps but it's not the solution," Marty concluded.

"If we can't cut his food off, what else can we target and where can we cut his supply line?"

On the 10th of June, a group of three horsemen rode up to a Gypsy encampment to the East of Salamanca and hailed the sentry.

"Hola, we are here to see Pedro the knife sharpener."

"Get off your horses and wait there."

The three did as they were told, keeping their hands in plain sight. It was midday, the sun beat down and the scent of lavender and hibiscus was overlain with woodsmoke and cooking.

A voice from behind them asked in Basque,
"What will Troy do?"
Antton grinned and replied,
"Bite your balls off. Hello Garai."
The three relaxed as Garai walked around in front of them his musket held in the crook of his arm.
"Come, the midday meal is ready," he laughed and slapped Antton on the back.

They joined Ryan and Linette at their caravan and the six sat around their fire to catch up.

"What brings you here?" Ryan asked after all the greetings were exchanged.

"We are going to disrupt the French supply lines to Salamanca and thought you and your friends might like to join in," Adam replied in perfect Spanish, much to Linette and Ryan's astonishment.

"Where have you been hiding?" Ryan asked him.

"Right under our noses," Antton replied for him.

"Where did you learn Spanish?" Linette asked.

"Before I entered service with Lady Caroline, I travelled as the valet for a Spanish gentleman who had a very attractive daughter," Adam replied with a blush.

"Oh! How romantic," Linette exclaimed.

"Not really. He caught us together one day and threw me out. I had to find my way back to England from Madrid with only a pound to my name and the clothes on my back." Adam winced at the memory.

Garai looked around in an exaggerated way then asked,

"So where's our illustrious leader? It's not like him to miss an opportunity to create a bit of mayhem."

"He has gone to find out where the best place to cut the supply line is and he asked me to give you this," Adam replied and handed a note to Linette.

Around the same time, Marty was approaching a Tavern in the medieval town of Ávila on the back of a mule and leading another four mules in a train behind him. Troy wandered along beside him. Marty was dressed as a trader and the mules were laden with fancy metal goods such as copper bowls, cauldrons, kettles, and such like.

He had grown a moustache and his skin had tanned to a similar shade to the locals. He wore a red traditional Barretina, a colourful neckerchief, white (but grubby) shirt, and black trousers tucked into high boots. In short, he looked exactly like you would expect a Catalan trader to look like.

The taverna had rooms to rent from the cheapest over the stables to moderately luxurious on the third floor, well away from the bar and kitchens. He climbed down from his mule and led the train into the yard where he talked to an ostler before unloading his animals and stacking his goods in a lean-to on the end of the stables. The ostler, for a half Real, directed him to a stall big enough to take all five of his mules, which had a stone water trough and several nets of hay hanging from the rafters. He rubbed each animal down with handfuls of hay to get the worst of the road dust and sweat off of them.

Once satisfied that his livestock and goods were all safe, he headed into the taverna to haggle with the owner over a room. This required a protracted and noisy exchange, which resulted in him getting a medium quality room on the second floor over the kitchens for the night for a hefty discount. Once settled, he returned to the bar to get an evening meal. It was full of French officers and a smattering of Spaniards. Troy followed at his heel.

He looked around for an available seat and saw one at the end of a common table that had five junior infantry officers and a civilian dressed in a French style black suit and high-necked white shirt. He was not their man.

He took the seat as it was the only one available and it would have stood out if he didn't. Troy made himself comfortable beside him. The French officers were chatting happily amongst themselves, secure in the conceit that there was no one else who could speak French. He gathered, as he waited for his meal to be delivered, that they were part of a relief force from Madrid that would replace troops that had been part of the siege of Cadiz. The besieging force had been starving, living off whatever shellfish they could harvest from the shoreline and boiled seaweed. The guerrillas were effective in ambushing any supply trains and foraging parties and the locals were aggressively uncooperative, hiding food, forcing them to raid villages to get anything to eat.

This confirmed that the siege of Cadiz was being lifted as Ryan had reported.

His food arrived and he was presented with garlic soup with a poached egg floating in it and fresh baked crusty bread. The wine was a rich red made from the tempranillo grape and was as good as anything he had tasted. He slurped his soup noisily gaining a glare from the civilian sat opposite him. The soldiers changed the subject and were speculating on what they would be doing once they got to Salamanca, they obviously had no clue as their speculations were wild and extremely diverse.

The main course arrived, a spicy sausage and bean casserole, wholesome peasant food flavoured with thyme and chilli. He ate in silence, quietly observing the room. As well as the infantry officers there were Hussars with their fancy uniforms and bangs and Lancers in green uniforms with a red bib. Both sported spectacular moustaches, which had been waxed and twirled to perfection. From the talk he overheard, they would all be moving out in two days.

The French civilian opposite him saw him looking leaned forward and said in terrible Spanish,

"They look magnificent, don't they? They are the pride of France!"

Marty shifted his gaze to him, remembering he was a Spaniard in this guise.

"Si Señor, they are very handsome. If they fight as good as they look, they must be invincible."

The Frenchman frowned as he tried to decide whether Marty was being genuine or sarcastic. Marty continued to eat his casserole.

"You are a merchant?" the Frenchman asked.

"Si, I trade in pots and pans," he replied shortly.

"Where did you come from?"

Marty made a point of putting his spoon down, looked at the man, and replied slowly.

"I came from Toledo. It took me two days as my mules are lazy and only walk slowly. My dog is happy as

he can keep up easily and has time to catch rabbits. I have a sore arse and my head hurts." He took a sausage and dropped it to the floor where Troy sniffed it then wolfed it down in two bites.

The Frenchman left him alone after that, and he finished his meal in peace. The room got louder as the soldiers got drunker and he decided to leave them to it and went to his room.

The next morning, he was down for breakfast early and ate it as leisurely as he could. There was still no sign of their man. Now no trader would miss the chance to show his wares, so to preserve his cover, he got permission from the owner to set up a stall in front of the taverna. He spread a blanket on the ground, laid out his pots, and sat cross legged in the middle.

He had on show a mixture of high quality and cheap pots and soon had a few housewives looking them over. The cook from the taverna also came out after lunch looking for a new cauldron and got into a shouting match with the owner as she was looking at the biggest and best one and he thought it was too expensive. In the end, she won the argument and took the largest cast-iron cauldron he had, negotiating the price down quite aggressively.

"*Thank you, madam,*" Marty smiled at her as he pocketed the money, "*it will last many lifetimes.*"

"*It will if I don't beat that old fool to death with it first!*" she replied, still angry.

"*Is he your husband?*"

Her look softened,

"*No, he is a widower. His wife died five years ago.*"

"*And you?*"

She looked down at the black clothes she wore.

"My Juan was killed by a bull that escaped from the ring. It was heading towards a group of children and he distracted it away from them. Silly old fool was no matador and got gored for his trouble."

Marty understood the two being widowed could theoretically get married. He also knew that local customs would make that difficult. He was about to suggest something when he spotted a figure approaching on the back of donkey.

The man was obviously French, and his donkey was trotting along keeping up with a squad of cavalry whose horses ambled along at a medium walk. He held a parasol over his head in his right hand and the reins in his left. There was a brown valise slung behind his saddle with what looked like a fold up desk strapped to the top.

The horses stopped in front of the taverna, and their riders dismounted. The donkey headed straight into the yard despite the efforts of its rider, who alternately hauled on the reins and kicked it vigorously with his heals. Marty watched as the beast trotted up to the door of the stables and stopped, waiting expectantly.

The rider threw his leg over its neck and slid the few inches to the ground, took off his hat and wiped his brow. Dark hair, brown eyes, face tanned from exposure to the Spanish sun, it was his contact.

The ostler came out and saw the donkey waiting by the door and let out a hearty laugh,

"Ay Bajo, you are back!" He looked at the Frenchman, who just stood there looking annoyed and explained,

"This is his second home. He is waiting to go to his stable and get his hay."
Maurice Chastain looked like he wanted to kick the beast but instead folded up his parasol and retrieved his valise and table. He turned to go into the Taverna. The pot trader, who had gathered up his unsold goods and blanket and made his way into the yard to put everything back into the lean-to, staggered as he tripped over the trailing end of the blanket and crashed into him.

The two ended up in a tangle surrounded by pots and pans. The trader was the first to his feet, bowing and apologising as he helped Maurice to his feet.

"Clumsy oaf!" Maurice swore and pushed him away. He gathered his belongings and stomped into the Taverna; this day couldn't get any worse.

Maurice finally made it to his room, a cheap one on the first floor over the kitchen as that was all his allowance would run to. He was unhappy. His arse was sore from riding that damn donkey. He was bruised from the collision with that stupid costermonger and his contact hadn't showed up. *It is typical of the English to be late,* he muttered to himself as he put his bag on the bed, then took off his coat.

A piece of paper fell to the floor, which was odd as he couldn't remember having put any papers in his pockets. He bent, picked it up, unfolded it and read,

Greetings, I will come to your room at midnight.

S

Then it dawned on him.

Maurice sat by the fire facing the door, waiting. He was very nervous; his visitor's reputation had preceded him and not all of what he heard had been complimentary. He tried to sit still but his nerves made him want to pee.

There was a scratching noise. At first, he thought it must be a rat, he expected there were many in this excuse for an hotel. Then he heard it again and it sounded like it was coming from the window. He got up and walked slowly over and peered through. He nearly had a heart attack when a face appeared and mouthed,

"Open the window."

Getting over his surprise, he unlatched the window and pushed it open. The costermonger was hanging by a rope and quickly maneuvered himself through the opening into the room.

"I thought I was going to have to let myself in," he said in greeting, *"Martin Stockley, how do you do."*

Maurice shook the proffered hand and realised it was like looking in a mirror.

Marty had concluded that climbing down from his room was a lot less likely to be spotted than sneaking around the corridors. Now Maurice was in a state of shock at his appearance at the window. He smiled his most friendly smile and guided him back to his chair.

"Relax, no one knows I am here; you are quite safe."

The resemblance between the two of them was amazing. There were minor differences, but they could easily be brothers. He estimated that dressed the same, he could pass for Maurice even close up.

"I am sorry I am forgetting my manners. Maurice Chastain at your service," Maurice stuttered in a high-pitched voice.

The pitch of his voice surprised Marty. It was at least an octave above his and kind of squeaky.

"Will you take over from me here?" Maurice asked.

"No, there has been a change of plan," Marty replied, *"I want you to continue to carry out your duties as you have been ordered by the Ministry of Finance with a small exception: when you get to Soult's headquarters, I want you to make a floor plan and identify the offices of the supply corps, Soult's office, and his secretary or aid's office."* He let that sink in then added, *"Once you have done that, I will take your place for one afternoon if I can find what I need. If I need a second afternoon, we will work that out at the time."*

"Can I help find what you are looking for?" Maurice asked.

"No, the less you know the safer you will be," Marty replied, then asked, *"did you bring the clothes for me?"*

Maurice went to his valise and took out a package wrapped in brown paper and tied with string.

"These are identical to mine from the same shops," he informed Marty.

"Are they new?"

"No, I wore them for a week and had them washed. They do not look new anymore,"

"Where will you be staying in Salamanca?" Marty asked.

Maurice dug out a piece of paper from his valise and passed it to Marty. It had an address in the Plaza de las Cigueñas written on it.

"They have allocated me an apartment there. It is relatively close to the Palacio de Monterrey where Soult has his headquarters."

"We will need a place to exchange information. Find a café or taverna near to your apartment and I will contact you there."

Marty spent the next half hour explaining how to encode a message and found Maurice a quick study.

It was time for a change of persona. Marty sold off the mules and stock to a trader in a Riocabada and transformed into a Spanish gentleman scholar. He thought this was a particularly apt disguise as Salamanca was a university city. He wore a fake goatee beard and a pair of blue tinted eyeglasses which were very fashionable and hid his eyes. His hair was pulled back in a ponytail as was fashionable amongst Spanish gentlemen. He dressed in the latest fashion and exuded personal wealth. He took a room in a good Taverna to overnight before moving in on Salamanca.

"I almost didn't recognise you," a familiar voice said.

Marty jumped. He hadn't heard Linette come into his room and his hand was lifting a pistol before his brain registered who it was. He glowered at Troy, who just laid there waging his tail a stupid grin on his face.

"You are going to get yourself shot if you keep doing that," he admonished her then swept her up in a hug. *"How are Ryan and Garai?"*

"They are well and send greetings."

"When did you arrive?" Marty asked.

The Dorset Boy Book 8: La Licorne

"Two days ago. I let them know I was waiting for my husband." Linette smiled. *"I am staying at a hotel down the road."*
"You had better move in here. It would seem odd that we are staying at separate establishments."
The two were used to working together and their respective partners trusted them, so cohabiting was not a problem.

Soon, Linette had moved in and Marty was surprised at the number of trunks she brought with her. It took two servants and a carriage to move them from one hotel to the other. He had her leave all of them except the one she needed for that night in the carriage as they would move on in the morning.

They left for Salamanca after coffee, the carriage and four making good time. Linette revealed that two of the trunks were for him. She had been shopping. The trunks were stacked on the roof and Troy shared the cabin with them. He would have happily run alongside but it was a five-hour trip and that was too much even for him. As it was, they arrived before it got too hot.

Linette had contacted their local agent and he found them a house to rent. It was near the University on the Calle Tavera. It was furnished and was just the kind of house a couple like them would take.

Once installed, Marty set about making himself as unexceptional as possible. He established a routine where he left the house and walked to the university every morning. He varied his route, but he just happened to pass through or near the Plaza de las Cigueñas every day.

On the third morning, he stopped at a café and had coffee and churros. He struck up a conversation with the owner and a French clerk of the Ministry of Finance.

"I made contact. He took about ten minutes to realise who I was," Marty told Linette as he stripped off the beard with a relieved sigh as they prepared for bed.

"That damn thing itches like hell," he complained.

Linette laughed, "this is the first time you have used such a disguise, non?"

"Alright for you. All you have to wear are wigs," he grumped.

"Mai oui, but they can be hot and uncomfortable too," she replied and asked, "has he done the plan yet?"

"No, he says he needs another two days. He told me Soult is here at the moment but plans to leave for Ciudad Rodrigo on Friday to inspect the garrison there. Maurice is scheduled to go with his entourage. If that is true, I will assume his identity on Saturday and pay the offices a visit," Marty explained.

"Ah, so he will have, as you say, a cast iron alibi!"

"Yes, I just hope I can imitate his voice. He sounds like he's been kicked in the balls."

On Thursday, Marty picked up a newspaper that had been left on the chair that Maurice vacated as he walked up to the café. He made a show of reading it as he drank his coffee but what he was really interested in was the detailed floor plan of Soult's headquarters concealed between its pages. That, however, would have to wait until he was somewhere much more private.

He walked to the university as usual after finishing his coffee and went to the library where he picked a book at random from the antiquities section. He found a spot in a corner with clear views of all approaches and settled down to study the map. It seemed that Soult had taken over a room called the Salon Principal on the top floor; his secretary had an office in an anteroom. He memorised the map then folded it and slipped it into the spine of the book, which he returned to the shelf, just in case he needed it at a later date.

Soult left the city on Friday with a huge escort that made his departure unmissable. Their exit out of the town and across the Puente Romano (Roman Bridge) was noisy and designed to make an impression. Maurice was visible sat on a baggage cart at the rear of the column eating the dust kicked up by the horses ahead of him.

Saturday came and at midday, 'Maurice' entered the building as most people were leaving to take advantage of the fact that the boss was away. He walked confidently through the entrance and up the stairs that led to the third floor where Soult's office was located.

The second and third floors seemed to be deserted and the door to the secretary/aid's office was locked, which didn't stop Marty for more than about ten seconds. He entered and re-locked the door behind him. If the secretary turned up for any reason, he would be in trouble as there was only the one door.

He started his search from the bottom up, that is with the bottom drawer of the desk, then the next up and so on. He found some interesting orders, which he copied, but nothing on logistics, so he moved onto the cupboards. The first produced nothing, nor the second, but the third turned out to be where they stored all the maps.

Soult's clerk was a methodical type, and all the charts were annotated with the region and date. He selected the ones for the regions north of Salamanca and the border region. Routes were highlighted with notes on the strength and location of garrisons at key points. After about an hour, he realised that to inconvenience Soult, he had to do two things, blockade the ports along the North Spanish coast, especially Bilbao and Santander, and cut the roads that crossed the border at Irun and Roncesvalles forcing any supplies to travel tricky back roads through Basque country where they could be ambushed in the mountains.

He copied the parts of the maps he thought necessary and checked his watch. It was five o'clock already! He had to leave; the French were notorious for keeping their hours. He listened at the door and could hear no one outside, so he unlocked the door and eased it open.

The corridor was clear but the door to Soult's office at the end, just a few feet away, was open a crack. Marty quietly closed and locked the door to the clerk's office, then walked silently up to the office door and peeped in.

"What the hell are you doing here?" he hissed as he recognised the figure in an infantry uniform.

"Merde! Do not do that! I nearly wet myself!" Linette whispered back, clutching her breast in shock as she jumped. She was dressed in the uniform of a subaltern of the 39th Regiment and would pass casual

inspection with her blond hair tucked up in a uniform hat.

"I knew you would need help," she snapped, annoyed he had been able to sneak up on her. *"You were locked in that room for hours."*

Marty looked at her in surprise.

"How long have you been here?"

"About ten minutes less than you. I knew where you were because you weren't in here," Linette replied smugly.

"Whatever. We need to go," Marty told her as he bit back a retort that he knew would just start an argument, *"you can explain later!"*

Linette just grinned at him and waved a sheaf of papers which she tucked into her jacket.

"Well, come on then, and don't forget to lock the door behind you." She smiled as she swept past and out into the corridor.

The two exited the building. Marty had to admire the way that Linette managed to imitate the way a man walked and avoid swinging her hips. Considering the differences in the male and female anatomy, it was an accomplished piece of acting. Especially as she normally had, what a French officer once described as, a seven-jewel movement (referring to the movement of an expensive watch).

She led him to a deserted stable at the back of a large empty house and produced a change of clothes for both of them. They quickly changed personas and emerged as the gentleman scholar and his wife through a different door in a different street.

Back in the house, Marty pulled out his copies of the maps and Linette her papers and they started to compare notes.

"Soult keeps a lot of notes and I made copies of some I thought would be useful. See this one; he is concerned that his supply of powder can be disrupted by guerrilla attacks and orders his supply corps to stick to the main coastal route from Bayonne. The only other way they are getting powder or any other supplies from the North is from the ports."

Marty pulled out the applicable map.

"They come over the border here at Irun then cross the river Bidasoa via one of these two bridges," he surmised as he studied the map. "If they are destroyed then they would have to route via Bera or Landibar, which puts them into the mountains and Basque country."

"Well they are very well defended. Soult has realised that the bridges are a weak spot and has detailed a battalion to defend them," Linette added.

"From an attack by land," Marty pondered, "but what about an attack from the sea? If we can destroy the bridges then they will have to take the other route and then Ryan and his gypsy friends can have fun ambushing the convoys in the mountains.

Linette looked at him, knowing that he had something in mind but decided to give him the bad news anyway,

"There is a battery guarding the entrance to the bay and river, any ship you sent in there would be blown to hell and in any case, there is a boom across the river to stop anyone from sailing up it, controlled by the military."

"Looks impossible doesn't it?" Marty grinned.

Chapter 16: Bombastic.

In Gibraltar, Marty had the Flotilla gathered for a briefing and sat on the edge of the table at the front of the room where his officers of ship and marines were gathered.   He looked at his pocket watch. He was expecting two more people to arrive.   Bill and Adam were serving coffee and churros when there was a knock on the door and a marine sentry announced,

"Commander Cocks and Captain Fairmont of the Engineers Sah!"

A middle-aged commander stepped into the room and bowed to the assembled worthies. He was followed by a short, stocky army captain in the uniform of the Engineers.

"Gentlemen, welcome, please take a seat and grab a coffee." Marty smiled, "Commander, it's very good of you to divert from your return to England to help us."

"I saw your Flotilla with Cochrane at the Basque Roads; you were a credit to the service. If I can help in any way, then I will, sir," Cocks replied, dipping his head in salute. He refrained from criticising Admiral Gambier but the fact he didn't mention him spoke volumes.

"For you who do not know Captain Cocks, he commands the Thunder, an eight-gun bomb ship. Captain Fairmont is on General Wellesley's staff and he and his men are demolition specialists," Marty said by way of introduction, which just increased the anticipation in the room.

"Now I expect you are all wondering what this is all about and what could warrant recalling Lieutenant

Thompson and Linette from their work in Spain," Marty paused, looked at the expectant faces, then grinned as he continued,

"To be effective, a modern army needs a number of things; soldiers, horses, food, clothes, shelter, swords, guns, and the means to make the guns go bang. Take any one away or reduce its availability then you reduce the effectiveness of the army. Hungry troops don't march or fight well. If they have no clothes, they get cold and sick. Take away the horses and cavalry are just infantry that doesn't know how to march." That got a laugh as all sailors held cavalry in some contempt. Marty let it run for a few seconds then continued, "but take away their weapons or the means to fire those weapons and you don't have an army but a large crowd of civilians."

James raised his hand, and Marty nodded at him to speak,

"Could we even hope to cut the food supply to the French army? They are expert foragers and cutting the food supplies just means they will steal it from the locals who will be the ones to suffer."

"Exactly," Marty agreed, "we made that mistake with Messéna, thinking that we were starving his troops, but they were far better foragers than we gave them credit for."

"So, are we going to steal their clothes?" Paul la Pierre the captain of marines joked.

"That would certainly be fun and probably entertain the locals, but no. We are going after their powder supply."

"Boom!" Midshipman Trevor Archer of the Eagle laughed setting off the rest of the room.

Marty stepped over to a large easel covered in a sheet and pulled the cloth aside. On it was a reproduction of the map he had made in Salamanca that had been redrawn at a much larger scale by John Smith. It depicted the Bidasoa estuary and the bay of Hondarribia, the river and the bridges at Irun and Behobia.

Marty gave them time to look at the map then continued,

"Our friend Soult is no fool and is well aware that if these bridges are cut, he will have to route his supply columns through the mountains over here," Marty pointed to the border, which curved around the mountains near Bera.

"And that is our country," grinned Antton who, along with the rest of the Shadows, sat at the back of the room, "if they go through there, we will cut them to pieces."

"And if he tries to bring it in from Madrid, the guerrillas will do the same," Marty concluded.

"I can imagine then that the good marshal has taken steps to protect those bridges?" Captain Cocks chipped in as he realised that comments were encouraged.

"Yes, he has a Battalion of Infantry and two batteries of artillery defending them," Marty revealed.

"So, a land assault will be difficult," Paul concluded, his head on one side as he expected Marty to have a plan.

"Quite," Marty agreed, "which is where Captain Cocks and the Thunder come in, but before we go there, let me fully explain the defences around the bridges and the bay."

He went on to describe the defensive force around the bridges and their disposition as they knew it from the notes that Linette made in Soult's office and information from their spies. He described the location and strength of the battery positioned on Punta Xaxiarri that dominated the bay and entrance to the estuary. Finally, he told them about the boom that was strung across the entrance to the bay of Txingudi. It was in three parts; fixed booms were strung from the shore on either side out to pylons that had been driven into the bottom in the middle of the entrance. The pylons were one hundred feet apart, creating a gateway that was closed by a moveable boom that was opened and closed by a rowed boat that towed one end out of the way of any incoming ships.

The local fishing fleet moored in the outer roads and did not enter the bay, that was reserved for the occasional French merchant ship that called in and was currently home to four Spanish hulks that had been requisitioned by the French and were used as store ships.

"As I see it, we need to complete a number of tasks to blow these bridges up. First, we need to neutralise the battery on Punta Xaxiarri. Once we have done that, we can bring the Formidiable, Thunder and Hornfleur into the bay," Marty explained.

"Then the Thunder can barrage the bridges and blow them up?" Angus Frasier piped up.

"Unfortunately, not," Cocks replied. "The range to the second bridge is around our maximum and dropping sufficient bombs accurately enough to destroy the bridge is impossible."

"Which brings me to phase three," said Marty regaining their attention. "As soon as we have control of the bay, a team will enter the estuary and take over the boom, opening it and keeping it open to allow the Hornfleur's landing boats and two cutters with half of Captain Fairmont's men to pass through and make their way up the river to the first Bridge.

The Formidiable and Hornfleur will lay down a barrage targeting the first bridge and the banks either side. This will make the French think that we are trying to destroy the bridge with our cannon. Under cover of that barrage, the marines will set up on either bank to provide protection for the engineers so they can set the demolition charges." Marty paused and took a sip of coffee, giving them all time to absorb what he had said.

"At the same time as all of this is going on, the Thunder will start a barrage on the second bridge. Their mortars have the advantage of being able to shoot over hills and their shells are explosive, but they will need spotters who can relay the fall of shot back to them so they can adjust their aim."

"We have a system of flag signals that we use to adjust our aim. I need at least one man in sight of the target and as many relay stations as needed to get the message back," Cocks informed them.

"It is not practical to get boats all the way up to the second bridge so the demolition team will have to come in overland from Pasaia where we will drop them off on our way to the bay. Ryan and his guerrilla friends and a contingent of marines will provide the escort and secure the bridge while the charges are set."

Marty looked at the impeccably dressed captain of engineers and added,

"I am afraid that your splendid red uniforms will have to be foregone in favour of blending in with the guerrillas. I hope you can go along with that."

The captain looked somewhat pained by the idea, but he had been chosen because he had a broad streak of practicality in his nature and nodded his acquiescence.

What followed was an extensive and thorough planning session where every contingency they could imagine was examined and taken into account.

Marty introduced Fairmont to the clockwork timers the tool-shed developed. They refined them over the years and developed their own much more robust wheellock mechanism that was much less likely to go off if it was knocked.

"Why haven't we seen these in use in the Army?" Fairmont asked as he examined the detonators.

"The powers that be deemed them too dangerous for general distribution. They are terrified they will get into the hands of the enemy and make it too easy for them to set bombs in the capital," Marty explained.

"I've seen a number of devices since I have been in your compound that would be of great benefit to the engineers. For example, those grapnels you fire from swivel guns would be very useful in a siege," Fairmont replied.

"Well now you have seen them, I'm sure you can replicate them," Marty grinned, "You can take a couple with you as examples if you like."

Fairbrother looked at the timer and raised an eyebrow in question. Marty shook his head, "not one of those."

"But we can use them on this mission," Fairbrother stated with a hint of annoyance in his voice. Marty sympathised, knowing how annoying it was when another branch of the same force had toys that you weren't allowed to play with.

The mission was scheduled for the end of September. Arthur Wellesley had his own reasons for that which he was keeping close to his chest, but Marty suspected that he wouldn't be advancing out of Portugal until at least next summer, so he wondered at the timing. But his was not to wonder why, and he trusted the instincts of the great man implicitly.

The engineers trained getting on and off the boats with the marines, who teased the 'crabs' as they called them unmercifully until they got it right. Marty knew that some firm friendships had grown up in their common endeavour especially when a couple of the engineers had fallen overboard and were fished out by a number of marines before their heavy equipment dragged them to the bottom.

The fact that almost all the engineers couldn't swim hadn't occurred to him, and he set up lessons for those who wanted to learn with a couple of his more amphibious marines as instructors.

By September, they were ready to go. The Hornfleur, Formidiable, and Thunder set off for the Bay of Biscay. The Eagle and Alouette left earlier and would range up and down the coast from Santander to Bilbao to intercept any French merchant ships with orders to take, sink, or burn everything they saw. The Eagle would drop Ryan and Linette near Bilbao so they could rendezvous with the guerrillas and gypsies.

The wind was from the Northwest, which meant the journey North took longer than they expected as the Thunder couldn't sail anywhere as close to the wind as Marty's ships. However, they eventually reached their turning point and swung around into the bay as the wind picked up, an autumn storm was approaching.

Marty stood on the quarterdeck, wrapped up in his waterproof canvas coat with his hat tied to his head. The spray and rain combined to make life miserable, and no matter how good the coat, it still ran down the back of your neck but at least now they had made the turn the wind was on the larboard quarter.

He looked around at the Hornfleur, which was two cables behind, and he could just make out the Thunder behind her. It was lucky that the Thunder wasn't one of the old bomb ketches, which would have had a terrible time keeping station but a custom-built merchant ship with a reinforced hull.

Paul la Pierre appeared at the steps to the quarterdeck, and Marty beckoned him up.

"How are our engineers holding up?" Marty asked.

"Let's just say we are running out of buckets," Paul grinned in reply. The truth was the majority of the 'crabs' were suffering acute sea sickness due to the erratic motion of the ship. It was probably worse on the Hornfleur.

"Is Shelby attending them?" Marty asked, concerned that a vital part of his force was effectively disabled.

"He is, but there's not much he can do," Paul replied then ducked as a shower of spray hit them.

"If we weren't running behind schedule, I would seek a sheltered bay to ride this out, but as it is, we will just have to go with it. We need to be at Pasaia tomorrow morning to rendezvous with Ryan, Linette and the guerrillas.

The next morning found them off the lighthouse at Faro de la Plata following the Formidiable around the point into the bay. The intention was for the Formidiable to heave to off the Puntas de san Pedro and ferry her marines and engineers onto the beach at San Juan. The other two ships would stay out further in the bay ready to resume their journey as soon as the Formidiable made her way back out.

The coastline was, to say the least, rocky and the entrance to the bay was bracketed by rock spurs that stuck out waiting to catch the unwary. The gap was just a cable wide and Marty had two men swinging leads in the bow. Under just spanker, foretopsail and Jib they crept in, getting out with the wind from the Northwest would be harder.

"Back the foresail!" Marty ordered and the ship slowed but didn't stop. "Damn, bring her into the wind and drop anchor," he ordered as he watched the rocks at Puntas de san Pedro creeping closer. Wolfgang was ready for this and the anchor prepared as a precaution.

A glance to the North showed the other two ships emulating them.

"What's the holding like?" Marty asked as he watched all the sails being taken in.

"Rocky with patches of sand," Wolfgang replied, "the hook is holding firm for now."

"Men on the shoreline," called the lookout. "It's Mr Thompson," he added as he recognised the lieutenant.

"Get the boats alongside and manned. Assemble the shore party!" Marty ordered. "Wolfgang, you have command I will go ashore and speak with Ryan."

"You are going to have trouble getting out of there," Ryan greeted Marty as he stepped ashore.

"Good morning to you too," Marty replied, "that's why I came ashore."

He turned to watch the marines and engineers walking up the beach. A couple of the engineers fell to their knees and kissed the sand.

"They had a really rough passage and most of them have been as sick as dogs. A bunch of feeble engineers are no good to anyone."

"So I can see," Ryan agreed, "what do you propose?"

"How secure are you here?" Marty asked.

"As safe as we are anywhere. We have lookouts posted on high ground and will get early warning of any approach."

"Good, then we will let the men rest until this storm passes. I will let the ones on the Hornfleur come ashore and stretch their legs. They will soon recover their strength with firm ground under their feet," Marty decided.

The bay was sheltered and once the buckets of puke had been cleared away and the decks washed to rid them of the smell, the engineers started to recover. Hot food could be prepared as the galley fires were lit.

The weather improved after two days and the wind swung around to the Southwest, perfect for exiting through the tricky mouth of the bay. Around three hours before dusk, Ryan got the shore party divided up into two sections. The first, under Sergeant Bright, would march to the battery and neutralise it, the second would march the ten miles to the bridge to be in position to attack. A separate squad of specialist marines from the Thunder accompanied the bridge team and would set up a signal relay to direct the Thunder's mortar.

It was a lot of men and they had a ton of powder to move on the backs of mules and donkeys as well. Ryan was worried as there was a lot that could go wrong, being spotted by a French patrol being the first of his worries.

Bright, his twenty men and a pair of local guides made their way along the coast on paths last used by sheep or wild animals. The going was hard, and the terrain turned a ten-mile march into closer to twenty. They were travelling light with only a day's rations and thirty cartridges per man in a small pack.

Two of his men ranged out ahead on point with the guides, they were specialist scouts, the rest of his men were strung out in a line and maintained a fast walk which they could keep up all day if necessary. They stayed off ridges where they could to avoid being silhouetted against the sky and when they did have to cross, one did so at places where the terrain could help hide them.

It took five and a half hours to reach the hill behind which the battery was situated. They stopped to prepare for their assault and to give the scouts time to recon the position. The men checked their Baker rifles and pistols drawing the old loads and reloading them to ensure the powder was dry. Knives were loosened in their sheaths and crossbows strung.

The first part of the attack would be made as quietly as possible so they could surprise the gunners and overcome them without a fight. The scouts returned.

"Two sentries and two lookouts. The lookouts are just over the brow of the hill so they can overlook the bay and its approach while staying out of the wind. One sentry is sitting on a rock overlooking the track up from the bay the other is already taking a permanent nap," the scout reported.

"Tender souls, these French," Bright grinned, "nice for them and nicer for us. Barker and Corbett, silence those two lookouts. You take down the remaining sentry," he ordered two men stood waiting nearby with loaded crossbows and the scout.

The lookouts never heard the crossbow bolts that hit them in the back of the head killing them instantly and the sentry gasped for air for less than a minute before he bled out from a slit throat and carotid artery.

The gunners for the four twenty-four-pound cannon were lolling around their camp, chatting, snoozing, smoking, and drinking coffee.

Their officer was asleep in his bivouac while his batman polished his boots. The little servant froze as he felt the cold hard muzzle of a large bore pistol press just behind his ear and a voice whisper 'shhhh'. Pressure from a hand on his neck stood him up and he was guided backwards behind the tent where he was pushed to his knees, tied up and gagged.

The back of the tent was slit open with a razor-sharp fighting knife, a tap with a cosh and the officer stayed asleep. He was pulled through the slit and joined his batman on the ground hogtied and gagged.

The gunners were laughing at a joke a sergeant had made at the expense of one of his men when suddenly they were surrounded by men in dark grey coats and black forage hats. The click of twenty rifles being pulled to full cock got their attention.

Below them in the bay, a small fishing boat scuttled into the mouth of the river under full sail with Midshipman Jon Williams at the helm. He was dressed as a fisherman and there were two men visible on deck as you would expect. The boat ran through the gap in the beach and up to the centre of the boom.

"Hello, the boom boat!" he called in Spanish.

A head appeared from the cabin built on the deck of what, in another time, would have been a medium sized fishing boat but now had no mast and was powered by ten oars.

"What do you want?" the fat French sergeant snapped in bad Spanish.

"I was asked to deliver this to you," Jon replied and held up a closed basket and two bottles of wine.

"To us?" He stepped out, took the wine in one hand and the basket in the other. He looked down into the fishing boat at the two fishermen noting their swarthy looks. Antton and Matai grinned back at him, and Matai gave him a mock salute as they pushed off and started to sail away.

"Fifteen, sixteen, seventeen, eighteen, nineteen, twenty," Jon counted out loud then ducked.

The cabin seemed to swell then the roof lifted off followed by a cloud of smoke and a loud bang. Seagulls screeched in protest and flew up from their perches on the boom. As the smoke blew away, all that could be heard were the moans of wounded men and the cries of the birds.

The fishing boat turned and ran up alongside the smoking boat and its wrecked cabin. A few timbers splashed into the water around them. Four more men appeared from the cabin and all seven leapt aboard the smouldering boom boat.

Coshes and clubs rose and fell silencing the groans of the wounded remnants of the French crew who had taken the full force of the pot grenade hidden inside the basket.

Yeovilton, the Formidiable's misshapen gunner prepared the device by packing musket balls around a cartridge of powder inside a gallon wine jug sealed with a cork tied in place with waxed twine. It had been initiated by one of the Flotilla's infamous clockwork timers that Antton had set before replacing the bung and tying it in place before handing the basket to Jon.

The result, as it went off in the confined space of the cabin, was devastating, killing or wounding all the boats eleven crew.

"They didn't even have anyone on watch," Jon observed as they dumped the bodies into the fishing boat then released the boom from the mooring pile and let it drift down on the sluggish current to open the river to the Flotilla's assault boats.

Jon scanned the shore the best part of a cable away to see if they had attracted any attention. An old man and a young boy sat on the wharf at the end of the boom on the Spanish, East bank, fishing. The old man was cackling with laughter, rocking back and forth as he watched. The boy was jumping up and down, punching the air. Jon waved.

On the Formidiable, Marty saw the Punta Xaxiarri approaching and wondered if Bright and his men had managed to neutralise the battery. He took up a telescope and trained it on the hill. The French flag still flew proudly, and no challenge was signalled. Well, he expected that as they hadn't made any move to enter the bay and if it were still in French hands they would wait until he made the turn.

"Bring us to quarters, Wolfgang," he said quietly to his first.

Before Wolfgang had a chance to shout anything through his speaking trumpet, the men were already moving. They all knew where they were and what they were about to do and had been quietly getting the ship ready for the last half hour. Consequently, the ship was ready, and the guns run out in a record five minutes.

Marty grinned as Wolfgang barked out a couple of orders for forms sake. He was incredibly proud of his men at that moment. He looked at the hill again and now he could see figures moving around.

Are those grey or blue coats? He thought and was about to ask Wolfgang for a second opinion when the French flag dipped three times. He let his breath out in a whoosh.

"The battery is in our hands, take us into the bay if you please," he ordered Wolfgang.

Wolfgang ordered the course change to take them around the point then ordered the guns loaded with ball. The leadsman in the chains called out,

"Five fathoms, sand and shell,"

"Take us in to three fathoms and anchor as planned," Marty instructed.

The leadsman called the depth, and the bottom gradually shallowed, staying sandy with good holding.

"Three fathoms!"

"Hard to port. Prepare to anchor!"

The bay had a sandy beach through which the river emerged. Behind it was an inner bay and river with the town beside it. According to their intelligence, there was only a small garrison in the town as most of the local troops were defending the bridges.

There were no French country ships in the inner bay, and no one came out to the beach to take a look at them apart from a few children.

The Thunder anchored fifty yards behind the Formidiable and the Hornfleur fifty yards behind them. The Hornfleurs boats were being lowered into the water from their davits even as their anchor splashed into the water.

The Formidiable's cutter and barge were brought around to the side and the risky business of loading a ton or so of powder commenced.

Marty scanned the beach and saw that the children were waving. He waved back and had a momentary pang. He missed his children. James was about the same age as they were and had started school by now. He hoped he was coping with being away from home.

Wrenching his attention back to the job at hand, he looked down the deck. The hands were hoisting a net full of powder casks over the side into the cutter. Once they were down, the net was unhooked from the tackle and the deck crew started on the net for the barge. It was up to the boats crew to organise it once it was down, and they worked quickly and professionally under the command of the midshipmen.

He was sorely tempted to jump into a boat and go with them, but he had to let his men do their job. With a huge effort, he forced himself to relax and put on an outward show of confidence. This was by far the riskiest mission he had them undertake without him being physically in the lead.

Shelby, the ship's surgeon/physician, came to the foot of the quarterdeck steps and looked up expectantly.

"Come ahead," Marty said by way of invitation and Shelby took the few steps up to the hallowed ground of the quarter deck.

"All well?" Marty asked.

"Yes, the engineers are mainly over their seasickness and we have an unusually small amount of sick men on report at the moment," Shelby reported.

"The prospect of an action will do that more times than not," Marty smiled and then lapsed back into introspection.

Shelby eyed his captain thoughtfully.

"They will be alright, you know. You have trained them well."

"What? Oh yes, I know but it's hard to stand and watch them go into action without you."

"Young Williams has good men with him."

"Yes, the shadows decided they would go with him as his crew. They were a little put out that they wouldn't be part of the main event." Marty smiled.

In the background, Wolfgang could be heard ordering the spotters up into the tops where they could observe the fall of shot when the barrage started. Marty watched the men running up the ratlines, so sure footed, like barbary apes.

"The boats are ready, sir," Wolfgang reported a minute or so later.

"Begin the barrage at your convenience," Marty ordered.

The gunners had estimated the range and had set their guns accordingly. The gun captains looked to the quarterdeck expectantly.

"By ripple broadside, FIRE!" shouted Wolfgang through his trumpet and starting with the foremost eighteen-pounder the guns fired one after the other from fore to aft. A ripple broadside put much less strain on the fabric of the ship than a full broadside and for the purposes of this action was just as effective.

As soon as the guns started to fire, the boats pulled away from the other side and got into line astern until all six boats were rounding the stern of the Thunder and moving into the river.

In the hills overlooking the bridge at Behobia, Ryan and his men watched and waited. The spotters and signal relay men had set up earlier and were ready to direct the Thunder's barrage.

Ryan lay on his belly beneath a bush, his telescope panning across the bridge and the area on the North bank where the majority of the force guarding the bridge were encamped. There was a platoon or so of infantry stationed on the South bank manning a checkpoint with a lifting pole.

A squad of cavalry patrolled the road around the wooded hill where the guerrillas, marines, and engineers were hidden. Ryan detailed a man to keep an eye on them and just as he left there was the sound of distant cannon fire.

A few French soldiers stood and looked towards the coast but there were hills between there and the camp, so they saw nothing. If they had looked up, they would have seen the black dot of a thirteen-inch mortar shell arc up into the sky from the bay, grow larger as it approached, and descend to explode two hundred yards upstream from the bridge.

The signal men relayed the fall of shot and the required adjustment. A minute and a half later, a second shell exploded just fifty feet from the bridge and level with its parapet. The French soldiers dove for cover. The third exploded right over the middle at around twenty feet. The blast radius of the shell was such that it destroyed the checkpoints on either side, killing many of the men.

The shells started coming in around every eighty second after that. The Thunder had two teams of gunners working the one gun and by its nature the mortar didn't heat up its barrel as much as a cannon.

Ryan let them pound the bridge for five minutes then instructed the signalman,
"Start walking the barrage to the North. Let's see if we can get them to run away."
"That will certainly make life easier," grinned Lieutenant Richard Tamworth, the commander of the Engineers, who lay beside Ryan.
"Sir, the cavalry patrol is on its way back," a marine reported.
"I've got that," Linette said from his other side and slipped away, collecting a group of guerrillas as she left.

Marty was impressed at the rate of fire the Thunder could put up with their single mortar. Of course, with their seventy-man crew, they had ample hands to swing the ship on its springs and reload the beast, but all the same, a round a minute or there about was still impressive.
The Formidiable and Hornfleur were alternating broadsides. The Hornfleur would fire and while they were reloading, the Formidiable would fire. Thus, a hail of eighteen pound balls were pounding the area around the bridge around every forty-five seconds. Like the Thunder, they concentrated on the bridge itself for the first ten minutes or so.
As the lookouts reported the progress of their boats, they slowly started to shift their aim. The Formidiable to the North bank and The Hornfleur to the South pushing any French defenders away from the Bridge.

By the time Paul la Pierre and Captain Fairmont's joint force of marines and engineers reached the bridge, it was looking ragged with most of its parapet knocked away and chunks missing from its deck where balls had gauged it. However, the basic structure was still intact, the piers undamaged. They had work to do.

"Ready the marines!" he called out and three of the Hornfleur's boats swung towards the North bank and the other towards the South. The Formidiable's two boats with the majority of the engineers on board and the powder headed straight for the bridge itself.

Marty was surprised when Fairmont told him how long it would take for them to set the charges. He assumed they would just pile or tie the casks around the piers and set them off. But Fairmont, backed up by his own gunner, told him that wouldn't even scratch them. They had to drill the piers and get the charges inside so the explosive would force the masonry apart. If they just strapped the casks around them all the force would go outwards.

The casks contained long cartridge bags of powder that would be fed into holes the engineers would drill using iron bars and sledgehammers. This was exactly the same technique used by engineers to blast tunnels through mountains. The charges would be linked with fuse to a central point where it would be ignited by a timer. Fairbrother planned to have a slow fuse set as a backup in case the timer didn't work.

This meant that the marines and the gunners had to keep the French away from the engineers for as long as the three hours Fairbrother and his men estimated they would need to do the job properly.

Linette and her band of Spanish cutthroats were set up either side of the road leading to the bridge from the South. The Thunder's one mortar was concentrating on keeping the main French force away on the other bank, so it was relatively peaceful there.

They heard the horses coming at a canter- that was perfect. They had set up where the road was bracketed by a pair of good strong trees on a bend in the road. As the cavalry rounded the corner they ran straight into the thin, strong rope that was strung between them.

The first two ranks and the officer were swept out of their saddles. The following eight ranks pulled up in confusion, horses rearing and men fighting to stay in their saddles. Muskets barked and more men fell. A second volley of pistol shots and the Spanish rushed from the trees, long knives glinting wickedly in the sun.

Linette was in the thick of it. She ran from cover straight at the officer who was getting to his feet. He saw her coming and pulled his sword but hesitated as he saw it was a beautiful woman. Linette had no such doubts. She shouted in French,

"Help me!" which confused him even more.

She threw herself into his arms and as she did, brought her knee up into his balls.

He squawked and doubled over; her knife came down penetrating the back of his neck just below the skull.

"Nicely done!" the nearest guerrilla complimented her as she retrieved her blade.

It had taken the French time to realise what the hell was going on, but they soon identified that the incoming fire was coming from the bay. The commander, Major Hercule Clarrion, sent scouts to give him an assessment and called in the commander of horse artillery.

"Captain Ravel, get your guns away as quickly as possible and set up to respond to those ships."

Ravel saluted. He was a veteran, knew that he had to keep his guns out of direct line of fire from the ships and far enough away that their secondary armament couldn't be brought to bear.

He had three sixteen cm (6.4 inch) howitzers, which would be ideal. They were parked away from the main camp with the rest of his guns and he took off at a flat run to get there as soon as he could.

He reached the compound,

"Sergeant Bantégnie, get the howitzers and caissons hitched up immediately, as much ammunition as we can carry!" he ordered his Sergeant Major, who spun on his heel and started bellowing orders.

He ran to his tent and dragged a map of the local area out of his campaign desk. It had been created by his own cartographer and had the contour lines drawn in as well as all the roads. He drew an arc around a point in the bay where he estimated the British ships were anchored. The arc described the maximum range of the howitzers and he soon identified a low hill near the hamlet of Dongoxenborda, the rear side of which would put him within three kilometres.

Cannonballs were landing amongst the infantry's camp sending men running for their lives when he emerged and headed over to the guns. He mounted the forward left-hand horse of the lead train and spurred it forward, leading his men from the front.

Ryan led his men down the hill to the bridge, they met no resistance and the mortar was maintaining a screening fire a cable to the North. The Marines rushed across and set up defensive positions in an arc, digging holes and piling the earth up in front for cover. The guerrillas took up positions on the South bank.

The engineers started work on the piers. Of the two bridges, this was the narrower and slightly shorter of the two having just the two piers as opposed to the four of the other. The plan, however, was the same and that was to take down two piers and open up a gap that wouldn't easily be bridged.

Men stood in the water, up to their waists in some cases, and started drilling. One man would hold a yard-long iron rod and two others would take it in turns smiting the end with sledgehammers. In between strikes the drill man would rotate the rod a quarter turn. They would keep this up for an hour until they had a hole deep enough for the charge.

All the time that was going on, Ryan, Angus, Fairbrother, and the Marines waited for a French probe or counterattack.

Marty looked at his watch.

"Almost one and a half hours, Wolfgang. I wonder how they are getting on," he said to his first.

Wolfgang didn't answer. He knew Marty was just worrying out loud.

A puff of smoke appeared in the air behind the Thunder followed almost immediately by a sharp crack. That was followed by a second then a third closer to the

Formidiable. Marty knew exactly what they were as he had seen them before back when he was a mid.

"Howitzers!" he shouted, "Lookout! Can you see where they are shooting from?"

A second salvo came in and it was clear they were targeting the Formidiable.

"No, sir! Can't see any smoke nor nothin'," the lookout shouted down.

The third salvo was very close, and bits of shrapnel dug chunks out of the deck.

"All men not needed for manning the guns, get below!" Marty ordered.

"Captain, Captain Cocks is hailing you," the quartermaster called.

"Thank you, Stan," Marty said and walked to the stern rail.

"Yes, Captain?" he called.

"If you can pinpoint those guns, I can drop a shell or two on them to sort them out," Cocks called across.

Chapter 17: Sortie

Marty was rowed in his gig to the boom boat, the small craft practically flying across the water. Troy stood in the prow, Wilson, Roland, John Smith, Chin, and a random sailor manned the oars and Sam the tiller. They pulled up beside the boat,

Antton, Matai, get over here, you," he indicated the random sailor, "get over there."

Now he had all his Shadows except Garai, who was with Ryan, he was ready for anything. As they rowed to the shore, he briefed them on their mission. Find the Howitzers and stop them.

He had thought about what Cocks said, but that would be his last resort. Even a five-minute break in the barrage at the bridge would let the French mount a serious counterattack. Even so, time was of the essence as there was only so much punishment the Formidiable could take.

They reached the north shore and leapt onto dry land, each of them carried a satchel, a rifle, or in Marty's case, his Durs Egg Carbine, an ammunition pouch, at least two pistols, and an array of edged weapons.

Now that they were on shore, the sound of the naval guns was not so overpowering and the further in land they got the greater the chance they would hear the howitzers. They moved at a dog trot, easy to maintain but covering distance quickly, towards the nearest hill behind the village of Hendaye.

They followed a steep and rocky track, that was no more than a game trail, for two miles to the top and stopped to look around.

There were no guns but now they could hear their fire from the North. Marty took out his small telescope and examined the hills in that direction. His eye, practiced at picking up the merest hint of a sail or a movement on a distant horizon, picked up the silhouette of a soldier stood with a telescope to his eye atop a hill a mile or so distant.

"A spotter!" he exclaimed and the others, noting the direction his telescope pointed soon picked up on it as well. John Smith, whose eyes were notoriously sharp, picked him out without aid,

"French horse artillery from his uniform," he commented, noting the dark blue uniform coat and tall brown hat.

"Come on, let's get to the base of that hill," Marty said impatiently.

It was a short jog, but Marty was aware it had taken close to forty minutes to get this far since leaving the ship. The poor Formidable had suffered at least another twenty salvos in that time and Marty was getting increasingly worried for the safety of his ship and his men.

The firing stopped. They couldn't know it, but the French had run out of ammunition and their barrels were so hot they needed to give them a respite.

The team hit upon the road that lead to the back of the hill just as three caissons drawn by four horses came around a bend. Marty stepped out in the road, forcing the lead rider to pull them to a stop.

"Where are you going?" he asked

"That is none of your business. Get out of the way or you will feel my whip," the rider snapped impatiently.

"You are an impertinent fellow. Do you know who I am?" Marty replied with all the arrogance he could muster.

"I don't give a fuck who you are. If you don't get out of the way so I can deliver this ammunition to the battery, the captain will shoot you himself," the rider shouted and spurred the horses forward, causing Marty to have to dive into the ditch to get out of the way.

"Impatient fellow," John commented as he helped Marty to his feet and handed him his gun and packs.

"Yes, very rude," Marty grinned. "Did you do it Antton?"

They jogged up the road until they could see the guns set up in a paddock just behind the hill. The captain was gesticulating to the rider to get the caissons into position behind the guns. He looked impatient and was yelling at the man to get a move on. Marty noted that the caissons were much closer to the guns than was normal so they could reload faster.

Marty signalled and they moved along a low hedgerow that bordered the field. They crawled on their bellies to stay out of sight and discovered the thistles in that part of France were particularly prickly.

They spread out into a skirmish line some ten feet apart and waited.

"Five, four, three…"

They covered their heads with their hands and opened their mouths just in time as the caissons exploded with an enormous concussion. The hedge was flattened by the shockwave and they felt the heat pass along their backs.

Marty rose to one knee and cocked his carbine. A soldier staggered out of the smoke and he dropped him with a chest shot. Along the hedgerow, rifles barked as the boys picked off any French artillerymen that came into view.

Marty reloaded and when he looked up, the smoke had almost blown away. The scene was chaotic, the caissons and their horses were nowhere to be seen and there was a shallow crater where they had stood. The blast had knocked every one of the soldiers to the ground and the nearest gun had been blown on its side.

"At them!" Marty called and they pushed through the hedge and advanced at a walk shooting any soldiers they saw. Marty fired his carbine killing another then let it swing behind him on its shoulder strap. He pulled his double-barrelled Manton pistols sighted and shot another with his right.

An officer staggered out from between two of the guns and Antton shot him, dropped his rifle and pulled out a pair of pistols.

Sam was suddenly confronted with a huge sergeant brandishing a pike, screaming madly and intent on killing him. He dropped his spent rifle and grabbed his iklwa short spear from where it was slung over his shoulder, crouched and prepared to meet his man. A brown blur came in from the side and grabbed the pike in its jaws about two feet from the point. The weight of the seventy-five-pound dog on the end of the eight-foot pole turned the sergeant around allowing Sam to deliver a killing stab with the iklwa into his side.

It was all over. Any soldiers that weren't dead were wounded and John and Wilson were busy spiking the guns and setting charges to blow their trunnions off. Chin had taken off up the hill to deal with the spotter and was last seen pursuing the man in a roughly Northern direction.

Marty walked up the hill to see what was happening in the bay and as he climbed, he got the impression that there was a smudge in the sky. The higher he got, the more fear gripped his heart, as the smudge became a column of smoke he scrambled in panic to the peak.

As he crested the hill, the awful truth was laid out before him. There in the bay, his beautiful ship lay burning, her guns silent. Small boats surrounded her, and the beach was full of men but there was no doubt the Formidiable would burn to the waterline.

Marty fell to his knees. He had failed to stop the guns in time. He felt a wrench in his gut like he had been stabbed. A sob broke from his throat and tears ran down his face. He couldn't tear his gaze away. He had to watch with the morbid fascination of one witnessing a funeral pyre. Troy pushed his head under his arm and whined.

"Oh shit!" Wilson's voice cut through the silence from behind him, then his men were around him. They all knelt and watched their ship die.

"They must have flooded the magazine," John commented as the main mast fell along the deck.

"Yea, she would have blown by now if they hadn't," Wilson agreed.

Flames reached up into the air, and Marty noticed that the Thunder had moved out into the bay away from the conflagration and was still firing. So was the Hornfleur. He stood and turned in the direction of the bridge. He could just about see it from there and he raised his glass to see what was going on.

The marines had set up a defensive line around the approach to the bridge on the north bank. He could see puffs of smoke as they fired at any French who tried to approach. The Hornfleur was laying down her barrage between the marines and the French camp but they could see that the French were forming up to make an attack. They had sufficient numbers to overwhelm the marine line, and with the loss of the Hornfleurs guns, the gap between salvos was enough to let them think they could do it.

He made a quick decision.

"Come on, boys, we need to help the lads at the bridge," he shouted and started off down the hill. He was mad as hell and wanted to kill as many enemies as he could to expunge the guilt, he felt for failing his ship.

He stopped as the logical part of his brain kicked into gear.

"Chin, you are our fastest runner. Get back to the beach where our crew are and get them into the town. Tell them to loot and burn everything. I want the commander of that French force to be distracted not for us to get into a pitched battle. So, as soon as the French turn up, they are to retreat and get onto the Hornfleur and Thunder.

We will set up a diversion or two as well. Come on, the rest of you, we have work to do."

Marty led them towards the port, the bridge was too far away for them to get to in time. He hoped they would find something to enable them to help the men at the bridge. They were about halfway there when Marty suddenly called a halt.

"Listen!"

They stood for a whole minute then there was a loud crack in the direction of the bridge and a dandelion head of smoke in the air.

"The Thunder is targeting the Irun bridge; they must have blown the other one already!" Marty exclaimed.

Around forty-five seconds later, the Hornfleurs broadside howled over their heads.

"That should hold them," John wryly observed, "one of them big bugger's worth a bloody broadside."

"Come on, let's see what other damage we can do," Marty said, still intent on extracting some revenge.

They reached the port and had to fight their way past a stream of refugees from the town. The civilians were carrying what they could and looked terrified.

Marty had a pang of conscience; he didn't like waging war on civilians, and he had unleashed hell on them in his grief. Well, there wasn't anything he could do to stop it now, he just had to live with it.

They finally reached the merchant docks and started searching the warehouses. They mainly held trade goods; wine, hams, leather goods, cloth, timber, stone and finally one that was full of military supplies. Nothing explosive but things that made life bearable for the foot troops; uniforms, boots, blankets, tents, cooking equipment, and so on.

They started a healthy blaze and soon flames could be seen breaking through the roof and coming out of the few windows. Unfortunately for the owners of the other warehouses, the wind was from the East and soon the next warehouse along was burning merrily as well.

They turned their attention to the hulks tied up alongside the dock. They were moored abeam of each other so you could walk from one ship to the next. A swift charge and the guards either fled or died. A smashed lantern in the right place and the middle ship was soon burning, and with them being tied alongside each other, the fire would soon spread to all of them.

"We need a ship to help get the crew back to Gibraltar," Marty told them, and the men spread out along the dock looking for a likely candidate. The Formidiable had a crew of three hundred including the marines, and if they were split between just the Thunder and Hornfleur, would make the ships very overcrowded. Even a moderately sized cargo ship could carry fifty to a hundred men and relieve the crowding.

"Skipper!" Matai called and waved him towards the Eastern end of the dock.

Marty ran down towards him; there was a V shaped notch in the harbour where ships could be pulled up to have work done and sitting right there was what looked like a Corvette. She was old, probably built around 1790, was armed with a half dozen puny six-pound cannon but looked well-kept and ready to sail.

She flew an odd pennant, but Marty didn't care, she would do. He pulled a pistol and fired each barrel in turn into the air. That was the signal to the men to gather. Within ten minutes, the whole team was there.

They boarded and quickly searched her from one end to the other. There was a solitary watchman onboard,

"What is your name, sir?" Marty asked him politely.

"Gerome Gallette," the man replied.

"Tell me, I am intrigued, what is this ship and what is she used for?"

"She is the Jacinthe. She was a Corvette of the Serpente class. Her crew has been taken up by the army."

"You seem to know a lot about her?" Marty observed.

"Naturally. I was on her when she was commissioned in 1792. She was a privateer for a few years and then part of the Navy. Now she is or was the guard ship for the port," Gerome replied and gave a very gallic shrug. *"She is my home."*

Marty's conscience kicked him in the heart. He had done enough to civilians today.

"Gerome, we need to take her to get my men back to Gibraltar. I don't want to kick you off if you want to stay."

"Gibraltar, you say! Well I've never been ther. You know this old girl has a flat bottom and will roll like a pig on wet grass."

"If you can take it, I'm sure we can," Marty grinned.

They soon had her cast off and heading out into the estuary. Six of them could get a couple of sails set and keep her moving as long as Marty kept it simple.

"Boat approaching from upstream!" shouted John, who was manning the tiller. "Looks like the barge."

Marty ran to the stern; it was indeed his barge and as it approached. He hailed and stood on the rail waving an arm to attract their attention.

Midshipman Longstaff had the tiller and swung the barge alongside.

"Get everyone onboard and tie the barge off astern," Marty ordered. This would make life much easier.

"The cutter isn't far behind us sir," Eric reported and asked, "is she a prize?"

"Not much of one, but we need her to get the crew home. The Formidiable has been sunk," Marty told him.

Eric looked shocked then tears sprang into his eyes. Marty put an arm around his shoulders and said quietly,

"No time for that now, son. You need to be strong in front of the men. Now take over the foredeck and get the men organised for sail handling."

Eric sniffed, nodded, took a step back, and faced his captain,

"Aye, aye, sir!" he said and saluted before turning away.

Marty smiled just before hearing an enormous explosion. The bridge had gone up!

"Cutter and Hornfleur's boats approaching!"

"Get the Cutter here and send the Hornfleur's boats home," he ordered. They were back in business.

With the extra men, they soon got the Jacinthe (Hyacinth) out of the estuary into the bay. Marty ordered the Hornfleur to signal the recall and fire a cannon to get his men back. The beach was already piled high with loot and things that had been rescued from the Formidiable.

Adam came aboard in the gig along with Marty's weapons and sea chests. He had a couple of bandages around burns where he and a crewman had lowered the chest from the transom gallery and burning rigging had fallen on them. Marty was about to ask about the ships secret books when Adam volunteered,

"The signal and code books are locked in your weapons chest. If we were going to be taken, I couldn't think of anything on board that would sink faster."

"Thank you, Adam," Marty said with all sincerity and shook his hand.

Wolfgang was among the second wave of men taken off the beach many of whom were festooned in baubles that they had acquired in the sacking of the town.

"We can get two hundred on her comfortably and two hundred and fifty at a squeeze," Marty told Wolfgang.

"If they bring all that loot on, they will be cramped anyway," Wolfgang replied nodding to the beach where teams of men were industriously loading loot into boats.

All such activity was curtailed when a lookout hailed that a large column of French soldiers was approaching from the direction of the bridge.

"Get all the men aboard now. Leave everything that they haven't brought on already," Marty ordered, quietly relieved that the dilemma he had been struggling with was resolved for him. At least some of the civilians would get their belongings back even if their houses were smouldering ruins.

The lookouts reported that the bridge was destroyed, and Marty went to the top of the mainmast to have a look for himself. Three of the four arches were missing, and two of the three piers were reduced to stubs. The butchers bill for the action was; six men killed on the Formidiable and fourteen wounded, two marines and three engineers wounded from the bridge party.

The loss of the Formidiable would be answered for in a court martial. Marty and Wolfgang would have to face that later but right now, getting the men back to Gibraltar was the main priority.

Chapter 17: The reckoning

Gerome hadn't exaggerated, the Jacinthe rolled and gave up leeway like a barge, she was as un-seaworthy a ship as Marty had ever sailed. But she got them back to Gibraltar where they disembarked gratefully to the comfort of their base.

Marty sent a report to Arthur Wellesley, Admiral Hood and Canning and a letter to Caroline on the first packet home. He delivered his report to Admiral Sir Edward Pellew the current Commander in Chief Mediterranean who had recently replaced Admiral Cotton.

"Come in my boy and take a seat," Pellew greeted him as he made his report. "You seem to have lost your Frigate and returned with a crank corvette," he observed.

Marty handed him the sealed report and the admiral, who had put on a lot of weight, sat back in his chair and read. A steward came in and served coffee with a glass of brandy on the side. Marty waited and watched the admiral's eyebrows rise and fall as he made his way through the report. Marty drank his coffee but didn't touch the brandy.

"Well I must say, this reads like one of those modern adventure stories," Sir Edward stated as he put the report down. "Your people did well to take down both bridges."

"The second bridge turned out to be the easiest," Marty added as it wasn't in the report, "it was older and the fabric not as hard as the one at Irun. They had the holes drilled in half the time and demolished both piers and all three spans."

"Excellent, excellent. You know you will have to face a court martial over the loss of your ship," Pellew stated.

"Yes, sir. I am fully aware of that. Do you have any idea when that can be convened?" Marty asked.

"We have five captains in port, so in theory, we could hold one immediately, but I want to hear what Hood and Canning say before I do that. You were working under their orders officially." Pellew sipped his coffee, grunted, poured the brandy into it, and took another sip. "Much better. You will not get another ship until you've been cleared."

Marty smiled at the assumption he would be exonerated; however, he was not so sure.

"They would have to find one first. It would be better if it were French or Spanish built."

"That's the spirit. Make sure you keep me informed of your whereabouts," Pellew replied in dismissal.

Back at the base behind Rosia bay, Marty checked over the inventory of his remaining assets. Ryan was back in command of the Eagle; Linette had taken the packet back to England having been recalled by Canning for some reason or another. The Eagle and Alouette were patrolling the Northern Spanish coast to prevent any supplies reaching the French forces from that direction. The Basque guerrillas were in control of the mountain passes.

He had letters from Arthur and there wasn't anything urgent that needed taking care of that required him to go back to Lisbon.

He had a meeting with Francis Ridgley, their spy network was spreading nicely across the peninsula. For once in his life, he had nothing to worry about.

That's a joke, he thought and started to worry. When Marty worried, he turned to exercise, and the pace of weapons and close combat training increased dramatically.

It took two weeks for a reply to arrive from Hood and Turner and he had to assume that Pellew got his at the same time. It said that they could see that no blame could be laid at his feet and that he should start looking for another ship as soon as the court martial had been held.

That's easier said than done with every French ship locked up by the blockade, he thought, but he asked Francis to ask the network if there were any French Frigates laid up anywhere.

He received a sealed letter,

"The court martial is set for Wednesday," he told Wolfgang, "we both have to attend and be 'examined'. The other captains' reports will be read by the court in advance, but they don't believe they will need to call them in person."

Marty believed that unlike his previous court martial for losing a ship, this one wouldn't be rigged. When he saw the names of the captains who would attend, he was still not convinced, even if Pellew was chairing it.

Chairman, Admiral Sir Edward Pellew
Clerk, Mr. Arnold Prendergast, (Clerk to the Admiral)

The Dorset Boy Book 8: La Licorne

Captains: Sir Frederick Maitland, Thomas Hardy
Thomas Stains, Phillip Pippon and Gordon Philibert.

Wolfgang would be 'interviewed' first, Marty would
be second. They boarded the flag ship, HMS Caledonia
at eight bells of the morning watch and were greeted by
Pellew's Flag Captain Edward Longstaff.

"Sir Martin, welcome," he smiled and shook his hand
then turned to Wolfgang, "Mr. Ackermann, a pleasure to
meet you at last."

He gestured for them to accompany him.

"Mr. Ackermann will be interviewed first then you
will be called, Sir Martin. The court has had the chance
to read your reports and logbooks, so this shouldn't take
too long. The admirals are in attendance and keen to get
this over with. May I take your swords?"

Admirals? Marty thought and exchanged a quizzical
glance with Wolfgang as he unclipped his scabbard from
his belt, but they had no time to ask questions before
they were ushered into Pellew's office. Longstaff
knocked on a connecting door and announced to the
room on the other side that they were there.

"Mr. Ackermann, if you would be so kind as to
attend the court. Sir Martin, Beamish there will attend to
you for refreshments," he said, indicating a steward who
had appeared from what was probably the steward's
pantry.

The door closed behind them and Marty could hear
the dull rumble of voices through the wall but nothing
that he could make out.

"Can I get you some coffee or tea, sir?" Beamish
asked with a soft Southern Irish accent."

Marty asked for coffee, which was served so quickly they must have a pot made for the members of the court.

He sat and waited, then stood and walked around, his coffee untouched. He checked his watch, forty-five minutes. He sat again and tried to relax.

An interminable two hours later, the door opened and Longstaff came in and said,

"Sorry to keep you waiting, Sir Martin. The court will see you now."

He rose, straightened his coat, and tucked his hat under his arm. Then, feeling like he was walking to a firing squad, he stepped through the door into what must be the admiral's dining room.

The dining room table was across the room and the admiral sat with the five captains arrayed either side of him. The clerk sat on the end, a sheave of papers and an inkwell in front of him. A single chair was placed in front of the table, precisely in the middle and his sword was on the table in front of the Admiral.

"Captain Stockley, HMS Formidiable," Marty announced himself.

"Please be seated, Captain," the Admiral said and indicated the lone chair. As he sat, he caught a movement out of the corner of his eye and a glance told him that Admiral Hood sat to the side, a frown on his face. Beside him was Arthur Wellesley.

Pellew introduced the members of the court and read a formal statement as to why they had convened, then added,

"The court is aware of the special role you have in His Majesties Navy and that your duties take you beyond what most of us would consider normal. All here are sworn to secrecy and Admiral Hood, as the Head of Naval Intelligence, and General Wellesley are here to ensure that proceedings take that into account."

"Would you, in your own words, tell the court of the mission and events that led to the loss of your ship," Captain Hardy instructed.

Marty told his story, leaving nothing out. He didn't explain his decisions, just described the circumstances and what he did as a consequence.

When he finished. Maitland asked,

"Why did you not move your ship as soon as the Howitzer bombardment started?"

"If I had, we would have to stop our supporting fire for the men at the bridge. Given the number of French infantry in the camp, they would have been overwhelmed in short order. That would have led to the failure of the mission."

"You put the mission before the safety of your own ship?" Hardy asked.

"Yes. The mission was to stop or at least seriously restrict the French Army in the West and North of Spain's supply of powder and other supplies and thus their ability to fight."

Hardy looked to the clerk, who went through his papers until he found something and nodded.

"What is to stop them just shipping it in through Bilbao or Santander?" Stains asked with a sneer.

I expected that from him. He has an unsavoury reputation and is a follower of Gambier, Marty thought but replied,

"I have ships of my Flotilla patrolling the North coast. The blockade by the Channel fleet doesn't come down that far since Porto was retaken."

Pellew hid a smile behind his hand on the pretence of covering a cough. He was well aware of Marty's dislike of Admiral Gambier, who was in command of the fleet.

"You were at the Basque Roads," Stains commented, "you exhibited recklessness there. Now you seem to have, again, behaved in a reckless fashion resulting in the loss of your ship."

Marty took a deep breath and controlled his anger.

"If you mean that I supported a brave man whose only aim was to destroy the enemy while others stood by and watched. Yes, I did, my decisions and conduct were driven by the requirements of the mission. They were neither reckless nor spontaneous."

Stains looked angrily at Martin as his reply stung, and he attacked again,

"According to your first, you are working with a French woman, several Basques and Gypsies. These do not sound like the allies of a man of honour. So how are we to trust your judgment as an officer?"

Marty's expression turned to stone and his eyes went flat, but Stains didn't notice, and he continued scornfully, "How, in fact, can we trust the judgment of one who habitually associates with people like that?"

Marty took a breath, but Pellew beat him to the reply,

"Captain Stains, you are treading on very thin ice. This is an investigative court and offers you no personal protection if you offend Captain Stockley's honour."

"The Admiralty forbids duelling amongst officers," Hood added from the back of the room, "but I could always ask the first lord for an exemption in this case as this mission and Captain Stockley had his blessing."

Stains' look changed from contempt to worry as he realised he was indeed sailing into a potential storm and had no support from anyone else in the room.

Marty, however, had enough time to get control.

"Thank you, Admirals," he nodded to them in turn and made as politically correct a reply as he could manage. "I don't expect regular Navy officers, especially ones who are performing long term and necessary blockade duty, to understand the intricacies of the Intelligence Service. We make decisions and choices that must look strange to those outside of our community. As to honour," he fixed Stains with a gimlet glare, "I do what I have to do to make our great nation safe and to enable men like Viscount Wellington to do their job. Honour is a poor excuse to avoid getting one's hands dirty and there is as much honest honour and loyalty in a Gypsy as I have seen in some who should have more. I owe my freedom, if not my life, to those rogues, and yes they are rogues, but if you earn their respect and friendship, they will die for you."

The comment about honour was as close to calling Gambier a coward as he could get without saying as much and Pellew stepped in before it went further.

"Quite, now the question here is, did Captain Stockley lose his ship through negligence, cowardice, or incompetence?" He looked around at the Captains.

Hardy asked for the part when he decided to leave the ship to be read back,

"Can you take me through your decision process at that point please," he asked

Marty nodded.

"The first Howitzer shells came in and at first, we thought they were targeting the Hornfleur; I immediately asked the lookouts who were not monitoring our own fall of shot to look for their spotters."

Hardy interrupted,

"Why not look for the guns? They would make smoke when they fire."

"The French are well aware of that and know that if their gun positions are spotted, we will lay a broadside or two on them. Howitzers can fire in a high trajectory so can hide behind hills out of sight and still target something on the other side. It's the same technique that our ship-based mortars use, and their gunners are well versed in it. Most often, you will only see their spotters who observe the fall of shot and signal changes to the crews. The other thing here was with the almost constant noise of our three ships firing we couldn't hear their guns either."

"I see," Hardy nodded, "pray continue."

"When they reported they couldn't see any we checked the chart and worked out the maximum range they could be firing at. There were three hills big enough in that area where they could be hiding.

Our lookouts were telling us that the men on the bridge were still drilling. The decision in my mind was clear. We had to keep up our barrage to enable them to complete their work. Even if we pinpointed the howitzers, Thunder had to keep supporting the team on the other bridge until that bridge was blown and the team gotten away, they couldn't stop either.

I had part of my personal team on the boom boat already, so I gathered the others and we took my gig to gather them up to find and destroy the French guns. I knew we were leaving the Formidiable to a beating, and it was the hardest thing I have ever done, but the mission had to come first."

"You are absolutely sure you destroyed the guns?" Pippon asked.

"Yes, we spiked them and blew off the trunnions, killed or wounded the gun crews."

"Why didn't you return to your ship when you realised the Formidiable was burning?" Stains asked.

"We were almost two and a half miles away and by the time we saw what had happened, she was already ablaze from stem to stern and the crew on the beach. I had an urge to get revenge and I gave into it," Marty answered frankly.

"You burnt the warehouses," Pellew commented.

"Well, we only intended to burn the one with the military stores in, but the wind picked up and the blaze spread to several others," Marty replied. "We did intend to burn all four hulks though."

Pellew called a halt to the proceedings, saying they needed to conclude and make a judgement. Marty was taken from the court. Longstaff took him to his quarters, where Wolfgang had been waiting, and invited them to luncheon with him. Arthur joined them with Hood.

"Well I think that went rather well," Arthur reassured him when he saw that Marty and Wolfgang still looked worried.

"The captains will discuss what they have heard over lunch and decide if they need to call any other witnesses," Hood informed him.

"That captain, what was his name? Stains? Didn't seem to like you, Martin," Arthur observed as he got stuck into a bowl of chowder.

"Ha! That's because he is a follower of that dolt Gambier," Hood barked with a laugh.

"Aah, I recall something about a court martial brought over accusations of cowardice; by Cochrane wasn't it?" Arthur mused, mopping out his bowl with a heel of bread.

"Well founded ones, the man's shy," Marty growled. He still got angry when he thought of the treatment his friend had received at the hands of the politicians.

"Well that's as maybe but he is very well supported and to all intents, un-touchable, even by you," Hood admonished him.

Longstaff steered the conversation to less contentious subjects and lunch proceeded on a more even keel.

Marty had little appetite and picked at the excellent fare delivered by the stewards. His stomach was clenched with nerves. No matter what Hood said, if this board found him negligent or incompetent, he would be placed under arrest and face a bigger and much more public court martial back in England. He told himself if they did, he would resign his commission. He could still help Arthur in a private capacity.

Longstaff left them over coffee and went back into the room where the court was held.

What is keeping them? Marty fretted as the others sipped coffee, even Wolfgang looked reasonably relaxed now he had eaten. He got up to start pacing when the door opened and Longstaff announced,

"Sir Martin, Mr. Ackermann, would you both please attend the court. M'lord Hood and General Wellesley, if you would be so kind as to wait here. Hood's eyebrows went up at that and Arthur looked annoyed, but they respected the wishes of the court and stayed seated.

When they entered, there were no chairs set in front of the court, so they stood side by side in front of Pellew. Their swords were laid across the table, so neither hilt nor point was towards them.

"Gentlemen, we have discussed and debated the evidence presented to us by your witness, reports, and the reports of the captains of the Thunder and Hornfleur," Pellew opened.

"This was a most unusual action with a most unusual goal, which you were tasked with because, as evidenced by Admiral Hood, it is exactly the type of mission your Flotilla was created to carry out." He looked around the table, "a Flotilla most of us here had not heard of before now. Your record as a captain is, to now, exemplary and would challenge Cochrane for its audacity. However, you have lost your ship and must be judged on your conduct in this instance." He paused and took a sip of the tea he had in front of him.

"It is the opinion of this court that you, Lieutenant Ackermann, behaved in an exemplary fashion and carried out the orders of your captain with alacrity and courage. You fought your ship to the bitter end, which resulted in the successful completion of your mission." He turned Wolfgang's sword, the hilt toward him.

"This court finds that you bear no blame for the loss of your ship and that your record will show you fought with honour and courage."

Wolfgang took his sword and clipped it to his belt.

"Captain Sir Martin Stockley. You left your ship while it was under attack by a shore battery, declining the opportunity to move it out of harm's way so it could continue to support the team attempting to demolish the bridge.

The question has to be asked whether the loss of a frigate to achieve the demolition of the bridge was a worthwhile exchange. Here we have to rely on the testimony of General Wellesley, who has revealed to us in strictest confidence his plans to eject the French from the Peninsula and the importance of restricting the French's ability to fight."

Pellew looked Marty in the eye.

"It is, therefore, the conclusion of this court that you acted in the best interests of the mission and that your sortie to silence the battery was carried out successfully. However, it was not completed in time to save your ship.

You cannot be held to account for that as the physical distances involved meant that it would have been a close-run thing even if you knew where the battery was in advance.

Your record will show that you hold no blame for the loss of your ship in so much as you acted in the best interest of the highly important mission you were upon. You did, in fact, act with courage and initiative to try everything you could to save her."

He turned Marty's sword, the hilt toward him.

"You have been exonerated."

The Dorset Boy Book 8: La Licorne

Marty breathed for the first time since Pellew started speaking and took up his sword to the gentle applause of the other captains with the exception of Stains.

Chapter 19: Chasing a Unicorn

Francis Ridgley hurried down the road that led to Rosia bay. It was October and, for Gibraltar, was cold being only thirty-five degrees Fahrenheit.

"Damn unseasonable," he grumbled to himself as he shrugged his coat collar further up his neck and wished for a scarf. It wasn't the cold so much as the damn wind which, coming from the Northwest, was biting and carried the hint of rain.

He rounded the corner to the Flotilla's home base and approached the gates where he was greeted by the marine sentry,

"Afternoon, Mr, Ridgley. Here to see the captain?"

"Yes, is he in?" Francis replied, giving the man the chance to do his job even though he knew exactly where Marty was.

"In his office, sir, with Lieutenant Ackermann. You know where it is." The guard opened the gate and let him in.

Francis wasn't fooled at the ease of his entry; he had witnessed what happened to anyone who tried to enter without an invitation or known to be part of the team. Just the week before, he was about to leave when there was a commotion at the gate. By the time he got there, a finely dressed man was face down on the ground with his hands tied behind his back, a pair of marines covering him with their muskets.

Francis hadn't interfered, he didn't know the man but as there were a number of East Indiamen in harbour. He assumed the gentleman was from one of them from the cut of his clothes.

Captain la Pierre had been called and he quickly ascertained that the man was indeed a tourist, someone important, at least in his own mind, and had wanted to see the base as it looked like there was something interesting going on. The something was weapons practice and he had been attracted by the clash of swords. As it was common practice at normal army bases to let people wander in to watch the drills, he had assumed he could do so here.

He had made the mistake of using the, "do you know who I am?" ploy to the marine, which had gotten the reply, "no and I don't give a fuck who you are," after which the outraged man had tried to push his way past.

Now he was covered in dust and being hauled roughly to his feet. He had gotten entry to the base by being dragged in under arrest and interrogated. They never missed a chance to practice. A message was sent to his ship to verify he was who he said, and he was delivered back to the ship in irons and given into the custody of the captain.

"Come," Marty called at the knock on the door and Francis entered. He walked straight to the fire and lifted his coat tail to get some heat on his backside.

"It's bloody perishing out there," he complained then helped himself to a cup of coffee from the tray on Marty's desk.

"Good afternoon, Francis. Would you like a cup of coffee?" Marty asked with a raised eyebrow. He knew that Francis must have something interesting to tell them if he behaved like this.

Francis just grinned and sipped his coffee which he had served up with cream and four spoonsful of sugar. Marty poured him and Wolfgang a cup each and settled back to wait for the pronouncement.

"Well aren't you going to ask me why I have braved the elements to come and see you rather than just send a messenger?" Francis asked.

"No, we were just going to wait you out," Marty replied with a smirk.

"So, you don't want to know about the Pallas class frigate that ran into Cartagena less than a week ago and is undergoing repairs for storm damage?"

Marty sat bolt upright and Wolfgang nearly choked on his coffee.

"A week ago? Are you sure?" Marty asked suddenly very attentive.

"Thought that would interest you as you so carelessly lost your last one," Francis crowed in triumph. He had their attention now!

"The ship in question is the Licorne. She got caught in a storm running in from Mauritius. She is also very short handed as they had fever onboard in the West Indies."

"The storm that came through here a week ago?" Wolfgang interrupted.

"And which they used to pass through the Straits unobserved," Francis finished. "Apparently he was heading for Toulon but the damage to his upper works was bad enough he stopped at Cartagena for repairs."

"And you know this because?" Marty asked.

"I have an agent in the harbour master's office who sent me a coded dispatch as soon as they docked." Francis grinned and stole a biscuit.

"What do we know about Cartagena?" Marty asked.

"I'll get the master. There's not a port along this coast he hasn't sailed into," Wolfgang offered.

Marty nodded and the wiry German left the room.

Marty pulled a chart from under the chart table that doubled up as a small meeting table and spread it out. It was a large-scale map of the Mercia coast and Cartagena was clearly annotated on it.

"What are you thinking?" Francis asked as Marty pondered.

"That we can take her one of two ways. We can wait for them to finish the repairs then ambush her when she leaves for Toulon or we cut her out."

The door banged open, letting in a gust of frigid air, Wolfgang, and Arnold Grey.

"Wolfgang told me we might have a chance of getting a new ship!" Grey exclaimed as he took off his coat and scarf.

"Maybe. It depends on whether we can cut her out or try and take her at sea," Marty replied, "she's in Cartagena."

"Oh, that makes cutting out a problem then," Arnold frowned and when everyone looked at him expectantly continued. "Cartagena harbour is one of the best protected in the Mediterranean. The entrance has seven batteries and three forts or castles covering it, which you have to get past to get in and out."

Marty raised his eyebrows; he knew Cartagena was a tough nut, but this was something else. Arnold was busy marking the batteries and forts on the map using drawings and notes from his logbook as a reference.

Marty looked at the map as more details were added. It was obvious that they could never force entry to the harbour or crash an exit. He thought about the problem: he was rich in men but poor in ships. The Eagle and Alouette were patrolling the Northern Spanish coast, which left him the Hornfleur and she wouldn't fool anybody.

He needed to get at least a hundred men into Cartagena, steal the ship, and sail her out past all those guns without getting blown out of the water. He had an idea.

"Do we still have those prizes James sent in?" he asked.

"Yes, Fletcher is still negotiating with the agents, why?" Arnold replied.

Marty didn't answer but asked Wolfgang,

"Do we have a current code book for the semaphores?"

"Yes, the one we took last month hasn't been replaced yet as far as we know."

"Are you thinking of trying another Trojan horse?" Wolfgang asked.

"Not exactly." Marty smiled.

Three days later, two of the prizes and the Hornfleur sailed out of Rosia Bay and headed East into the Mediterranean. Once out and away from land, they flew French flags. The day before, a cutter, borrowed from Admiral Pellew had left with Midshipman Hart in charge and had also headed East.

The Dorset Boy Book 8: La Licorne

When Marty told Pellew what he intended, the old boy was amazed at the audacity of the plan, but as Marty filled in the details Pellew converted to a believer and willingly given up the cutter to the cause. Mind you, there would be hell to pay if they didn't bring it back in at least reasonable condition.

Stanley was having a great time. He had a command of his own, a team of good men that included Wilson and Roland from the captain's Shadows and a mission that was vital to them getting a new ship.   His destination was a signal tower on a point just to the North of the fishing village of Benidorm, and he had just one and a half days to get there.

Luckily, the wind was fair and came in over his quarter enabling the cutter to make its best speed. The sea was choppy, which was normal this time of year, but at his current speed he would be at his destination on time, if a little shaky in the knees.

It was his birthday the day before they left, and the captain had gifted him a new telescope as a present. He was incredibly proud of it and that the captain had even remembered his birthday.

They approached the narrow beach at the foot of the cliffs at the Playa de Mina before false dawn lit the eastern sky. Their way lit only by the waning moon.

"Are the marines ready?" he asked Sergeant Bright.

"Sah, ready and raring to go," the older man replied, phlegmatically looking down his nose from under the brim of his hat, which wasn't difficult as he was about a foot taller than Stanley.

"Ready the boats!" he called, refusing to let the sergeant intimidate him.

They dropped anchor in just two fathoms of water. The shore party got into the boats and rowed the short distance to the beach. The cliffs rose vertically up either side of them and at first glance looked unassailable, but Stanley had been briefed that there was a path that zigzagged up to the ruin of the ancient castle where the signal station was located. Like his captain, he led from the front and, like his captain, he had thought out in advance what his force needed to do.

"Scouts get up there and make sure there are no sentries still breathing by the time the rest of us arrive," he ordered, and two men slipped away into the gloom. He waited two minutes then moved ahead barking in a low voice,

"With me, men."

If he could have seen the faces of the men, he would have seen grins and looks of approval. The men liked an officer who led by example.

The climb was longer than he expected. The path that zigzagged up the cliff was worn smooth by generations of feet traipsing up and down to collect seaweed and shellfish in the bay, but there was still the occasional loose stone to catch out the unwary. They stepped carefully, making as little noise as possible.

They got to the top to find one of the scouts sitting on a rock making a show of waiting for them. The sun was just peeking over the eastern horizon and he was nicely backlit.

"All clear, sah," he reported, "the sentries all taken care of. There is a barracks set up in the ruins and the tower is intact.   Simms is keeping an eye on the barracks."

"Good, Sergeant, take all the men except the signallers and neutralise the garrison. Wilson, Roland, you are with me."

The two prizes and the Hornfleur also made good time towards Cartagena. The prizes were taken less than a month before and had come complete with their signal books, which was a major bonus. One hundred and fifty men were packed into them and another seventy-five in the Hornfleur, add to that the crews of the prizes, the ships would be burnt, and Marty had almost a full two hundred and fifty men with him.

"This is probably the craziest thing we have ever done," Arnold Grey grinned at Marty.

"No risk, no reward," Marty replied and looked to be relishing the prospect of pulling off the heist of the century. "If young Hart and his men have done their job, we will stand a good chance of pulling this off."

"It will all be in the timing," Arnold mused, as they went over the plan for the hundredth time.

They had taken a course that would allow them to swing around in a wide arc to approach Cartagena from the East as if they had come from Toulon, timed to arrive at or just before dusk. If all had gone well with the young Hart's mission, they should be able to enter the harbour without a fight.

They chose the signal tower near to Benidorm as it was around halfway between Valencia and Cartagena and the most isolated on that stretch of coast. Hart had to take it and hold it for a whole day at least. This was so they could keep it operating as if nothing was awry, inject their messages, and answer any questions from Cartagena that resulted.

Their timing was almost perfect. They arrived forty minutes before sunset and entered the mouth of Cartagena bay under minimum sail.

"Signal from the Fajarado castle, sir," Midshipman Williams reported and consulted the Spanish signal book. "Recognition challenge for today. I will answer him," he continued.

Marty just smiled, his mids knew their duties and he didn't need to tell them the steps. Flags flew up the masts of all three ships in answer to the challenge and Marty was a little relieved they were all the same.

"Response acknowledged," Williams reported after he saw the flags dip on the castle rampart.

Marty scanned the shore while they still had a little light. There was the Poladera Battery, built into the solid rock, more of a fort than a battery with the black muzzles of her forty-eight-pound cannon staring out at him.

As they crept in, Marty wanted to reach the anchorage after dark. He saw the lighthouse of Dique de Navidad, it's light just beginning to glimmer. He turned to the other shore and spotted the Battery of San Isidora, which was again more of a fortress than a battery with high stone walls through whose embrasures more forty-eight-pound cannon glared.

He was sweating, not because of the temperature it was barely thirty degrees, but with nerves. He had never been so nervous in his life, except maybe when he had married Caroline he had to admit.

Well I lived through that and I will survive this! he told himself sternly. Wolfgang was commanding the other prize with Second Lieutenant Phillip Trenchard and he had Third Lieutenant Andrew Stamp with him.

If this goes wrong, the French will bag the entire crew, he fretted silently while maintaining an outward appearance of calm.

They slid into the harbour and there was La Licorne. A recognition signal shot up, which they answered and then,

"She is signalling that we should come alongside and send over the replacements," Williams reported after deciphering the spelt-out message with Antton's help.

"Stanley's team has been successful," Marty crowed in relief, "get us alongside, Philip. Wolfgang will take the other side."

The deception, which was working up to now, was that a replacement crew had been sent to La Licorne, from Toulon. Orders to cover their arrival would have been received that very morning via the semaphore system.

As they approached, an officer illuminated by the deck lamps called across,

"How many men have you brought?"

I know that voice! Marty thought.

"We have seventy-five. The other ships have another seventy-five and some stores," he called back in a decided Basque accent.

Marty ran below to get a wide brimmed hat that could hide his face. He was already wearing a long pea coat that civilian captains wore to hide his weapons. By the time he got back on top, they were throwing the lines over to tie up alongside.

The men were on deck ready, so as soon as the two ships were tied off, they swarmed over the side with their bags in hand. Several who could speak French shouted greetings and struck up conversations with the French crew. Marty waited, he had gotten a clear look at the French captain and knew exactly who he was even though it had been many years since he had last seen him. The deck was swarming with the new crew and the Hornfleur was tying up alongside Marty's ship so more could bridge across.

Marty crossed over and walked towards the captain.

"Is this all the crew you have left?" Marty asked.

"No, one watch is on shore leave," he replied.

Marty glanced over his shoulder. All his men were aboard and were ready for the next order.

"Formidiable!" shouted Marty and all hell broke loose. Coshes and blackjacks appeared in his men's hands and French sailors fell to the deck unconscious or disabled. Marty stepped smartly up to the captain and punched him hard under the diaphragm, felling him like an ox. The deck lamps were extinguished apart from one on the quarterdeck and to cover any extraneous noise a group of his men started singing a rude French sea shanty.

"Tie him up and get him down to his cabin," he ordered a pair of marines, "Wolfgang! How is the clearance exercise going on below decks?"

"Almost done. We hit them so fast they didn't really have time to react," he reported.

"Good. Get the Hornfleur away and get everything off the prizes."

There was a splash and a minute later, a sailor ran up to them from the hatch to the lower deck.

"One of them went out through a port, sir! He wus swimming towards the shore last I saw of him."

"Damn!" Marty exclaimed, "that put's the cat amongst the pigeons. We will have to make do with what's onboard. Cut the prizes loose and set fire to them. Then prepare to make sail."

Marty hoped that La Licorne had been watered ready to sail on the morning tide as her fake orders had instructed. She should have enough provisions to get them to Toulon, which should be enough to get them to Gibraltar.

There was the brief sound of axes as the moorings were cut and the prizes let loose. The message was passed to the Hornfleur to follow them out.

Arnold Grey was busy fixing their position by taking their bearing to local landmarks. The Castillo de Concepcion was one, the Cathedral of Santa Maria another. Both were lit and recognisable in the dark. The third was the lighthouse.

"Get men in the chains testing the depth and lookouts all around. We are going to have to feel our way out." Marty ordered.

It was too early for the moon and the tide was just reaching its peak, not ideal conditions to be attempting to leave port. But they had no choice as once that sailor got to shore and raised the alarm they would never get out in daylight.

There was a steady Westerly breeze that filled their sails as she came up to her anchor and broke free. The capstan's clicking getting faster as the hook was pulled up to be catted. The men were working as fast as they could, given that they didn't know the ship, but she was designed by the same man as the Formidiable so that helped a bit.

"We have steerage," John Smith reported from the wheel.

"Steer towards the light," Arnold told him indicating the lighthouse they had passed on their way in.

"Well I weren't going to steer for the flipping Cathedral were I," John was heard to mutter.

"Set the foresails and the spanker," Wolfgang bellowed.

"Well if they didn't know somethings up already, they will now," Marty laughed as his First's voice echoed off the buildings around the harbour.

Just then a bell started to ring from the direction of the town, soon it was joined by others. Flames were coming through the hatches of the prizes and helped illuminate their way.

There was a crash and the ship stuttered in her movement.

"What the hell was that?" Marty shouted.

"Fishing boats, sir!" called the forward lookout, "came out of nowhere!"

There was shouting and swearing in Spanish from the water either side of them and Marty realised they must have run right through the middle of the fishing fleet as it was making its way out.

"Get a line to those men!" he ordered and soon three very bedraggled Spaniards were hauled up on deck.

"Please accept my apologies. I will pay you for the loss of your boats," Marty told them in Spanish.

"You are not French!" exclaimed the oldest of the three a gnarled specimen who must have been over sixty years old.

"No, we are British. We are stealing this ship," Marty told him.

The old fellow let out a wheezy cackle and was joined by his mates as he explained what was going on to them.

"They thought you were joking to start with, but I told them the French would never pay for any boat they ran down. Can we help you in any way?"

"Can you pilot us out of the harbour?" Marty asked.

"That will be our pleasure. It's a good joke you play on the French pigs no?" and he cackled again.

Marty led him to stand beside John at the wheel and gave himself the roll of interpreter.

"How much water does she need to swim?" the old man asked.

"About two and a half fathoms," Marty replied.

"Steer so the light is more to starboard. There are rocks along the shoreline."

But now every bell in Cartagena was ringing the alarm and the prizes were well ablaze. Marty could see the Hornfleur silhouetted against their light a cable behind them.

"You are being followed, senior," the old man said.

"It's ok, it's one of ours," Marty grinned in reply.

We might just make it yet! he thought, relaxing for the first time all day.

They passed the light and the old man asked them to steer due South. A salvo of guns was fired from the battery up on the hill. Marty had no idea what they were shooting at because none of the shot came anywhere near them. Then the battery at Podadera on the point fired and Marty saw splashes near the Hornfleur, the balls creating phosphorescent fountains.

"If you could go a little faster, we would all be very grateful," the old man said looking fearful.

Marty agreed.

"Make more sail! Set royals, and topsails!" he shouted.

The men were ready, and it took scant minutes for the sails to be set and the ship to pick up speed. The Hornfleur sped ahead as they piled on more sail as soon as the first shots splashed down. She came up beside them and Angus Frasier waved at Marty as they started to overtake them.

"Set the mains!" Marty called, laughing at the mids' audacity.

He stepped down into the cabin, where the former captain was under guard by a pair of evil-looking marines.

"Hello, Anton," Marty smiled and took off his hat, "they gave you a Frigate. How long did they take to forgive you losing a corvette to a prize crew?"

Captain Anton Rosier looked in astonishment at the man he had last seen as a seventeen-year-old midshipman sailing away in his ship in the Mediterranean before the battle of the Nile.

"Seems like you are destined to keep losing what is yours to me now, doesn't it?" Marty laughed. It was turning out to be a very, very good day.

At the signal station the next morning, they were just preparing to burn the whole thing to the ground when a signal came in from Cartagena.

Wilson decoded it and passed the message to Stanley who read it with a beaming smile.

"Send to Toulon. La Licorne fully re-manned and in all respects ready for sea.   That should set them thinking."

Chapter 20: The trouble with politicians

Christmas 1811 and His Majesties Ship Unicorn, a (now) forty-two-gun frigate newly acquired from the French, was in drydock at Chatham having her bottom cleaned and repaired ready for a layer of extra thick copper to be applied.

Her crew, those who wanted it, were on shore leave and she was under the command of fourth lieutenant Stanley Hart. Newly promoted as this ship warranted a fourth lieutenant. He only had a harbour watch of a crew but carried a fat purse given him by Captain Stockley, which enabled Fletcher, their purser, to bribe the yard into carrying out exemplary work ahead of poorer ships in the fleet.

The Unicorn, formerly La Licorne of the French Navy would be fitted out with twenty-eight, eighteen-pound long guns on her main deck, two monstrous sixty-four-pound carronades on her fore deck (instead of the four twenty four pound carronades the French carried) mounted in tandem on swivel mounts, ten twenty-four-pound carronades on her quarterdeck, and two long nine stern chasers in the captain's cabin.

Stanley was surprised when a carriage pulled up and liveried servants carried a full Christmas feast onto the ship, cooked it, and served it with plenty of beer and wine to the entire harbour crew.

The toast at the end of the meal was, "Sir Martin and Lady Caroline!"

At his London home in Grosvenor, Marty was having Christmas with his family. Lady Caroline, stunningly beautiful as ever and his four children were the centre of his world until his ship was ready to sail again. Snow in the peninsula effectively put the war there on hold and he could enjoy some down time.

He had persuaded Wolfgang to join them for Christmas dinner, which as usual was sumptuous and took up most of Christmas day. He declined to go to church with them and instead attended a Calvinist service in a nearby chapel. He now sat with James, Marty's eldest son, who was discussing, very seriously, the merits of different sail configurations to get the best out of a three masted ship in varying weather conditions.

"He will follow you to sea," Caroline sighed wistfully.

"What's wrong with that?" Marty asked, slightly surprised.

"Oh, there is absolutely nothing wrong with him going to sea. It's just that he is following your example a little too closely."

Marty raised his eyebrows in question. He sensed there was more to come.

Caroline pursed her lips and took a deep breath.

"He has turned out to be an excellent shot with that gun you got him for his birthday. We had game for dinner at least twice a week whilst we were in Cheshire."

Marty beamed with pride.

"Tom says he is very disciplined when he is shooting. Always knows where his dogs are and is very careful how he handles a loaded gun. He keeps his gun clean and well maintained."

"Well, so far I don't see a problem."

"However," she continued, holding a finger up to forestall further comment from him, "I caught him, with one of your duelling pistols, the small calibre ones you got from Adams.   He was practicing shooting a scarecrow. He stood back to back with it and paced out ten steps turned and fired."

"Like a duel!" Marty exclaimed.

"Exactly!" Caroline said in a tone that said she didn't approve. "I mean, really, he is only nine!"

After Christmas and Boxing Day had passed, Marty was getting ready to go down to Chatham when a courier arrived with a message from Turner.

Marty read it then sat back in his chair in disbelief.

"What's happened?" Caroline asked.

"The bloody fools!" Marty swore. "They have only gone and exchanged him!" and thrust the message towards her.

"Exchanged who?" Caroline asked, alarmed by his violent reaction.

"Dupreeh. They have let Dupreeh go back to France in exchange for some inconsequential son of a… the idiot politicians have let him go!"

Epilogue.

Turner sat in his office. There was still a second desk for Hood should he want to use it but increasingly the old admiral was spending his time at home. He sorted through the papers on his desk then sat back and stared at the painting of the battle of the Saints on the wall opposite his desk. He didn't really see it as his mind was going over recent events.

The son of Richard Ryder, the Home Secretary, had gotten himself captured by the French a year ago through his own utter incompetence. Worse, he had lost a valuable fifth rate and its crew. His father had initially bought him his commission and the fool hadn't learnt a thing in the two years he had spent as a lieutenant aboard a second rate.

A senile old admiral had promoted him to captain and given him the ship to flatter his father, it took just six months for him to lose it and get himself captured.

Spencer Perceval was the current Prime Minister and Ryder was his home Secretary and given the current unrest in the country needed all the support he could get. So, when the French asked for Dupreeh in return for the idiot son, Perceval handed him over despite the protests and warnings from both Naval Intelligence and Canning's Foreign Office Intelligence people.

James sighed. The country was almost in open revolt; international trade had collapsed, the price of staples like bread had gone through the roof, the people were agitating for the vote, and the Luddites were rioting and smashing machines.

His mind turned to his protégé. Marty had lived up to the potential he saw in the young shrimp of a boy all those years ago. From the day Martin had saved his life to his induction into the secret service, he had grown in every way. Now he was their most competent asset, trusted by Wellesley and Canning. He had built his Flotilla into an effective weapon and his network of agents into something that could challenge the French.

He had, however, made enemies. The worst of which, Admiral Gambier, was constantly trying to undermine him with the politicians. That led to a sudden thought, had Gambier been behind the swap of Dupreeh for Ryder?

The war on the Peninsula had to come to a head in the following year or the country would completely run out of money. Marty would have to play an active part in that and had set the foundation with the action to restrict Soult's supply of powder. He had lost a ship but, typical of the man, hadn't waited for the Navy to give him another and had just gone out and, with an absolutely audacious action, stolen himself an almost new one from the French.

1812 was going to be an interesting year. The king's mental health had deteriorated, and he was now as mad as a hatter. The people were demanding the vote and the war was coming to a head.

There was a knock at the door and his secretary announced Mr. Canning.

"Good morning, George," James greeted him and asked the secretary to bring coffee.

Canning settled himself and after he had taken a cup asked,

"How did Martin take the release of Dupreeh?"

"As one would expect. He was bloody furious," James replied.

"If they meet again, I have the feeling only one will walk away," Canning stated.

"Hmm, my money will always be on Martin," James replied.

"Mine too but it will be a fascinating encounter," Canning predicted then asked, "how did Lady Caroline take it?"

"Perceval has made an enemy of her. He will no longer be able to count on her block of votes," James informed him. "She will not do anything to hurt the service and will support any vote that we ask her to, but Perceval has lost her personal support."

Canning looked thoughtful.

"The exchange may have cost him more than he thinks then."

"Will you tell him?" James asked curious how Canning would use this information.

"Me? No. I never supported him. He is too right wing for my liking. No, he will find out soon enough. When do you get your admiral's pennant?"

Politicians are a cold-blooded bunch, James observed and was thankful that Canning and he were on the same side.

Authors Notes

The years covered by this book 1810 – 1811 were rather dry of action except in Portugal. But that gave me free rein to improvise, which is fun.

The major characters really existed as usual but the whole action to blow up the bridges is a figment of my overactive imagination, as was stealing la Licorne.

The action of the Lines of Torres Vedras was a real event as was the retreat of the French. The British managed to keep secret that they actually had three lines of defence; the French never had a clue, and we really did underestimate their ability to forage.

The siege of Cadiz was another real event and was one of the most pointless sieges in history. The British controlled the port and simply resupplied the city by sea. The French, meantime, were starving as their supply lines were constantly raided by Spanish guerrillas.

Now I know that someone will object to Caroline fighting a duel, but it is a historical fact that women did. Although, admittedly, most were between women. There have been women-only fencing clubs since at least the 1700's. British history is littered with strong women and while it was the social norm for them to defer to their husbands and fulfil a subservient role there were many who 'kicked against the pricks'.

A note on when people ate in the 1800's. Most people ate just two times a day and the first meal was taken around midday, called dinner and was normally the biggest of the day. The second (supper) was taken later in the early evening. Breakfast for the masses really

The Dorset Boy Book 8: La Licorne

didn't start until the early1900's although the upper class did partake, probably to show off their wealth. What we call lunch came about as the main meal got eaten later as industrialisation took over people's lives and a lighter meal was needed to fill in at the end of the morning.

Maurice, Marty's French double was, for some reason only known to my subconscious, based on a cross between Thomas Castaignède, the former French rugby player now a pundit, and Passepartout from Around the World in 80 days. The squeaky voice comes from Thomas, sorry Thomas if you read this but you do have a rather high register, and the image of Maurice on a donkey with a parasol came from Jules Verne's fabulous novel.

1812 is a much more significant year as it was the start of Wellington's campaign to push the French out of the Peninsula. Marty and the Shadows will have an active role to play, of course, so look out for book 9.

And Now an extract from Book 1 of The Scarlet Fox series by the same author!

The Scarlet Fox Book 1, Chapter 1: A change of profession.

The passage from Rotterdam was stormy. The lugger had all sail set and was heeled over in the wind, spray kicking up and over the bow. She was heading for Baytown, a well-known smugglers' village south of Whitby on the Yorkshire coast. They were intent on keeping their illicit cargo of Dutch Gin out of the hands of any revenue cutters in the area, so they drove her hard.

Ray and Scarlett Browning were twins. Their father, Smoker Browning, was the head of one of the two smuggling gangs that operated out of the bay, and the twins had been given responsibility for getting their valuable cargo safely home. At eighteen years old, they already had many years of experience between them and handled the boat with skill and more than a little daring.

Scarlett was the older by thirty minutes. She was beautiful by any standards with a mane of auburn hair and blue/green eyes that changed colour with her mood. At five feet eight, a little too tall to suit the fashion of the time, but she didn't care, marriage and romance were not at the forefront of her interests. Her body was shapely but well-muscled from the rigours of sailing boats in all weathers. She attracted the attention of many young men, but a sharp knife and a pair of pistols were usually enough to cool their ardour unless she found the attraction mutual.

Ray was out of the same mould as his father. Shaven head, piercing blue eyes, muscular, and athletic. He was renowned for his sailing and fighting skills and for being a fair, even-handed skipper. He was generally even-tempered but when he did blow, it was usually fast, violent, and over quickly. Unlike Scarlett, he was one for the ladies and had a string of conquests under his belt.

Smoker Browning begat eight children from two wives. The first, Anne, died from the flux after the birth of their second child. The first child died at six and the second got himself shot by a revenue man at sixteen. Smoker hunted him down and gutted him in revenge. His second wife, May, gave him the twins and two more boys, Will and Raif, who were sixteen and fourteen respectively. Scarlett got her looks from May, who was still a good-looking woman at the age of thirty-six.

The twins had their hands full. The wind had swung around to the Northwest, which meant they were having to tack to make any headway as it was almost dead against the course they needed to ply. The lugger's gaff-rigged sails let them sail close to the wind but they were still having to sail three sea miles for every mile gained towards home.

They had gotten to just over twenty miles from port when the lookout spotted a sail to the Northwest. A Revenue cutter found them and was bearing down on the wind, intent on an intercept. Ray didn't want a confrontation. For a start, if the cutter started shooting, their cargo would probably suffer even if they eventually got away, and anyway, they didn't want the cutter to get close enough to identify them.

It was two hours to dark.

"If we run South, we can lose them in the dark and overnight at Filey behind the point," Scarlett suggested.

Ray thought on that for a moment then agreed,

"Let's do that. He won't make much on us in a stern chase and if we look as if we are going to head out to sea before we wear, he might spend the next day looking for us in the wrong place."

They tacked and took up a course that would run them South down the coast, the cutter settling in behind them. With the overcast, dark came early and while the cutter could still see them, they eased out to sea. As soon as the darkness swallowed the Revenue boat from view, they performed a long, lazy wear to bring them around to the West.

Filey was a village that lived behind a peninsula that stuck out into the sea to the East which provided a natural shelter from any weather from the North. They slipped in cautiously, using the lights from the village as beacons, and anchored up for the night.

The next morning, the wind had swung more to the West and as soon as they could see, they eased out and headed North. The cutter was nowhere to be seen, and they slipped into Baytown before ten where the well-rehearsed team on shore had the cargo unloaded and concealed in short order.

Smoker greeted the twins in the kitchen of the family home where May had a hot meal waiting for them. The rich lamb stew was topped with dumplings and had carrots, onions, and turnip cooked through it.

"Expected you in yesterday," he said as they were mopping up the gravy with thick chunks of crusty home-made bread.

"That bloody revenue cutter jumped us about twenty-five mile out. We had to hole up by Filey," Ray replied.

"They are getting bolder, even sent a press gang into the village," Smoker stated with a frown.

"Did they get anyone?" Scarlett asked, concern written on her face.

"No, all they got was a beating," smiled Smoker as he recalled the brawl that ensued when the Navy press gang descended on the Ploughman pub. He paused, obviously thinking about something.

"I bin thinking we need to get into somethin' else besides smuggling to spread our interests and I think we will want to keep it in the family."

"What you got in mind, Pop?" asked Scarlett, intrigued.

Her father sat back and lit his clay pipe. He blew out a cloud of smoke and answered,

"Privateering."

Scarlett and Ray looked at each other.

"Why privateering?" Scarlett eventually asked after the silence stretched out as long as she could stand.

"Perfect for us. We can make a lot of money in a relatively short time with little risk if we do it right. It will be legal, and gold can't be traced."

Ray sat forward in interest.

"We will need a ship."

"The profit from this trip will pay for a Ketch and arm it. We will need to man it from the brotherhood to start with, and you can pick up more as you take prizes. There's plenty of men out there looking to make a quick profit."

Scarlett looked at Ray and asked the question they both wanted to ask,

"Which one of us would skipper it?"

Smoker laughed,
"Worried I'll split you two up?"
The looks on their faces were the only answers he needed.
"You both go. You are a good team and will watch each other's backs. In any case, I doubt I could split you up if I wanted to."

The following days showed their father hadn't waited to tell them before putting his plan into action; he had already started the process of acquiring a ship. He surprised them by taking them up to boatyard in Whitby where the hull of a new Ketch was well under way.

The Ketch was a relatively new design of hull having been introduced around ten years before in around 1650. They were mainly used as large fishing boats and cargo haulers but could also carry up to sixteen guns. They were fast and weatherly and could even make long voyages in open water.

Ray paced it off, she was around sixty feet at the waterline, a little longer than the usual fifty-five. Fully rigged, she would have a central mainmast and a short mizzen balanced at the bow by a twenty-foot-long bowsprit. She would carry square sails on the upper main and mizzen and gaff sails for the rest. She would be armed with sixteen eight-pound demi-culverin cannon.

As an armed ship, she would need a minimum of eighty men to sail and fight one side, but for the type of work they would be getting into, they would carry at least a hundred so they could man prizes without effecting the efficiency of the ship.

The men were busy talking about knees and ribs when Scarlett noticed someone standing on the other side of the yard, partially concealed by some crates, who seemed to be taking an unhealthy interest in them. She walked up to Ray and her father and quietly pointed him out, then she flounced off as if all this ship business was boring her.

Playing the empty-headed girl, she wandered away towards the gates. As soon as she passed behind a stack of timber, she pulled a pistol from inside the hand muff she wore on a chord around her neck and circled around behind him.

He was so intent on watching Smoker and Ray, he didn't hear her come up behind him until she cocked the pistol, pointing it at the back of his head.

"Hello," she said pleasantly, "are you having a nice day?"

The man, who she noticed had long, greasy, dark hair hanging down to the collar of his equally grubby coat, stiffened and slowly turned his head. He had a sharp featured face with a squinty, suspicious look about him.

"Now, why are you so interested in what we are doing?"

She stepped back a pace to make sure he couldn't grab the gun and kept it pointing straight at his face.

"Me, miss? I ain't watchin' no one," he stammered, noting that the pistol was rock steady and despite the friendly tone, the girl had a very stony look on her face, her blue/green eyes as cold as ice.

"Turn around and walk over there," Scarlett ordered, indicating with her free hand where she wanted him to go. He was surprised when he saw it wasn't towards the ship but to a screened off area where the shipwrights prepared some of the more intricate timbers. He started to get very nervous, on the verge of panic, when Smoker and Ray followed Scarlett into the work area.

Smoker signed to the workers to leave and once they were alone, he stepped over to a workbench and picked up an adze. He made a show of examining the edge, which was razor sharp.

"Well, if it ain't Michael Knight as I live and breathe!" he said, "you still snitching for the revenue?"

"Master Browning, I didn't expect to meet you here. I was just watching them building ships," Knight wheedled.

"Oh? A new interest of yourn, is it?" Smoker sneered in disbelief, "last time I saw you, your only interest was in selling information to the revenue so you could go whoring. I believe you were told if we ever saw you again, you would pay."

"You shouted that at him as he ran away, Pa," Ray added, hefting a heavy maul.

Now Scarlett remembered the man. He had informed the revenue when a shipment was being delivered, and he even showed them where they were. Three of their men were killed and they lost half the cargo. They only got it back after they raided the revenue compound.

"Shall I shoot him, Pa?" she said, cold anger blossoming in her chest.

"No, that be too good for this scum," Smoker snarled, "Ray!" he commanded and indicated a large block of wood.

Ray dropped the maul, grabbed Knight by the arms, and hauled him over to the block, easily overpowering the smaller man. He kicked him in the back of the knees forcing him to kneel and holding the back of the neck in an iron grip with one hand, forcing Knight's right hand out and down onto the block with his other. All the while, the pistol in Scarlett's hand didn't waver, even though she knew what was coming.

Knight started to gibber and sob in terror as he realised that retribution was nigh. He begged and cried, but all that did was disgust the Brownings and harden their resolve.

Smoker brought the adze down, Knight screamed, his right hand cleanly severed at the wrist, then Smoker took a piece of wood and dunked it in a pot of boiling pitch, which he smeared on the open wound, cauterising and sealing it.

"There, don't want you bleedin' t' death, now do we," he consoled him then nodded to Ray, who wrapped his hand in Knight's hair, pulling his head back.

Smoker pulled out his knife, stood over the miserable informant, and said,

"He deserves to carry the mark for the rest of his days."

He split his nose from top to bottom and carved a symbol into his forehead.

"Now everyone will know you for what you are," he snarled, "get him out of here!"

Ray dragged the stricken man out of the yard and threw him into the street. The workers in the yard didn't take any notice; they knew who Smoker was and owed the brotherhood their livings. A man stepped over the wretch as he landed at his feet and spat in his face. Everyone else carried on as if he didn't exist. He was a dead man walking. He would receive neither aid nor succour from anyone. He carried the mark of the traitor; this was the justice of The Brotherhood.

The Dorset Boy Book 8: La Licorne

Books by Christopher C Tubbs

The Dorset Boy Series.

A Talent for Trouble
The Special Operations Flotilla
Agent Provocateur
In Dangerous Company
The Tempest
Vendetta
The Trojan Horse
La Licorne

The Scarlet Fox Series

Scarlett

See them all at:

Website: www.thedorsetboy.com
Twitter: @ChristoherCTu3
Facebook: https://www.facebook.com/thedorsetboy/
YouTube: https://youtu.be/KCBR4ITqDi4

Published in E-Book, Paperback and Audio formats
on Amazon, Audible and iTunes

The Dorset Boy Book 8: La Licorne

Printed in Great Britain
by Amazon